Cast of Ch: D0843446

Eugenia Gates. A sharp-tongued secretary from New York City, Eugenia was planning on peace and quiet during an unexpected two-week vacation she was to spend in Mary Fredon's spacious apartment. Dead bodies and an amorous, self-assured army sergeant put an end to that.

Kendall Smith. The sergeant in question, he also claims that he was being lent the use of the apartment. His immediate goals are to gather a date for every night of his furlough and to infuriate Eugenia as much as possible. He almost succeeds at both.

Lucy Davis. An incorrigible snoop, she's asked by Mary to stay in the apartment as a chaperone for Eugenia and Ken Smith.

Mary Fredon. She accidentally lent her apartment to both Eugenia and Ken, apparently in shock after her husband ran away with the next door neighbor, but she returns in time to see a murder committed. An obsessive housekeeper, she's alarmed at her guests' untidy ways.

Homer Fredon. The straying husband, who's known to have an interest in antiquities.

Betty Emerson. The other woman.

John Emerson. The other woman's dashing husband, who seems more concerned about his missing eye than his missing wife.

Mrs. Budd. Betty's mother. She's staying with her son-in-law.

Suzy Howland. The Emersons' maid, she lends a hand at Mary's apartment at well. She sees people who shouldn't be seen.

J.X. Boxton. An undertaker, he also lives in the apartment building.

Mrs. Brindle. Another neighbor, she complained about strange noises in Mary's apartment.

Bartholomew Egbert. A pompous policeman with an exaggerated sense of his skills.

Books by Constance & Gwenyth Little

The Grey Mist Murders (1938)*
The Black-Headed Pins (1938)*
The Black Gloves (1939)*
Black Corridors (1940)*
The Black Paw (1941)*
The Black Shrouds (1941)
The Black Thumb (1942)
The Black Rustle (1943)
The Black Honeymoon (1944)*
Great Black Kanba (1944)*
The Black Eye (1945)*
The Black Stocking (1946)*
The Black Goatee (1947)
The Black Coat (1948)*
The Black Piano (1948)
The Black Smith (1950)
The Black House (1950)
The Blackout (1951)
The Black Dream (1952)
The Black Curl (1953)
The Black Iris (1953)

*reprinted by the Rue Morgue Press
as of January 2002

THE BLACK EYE

BY

CONSTANCE & GWENYTH LITTLE

The Rue Morgue Press
Boulder, Colorado

About the Littles

Although all but one of their books had "black" in the title, the 21 mysteries of Constance (1899-1980) and Gwenyth (1903-1985) Little were far from somber affairs. The two Australian-born sisters from East Orange, New Jersey, were far more interested in coaxing chuckles than in inducing chills from their readers.

Indeed, after their first book, *The Grey Mist Murders*, appeared in 1938, Constance rebuked an interviewer for suggesting that their murders weren't realistic by saying, "Our murderers strangle. We have no sliced-up corpses in our books." However, as the books mounted, the Littles did go in for all sorts of gruesome murder methods—"horrible," was the way their own mother described them—which included the occasional sliced-up corpse.

But the murders were always off stage and tempered by comic scenes in which bodies and other objects, including swimming pools, were constantly disappearing and reappearing. The action took place in large old mansions, boarding houses, hospitals, hotels, or on trains or ocean liners, anywhere the Littles could gather together a large cast of eccentric characters, many of whom seemed to have escaped from a Kaufman play or a Capra movie. The typical Little heroine—each book was a stand-alone—often fell under suspicion herself and turned detective to keep the police from slapping the cuffs on. Whether she was a working woman or a spoiled little rich brat, she always spoke her mind, kept her sense of humor, and got her man, both murderer and husband. But if marriage was in the offing, it was always on her terms and the vows were taken with more than a touch of cynicism. Love was grand, but it was even grander if the husband could either pitch in with the cooking and cleaning or was wealthy enough to hire household help.

The Littles wrote all their books in bed—"Chairs give one backaches," Gwenyth complained—with Constance providing detailed plot outlines while Gwenyth did the final drafts. Over the years that pattern changed somewhat but Constance always insisted that Gwen "not mess up my clues." Those clues were everywhere and the Littles made sure there were no loose ends. Seemingly irrelevant events were revealed to be of major significance in the final summation. The plots were often preposterous, a fact often recognized by both the Littles and their characters, all of whom seem to be winking at the reader, almost as if sharing a private joke. Certainly there are aspects of *The Black Eye* that one could say defy the laws of science. You just have to accept the fact that there are different natural laws in that wacky universe created by these sisters.

The Littles published their two final novels, *The Black Curl* and *The Black Iris*, in 1953, and if they missed writing after that, they were at least able to devote more time to their real passion—traveling. The two made at least three trips around the world at a time when that would have been a major expedition. For more information on the Littles and their books, see the introductions by Tom & Enid Schantz to The Rue Morgue Press editions of *The Black Gloves* and *The Black Honeymoon*.

THE BLACK EYE

CHAPTER ONE

THE APARTMENT HOUSE was one of those older buildings, but it had a look of dignity and reserve. There was an expanse of neatly clipped lawn at the front, edged with carefully barbered hedges, and a series of small iron balconies that decorated the façade from top to bottom were more elegant than absurd.

The taxi man carried my bags in and surrendered them to an elderly door-man, who escorted me to the elevator. He and the elevator operator appeared to accept me tentatively—on probation pending good behavior, I thought, and I and my bags were eventually ushered into Mary's apartment on the sixth floor.

The door closed behind me, and I stood for a moment surrounded by my luggage and fighting a chill sense of disappointment. I had hoped the place would be small and cheerful, and instead I looked down the length of a dark, unfriendly hall, which widened into a foyer at the end, where I could see heavy drapes hanging in the two archways. The hall was lined with closed doors, and I presently moved forward and began to open them. There were four bedrooms—one large one, with its own bath, which I supposed was Mary's room, and a second bathroom opening from the hall.

I closed Mary's room again and chose the most cheerful of the three smaller bedrooms for myself. It had a dull green carpet, mahogany furniture, and sun-yellow drapes—and I hoped that the drapes would cheer me up in the morning and fortify me for the gloomy hall.

I arranged my bags, unpacked a few things, and then washed up a bit and combed my hair. I was still feeling depressed, and it took a certain amount of self-urging to get myself to explore the rest of the apartment.

The foyer opened into a very large living room and a good-sized dining room, and the kitchen behind was narrow but long. The living room had huge windows and a pair of glass doors that opened on to one of the iron balconies.

I slumped down into an armchair and wondered why I felt so gloomy. After all, I had come out here for two weeks of rest and quiet—and if the apartment was large and somber, at least it seemed a perfect spot for solitude. I wondered idly what the rent was and how Mary was able to afford it. She had told me that she was broke—but that was an elastic expression, and I supposed that what I would call broke would be destitution to Mary. She intended spending the summer at her cottage in the country, but she was in retirement, with a broken heart, because her husband had flitted off with the woman next door.

I sighed and pulled myself out of the armchair. The living room seemed to frown at me from all its four walls, so I went through the glass door and out onto the iron balcony. I found that it was narrow but long, and neatly halved by a section of iron grillwork that was the same height as the railing. One half was at Mary's disposal, apparently, and the other half belonged to the adjoining apartment. It was understandable, I thought, grinning at the inadequate little barrier, that Mary's Homer had run off with the woman in the next apartment. Practically sitting in each other's laps, like that—if they used the balcony much—they'd have either to start a fight or cook up a romance. It was a wonder that Mary hadn't run off with the man next door—except that Mary was a practical soul, and if she'd wanted to do any flitting, she'd have had it, properly sanctioned in the courts first.

An elderly woman emerged from the other apartment onto her end of the balcony and, after inspecting the lawn below for a suitable interval, pretended to catch sight of me for the first time.

"Oh—oh, good afternoon."

I responded in kind, and she asked brightly, "Is Mary back?"

"No."

"I see. She's still at the cottage, then?"

"Yes."

"She hasn't sublet the apartment?"

"No."

"Oh—well—you're a friend of hers then. Staying long?"

"No."

"Well, of course accommodations are so hard to get, right now, I suppose you're glad to have the use of the apartment for a while?"

I sighed and reflected that perseverance such as hers really ought to be rewarded. So many people are sissy enough to give up after the first try.

"I'm very grateful to Mary," I explained. "I live in New York, and I met her there, last week, when we were both shopping. I wanted a complete rest for two weeks—it was an unexpected vacation—and I hadn't been able to get accommodations anywhere. I told her about it, and she suggested that I come here. She said it would be quiet and restful—that's what I'm hoping for."

"Oh, my dear!" the woman protested. "A young girl like you! You should be looking for gaiety—not quiet."

A man came through the glass doors behind her—a tall man, and unusually good-looking, and I wondered if he could possibly be the husband from whom the woman had run away—and with Mary's old Homer, too.

"My son-in-law, John Emerson," the woman announced with a certain amount of pride. "I am Mrs. Budd."

I nodded, and admitted that I was Eugenia Gates.

Mrs. Budd badly wanted to ask who Eugenia Gates might be, and while she considered ways and means John Emerson asked negligently, "Is Mary back?"

Mrs. Budd told him she was not, and that I was staying in the apartment by myself. "She wants peace and quiet, John."

John raised his nicely shaped eyebrows, and I sat down on one of the chairs and put my feet up on the other.

"My dear," Mrs. Budd said, "I'm afraid Mary wouldn't like that—I mean your feet on that chair, you know she keeps everything so exquisite."

I, took my feet off, removed my shoes, and put my feet back again. "Is that all right?" I asked.

John Emerson gave a short laugh. "Probably not—but Mary isn't here, and we won't tell on you. Do you hear, Mother?"

"No, no, I shan't say a word," Mrs. Budd said—and proceeded to blackmail me. "Do you live with your parents?"

"I'm an orphan," I said meekly.

"Are you in business?"

I nodded. "I'm a secretary. My father was a Kentucky colonel who lost his vast estates—so I had to go to work."

Mrs. Budd stared, but Emerson gave me a cool glance and observed, "You seem to have lost your Southern accent."

I ignored him and gave my attention to Mrs. Budd.

"My mother's blood was bluer than her native grass, and we feel that she really died of a broken heart when she had to give up her stables."

Someone called from inside their apartment, and Mrs. Budd reluctantly tore herself away but called back over her shoulder, "Don't go—I'll be right back."

There was a moment of silence, and then John Emerson stirred and lit a cigarette. "Allow me to pinch-hit for my mother-in-law. Now whom do you secretary?"

"A busy executive. He's busy fishing and golfing most of the time, but right now he's substituting for me at the office. I hope he doesn't get things into too much of a muddle."

"Did you ever hear of modesty?" he asked, laughing a little.

"I heard all about it. I had an aunt who had it quite badly."

I lay back and closed my eyes after that, and when the silence had lasted for some time I opened them again and saw that he had gone.

I went contentedly off to sleep, without further interruption, and when I woke up again it was dark. I yawned once or twice, and then pulled myself up from the chair and stumbled through the glass doors into the living room. I barked my shins three times before I found a light switch, and then I regarded the vast, imposing room with a shudder. I went through to the hall, and while I fumbled for the light switch there I tried fuzzily to remember which door led into the bedroom I had chosen for myself. I found the switch at last, and as the light glowed into an ornate fixture in the ceiling someone inserted a key in the front door.

I stood absolutely still and forgot to breathe as the door swung slowly inward—and then caught up with two or three quick gasps when a large soldier walked himself into the hall. He was carrying a bag, and when he caught sight of me he dropped it to the floor with a thump.

I took an involuntary step backward and asked sharply, "Who are you?"

"Sergeant Kendall Smith of the Army," he said formally, and removed his cap. "Mrs. Fredon was kind enough to offer me the use of her apartment during my furlough."

CHAPTER TWO

I LOOKED at the solid khaki length and breadth of the man and stammered, "But you can't—there's been a mistake of some sort. I mean she told me to use the place for my vacation, and I'm here for two weeks."

"Don't let it upset you," he said kindly. "There's plenty of space. Bedrooms for all."

I collapsed onto one of the hall chairs and had a moment of utter despair. I'd have to get out, of course—every minute of a soldier's furlough is precious, with no time to spare—but I hated to think of dragging back to New York. It was unlike Mary to create a mess of this sort, and I felt a spasm of anger for her.

The sergeant picked up his bags and said, "Don't look so gloomy—we soldiers need plenty of cheer in our dull lives. We can both stay here, and I'll go out and sleep on the lawn at night—be more homelike for me. When's dinner ready?"

I took a long breath and stood up. "Dinner isn't. But if you're hungry, I am, too, so let's go out and find a hash house somewhere."

"Good enough," said Sergeant Smith without undue enthusiasm. "Of course, when I saw you, I had hopes—but never mind about that. I'll just go and wash the stains of travel away."

He showed that he knew the place by flinging his bag into one of the bedrooms and then making straight for the hall bathroom. I sat down again and studied the toes of my shoes and wondered whether there was any way out except the dreary trip back to New York.

A telephone shrilled suddenly, and I got up and had to hunt around for a bit before I found it in a small closet at one end of the hall.

It was Mary. "Eugenia. I've just remembered—so stupid of me—about Ken, I mean. Has he turned up yet?"

"If you mean Sergeant Smith—yes. He's washing off the travel stains."

"That's right, Ken Smith—such a fine boy. But of course you'll need a chaperon, so I've arranged to have Lucy stay with you."

"Lucy Davis?" I croaked, and then cleared my throat to show I hadn't meant anything.

"My dear, she was the only one available. I knew that she'd planned just to stay at home this summer, and she had nothing much to do—and of course she was delighted. But listen, Eugenia—I'm devoted to Lucy, and all that, but she is an incorrigible snoop, so I want you to lock my bedroom door and put the key in that desk in the hall—you'll find a little pigeonhole drawer in the top part—and then I'll know where to find it when I get back."

I thanked her for the chaperon—not heartily, because I knew Lucy Davis all too well—agreed to take care of the bedroom situation, and then handed the phone over to Sergeant Smith, who had appeared at my side and seemed to be waiting for it. He talked and laughed with Mary for some time, while I went on into my bedroom and freshened myself up a bit. I was practically starving by that time, so I made it as short as possible, and when I came back into the hall Smith had finished with Mary and seemed to be trying to make a date with a girl named Alice. I gathered that he was having some difficulty, but he finally got it fixed for Thursday and hung up.

He turned to me and asked cheerfully, "All ready? Then I'll leave the rest of them until I get back."

"You'll have a busy evening."

"Ah no." He carefully double-locked the apartment door behind us and explained as we started down the hall, "The others are easy. Alice is the popular one—and look how well I did with her. This is Monday, and I got her for Thursday."

"Wonderful!" I murmured.

"Oh well," he said tolerantly, "you don't know Alice, or you wouldn't be so sarcastic."

He apparently knew the terrain well, for he led me straight to a restaurant where the proprietor greeted him like a long-lost brother. The two of them kept the conversation rolling throughout the meal, so I just sat and ate.

We were on the way back before I remembered that I hadn't yet locked Mary's bedroom, and I wondered if Lucy had arrived in the meantime, and if she had a key to the apartment.

She hadn't. We found her walking up and down the hall in a rage, with her face nearly as red as her curls. "I don't know what you think you're doing, Eugenia Gates," she howled at me. "I come over here to do you a favor, and you keep me waiting until I've worn a path in the carpet." She glanced over my shoulder and tuned in another station. "Hello there, Ken! Darling! How *are* you?" And fell on his neck and kissed him.

He backed up and said, "Lay off, Lucy. I'm practically engaged, and I'm the conventional type."

"But, Ken—my *dear!*" she shrieked. "Who is it? *Do* tell me—I simply can't bear secrets."

I went on into the apartment, and they followed, Lucy insisting that Ken get her a drink. She declared she knew that Mary had plenty of liquor around somewhere. Ken told her he wasn't going to touch Mary's liquor, even if he found it, and he wasn't going to look. By this time they were down in the foyer, and I realized grimly that the job of chaperon was going to fall to me, even though Lucy was at least twenty years older.

I shrugged and, slipping into Mary's bedroom, turned on the light. She'd taken care over the furnishing, I thought, looking about—it was quite impressive. The bed dominated everything—a huge mahogany thing with a canopy, and a drawer underneath—a genuine antique, I supposed. It was set up on a low platform, in a rather regal fashion, and I went over to inspect it more closely. I saw, then, that the drawer was slightly open, and I pushed it in, and had to pull it out again to free the heavy cream-colored spread. I slid it shut once more and thought how typical it was of Mary that in her apartment even antique drawers moved smoothly in their grooves. Every time I saw her— which was, when we had lunch together in New York—she'd give me what you might call Hints to the Housekeeper—and her apartment suggested that she knew what she was talking about.

There was a picture of Homer on the dressing table—framed in heavy silver, and certainly not turned to the wall, and I wondered whether Mary had been as hurt over his defection as I had supposed. He wasn't much to look at—even with all that sterling silver around him. Then I noticed another door in the room, but it was locked on the inside—it evidently led out into the foyer, quite near the kitchen.

I realized, with a sudden pang of conscience, that I was doing exactly what Mary had feared Lucy would do—I was snooping. I went quickly to the other door, removed the key, and stepped out into the hall. I could hear the other two still arguing the liquor question in the kitchen as I locked the door and took the key along to the desk in the hall. It was another antique, with lovely mellow lines and a soft glow on its surfaces that showed hours of careful polishing.

I opened the top, found the little drawer, and dropped the key in, and then turned away with a sigh of relief for duty done.

I went along to my room and took off my hat and busied myself with the rest of my unpacking.

I had just finished when Lucy pushed in without bothering to knock. She cast a dismayed look about the room and protested in the usual shrill squawk, "But, Eugenia, my *dear,* I always have this room. Mary always puts me here when I stay with her. I mean, it's like my own."

"I don't wonder you like it better than any of the others," I agreed. "I looked them all over and picked it out myself."

"But—?"

"So you'd better go and find the next best before Smith gets it."

"Oh." She tapped her front teeth with about two inches of crimson fingernail and then brightened. "Well, it's all right—I'll take Mary's room. I know she'd want me to have it."

"It's locked," I told her. "Mary said she was keeping it locked because Smith might throw one of his rowdy parties and a stray drunk might wander in and ruin that beautiful lavender carpet."

She looked at me blankly for a moment and then gave a sudden loud giggle. She dashed out of my room, leaving the door open, and yelled, "Ken! Where are you? Ken!"

I heard her open a door, and poor Ken's exasperated voice: "Lucy, get the hell out of here—can't you see I'm disrobing?"

"Oh, don't be a lemon," she said impatiently. "Listen, how about throwing a party? We've loads of room here."

"We'll discuss it in the morning. Good night, Lucy." A door closed firmly, and I figured that she'd been shut out. I heard her bang into the remaining bedroom, and then she had to come out again and drag her suitcase in, muttering furiously from time to time.

I went to bed and settled myself with a book, because I didn't expect to sleep too early, after my nap on the little balcony. I was mistaken, as it happened, because I went to sleep sitting up against my pillows, with the book fallen to my lap and the bedside lamp burning brightly.

I woke up at three o'clock with a stiff neck and a very active hunger. I didn't think there was any food in the place, but the pangs were so insistent that I decided to go and see if at least there were some cookies.

I got into a gown and my slippers and crept along to the kitchen, where I turned on the light. I hunted around until I found a box of soda crackers— which seemed a feast, when I had expected nothing—and I decided to go and eat them out on the little balcony and look at the stars.

It was nice out there—dark and quiet and peaceful, and I sat down, with my feet propped on the other chair, and munched contentedly.

After a while the glass doors of the other apartment opened, and John Emerson stood there—talking back to someone in his living room.

"You were completely mistaken," he said coldly. "It was that damned black eye."

CHAPTER THREE

I DROPPED THE box of soda crackers in sheer surprise, and John Emerson turned quickly and looked at me.

"Oh." He stepped out onto the balcony and closed the doors behind him. "You're up late, Miss Gates."

"So are you," I said, stretching an arm down for the cracker box.

"Well, yes—but I've been playing bridge, and that takes time."

"I've been reading," I explained courteously, "and that takes time too."

The conversation bogged down at that point, and I wondered why he didn't return to his living room and go on with the peculiar argument, until I realized that he probably didn't want to continue it while I was there, since I'd almost certainly overhear it. I decided that he was simply waiting for me to go. Most likely it was a girlfriend in the living room, and he was having an interesting tiff with her—and here I was interfering. Maybe they wanted to come out onto the balcony to make it up.

I sighed and stood up. "Well, all right," I said absentmindedly, "I'll go to bed."

He looked at me more fully and asked with a faint amusement, "Why? There's no particular hurry, is there? Suppose I leap the barricade, and we can talk for a while."

"Oh no," I said hastily. "I mean it's too late, and anyway, I ought to be getting some sleep."

I said good night to him and went in, thinking that perhaps it wasn't a girlfriend after all, but just his mother-in-law. And his wife had run off with Mary's husband. I shook my head and wondered what she looked like, that she'd have to pick poor old Homer to flit with.

I went to bed and to sleep and dreamed of a black eye that floated through the atmosphere in lonely menace.

I awoke to a lively clatter of dishes in the kitchen and a cheerful smell of bacon and coffee. I got up and hurried along to the bathroom—and then hurried right out again, because it stood in need of cleaning and tidying before I could bathe there. I cursed Smith and Lucy impartially for the mess of damp towels and dissolving soap and made up my mind to eat as much of their bacon and eggs as I could stuff into me, to get even. As it happened, it didn't work, because they had provided amply for me.

Lucy, with every red curl in place and her face painted on for the day, trilled a cheerful good morning at me. "I was just going in to see if you'd died. You'll get fat if you lie around in bed all morning. Ken went out and bought some supplies, and I cooked breakfast for us—isn't it fun? And we're going to throw a party."

I groaned, and Ken looked up at me.

"Don't be so grim. Don't you ever get any fun out of life? Look at Lucy."

I looked. Dyed hair, girdle and figure fighting it out, false teeth, and the age of fifty just around the corner, if it hadn't already caught up.

"Very nice," I said politely.

Lucy narrowed her eyes at me, and Ken said significantly, "If you were one of my privates I'd fix you."

"Sergeants are all the same. Bullies."

"It relieves your inhibitions to be a bully," Ken said, turning the gas off under the coffee. "Now if I were a lieutenant I couldn't do any bullying."

"I suppose that's why you're not a lieutenant."

He had picked up two plates of bacon and eggs and started toward the dining room with them, but he put them back on the kitchen table, turned to me, put his hands around my neck, and squeezed.

"Smile," he said ominously.

I smiled, and he released the pressure just before my eyes popped out.

"I love brute strength," Lucy said wistfully. "Don't you, Eugenia?"

I opened my mouth, but Ken loomed over me and waved a large finger under my nose.

"No more sarcasm. This family has got to pull together. Sweetness and light—at least on the surface."

We carried the food into the dining room and sat down at the table, which Lucy had arranged rather elaborately. Ken looked it over and said, "Ahh no, Lucy—you'll have to cut corners, or the kitchen detail isn't going to like it."

"Who's the kitchen detail?" I asked sharply.

"Well, you are," Ken said, "naturally. I went out and bought the stuff, Lucy cooked it, and it's up to you to do the dishes."

I shook my head.

"Listen, Sergeant. I was invited to this breakfast—but hereafter, bear in mind that I go out for all meals. I'm here to rest, and I intend to rest. I'm not even going to clean my room or make my bed—except once, and that's when I leave."

"Incredible," he said, staring at me. He raised his great shoulders and dropped them again. "I couldn't stand that, so I suppose I'll have to make your bed for you myself."

Lucy let out a yell of laughter. "But, Ken—how marvelous! Will you make mine too?"

"You girls are sissies," he said disgustedly. "We don't have any housework problems in the Army—the boys do it all themselves, and have plenty of time left over for other things. It needs a little organization and system, that's all. It would be downright damfoolish to go out for all our meals—it's too expensive, and the meals would be no good and insufficient. Now if you girls will only give me a hand we can have decent food and a clean house, and still have plenty of time for fun. Come on, we'll clear these dishes away first." He put on a frilled and embroidered apron that was hanging behind the door in the kitchen and started to wash whatever articles were within reach of his long arms. It was all Lucy and I could do to keep him supplied with dishes and to get them wiped, and in no time at all he had finished and was mopping up the pool of water he had made around the sink.

He removed the dainty little apron, which was now drenched and wilted, and made for the hall.

"Come on, girls—I want you to watch me, and I'll show you how a bed should be made."

He went to my room and started his demonstration by pulling all the bedclothes off the bed and starting from scratch. He put the bottom sheet on and stretched it so tightly that I feared it would rip, and then he started to fool around with the corners. He said you should always make square corners with your sheets, and that we'd better pay particular attention.

Lucy and I got bored after a while. She went in and made her bed, and I went along and made Ken's, and then we drifted back, but he was still working on his masterpiece, so we went off again and did a little dusting. In the end we found him dreamily regarding the neatly made bed, but I noticed that Mary's fancy spread was folded over a chair.

"Wonderful!" I said, peering around his elbow. "What about the spread? Shouldn't we put that on to keep the sheets clean?"

"You can if you want to," he said reluctantly, "but it seems all wrong to cover up a smooth job like that."

"All right," I agreed, "anything for art. We'll leave it the way it is."

"Good." He straightened up and turned away. "Now what else has to be done?"

"Not a thing, dear," said Lucy, and patted his arm. "Eugenia and I puttered around a little, and the place looks charming, so let's plan our party."

"What about the marketing?" Ken asked sternly.

I snatched up a book and fled to the little balcony.

It was nice out there, and I relaxed in one of the chairs and lit a cigarette. From inside the apartment I heard Ken bellow, "For God's sake, who did this?" and figured that probably he had discovered his bed, which I had made without square corners. I propped my feet on the other chair and looked at the adjoining section of the balcony. The thing was an architectural mistake, I thought, and a bad one. There was no privacy for either side, and it was a perfectly simple matter to step over the barrier and enter the next apartment for whatever fell purpose you might have in mind. However, I wasn't paying the rent, so I yawned and opened my book.

Three minutes later Mrs. Budd stepped out onto the balcony. She glanced at me, found me absorbed in my book, and said, "Don't let me disturb you, my dear—you go right ahead with your reading."

I said, "Thanks," and concentrated deeply.

She allowed two minutes to pass and then observed, "You know, you remind me of my daughter—she has hair like yours, that sort of golden brown. Such a pretty girl. And even though she says so herself, I know she never ran off with that old stick of a Homer."

CHAPTER FOUR

I LOOKED AT THE woman and wondered how any daughter of hers could have turned out a beauty. Her figure was clumsily heavy, and she had small eyes and a big nose. Her iron-gray hair was arranged in various rolls and swoops—and with all this, she had the audacity to wear a yellow dress and red shoes.

"I don't quite understand you," I said after a moment. "Why wouldn't your daughter be with Homer if she told you she was? Did she telephone?"

"No." Mrs. Budd raised her yellow bosom on a long sigh. "She sent a card from Binghamton, but there wasn't very much on it just that I was not to worry, that she and Homer had eloped and she was feeling fine."

"It does seem odd," I agreed. "Mr. Emerson is so attractive, while poor old Homer—"

"But that's it—exactly!" Mrs. Budd broke in eagerly, and it was obvious that she felt a tremendous relief in being able to talk of what troubled her— even to a total stranger. "John is attractive, and I know he liked the women and all that, but he was a good husband to Betty. She used to get furious when he paid any special attention to some woman, but I kept telling her that she should overlook those things and keep her home together. She had no patience, though she always said she'd sooner he overlooked a few of her faults, and she wasn't going to be bothered keeping a second-grade home together. I thought and said that she was wrong—but she wouldn't listen. Of course, I know she'd have left him before if it hadn't been for her little girl."

"There's a little girl?" I asked, surprised.

Mrs. Budd nodded. "She's at camp just now. But whenever Betty talked of going to Reno she always planned to take little Eleanor with her. Every time she got really serious about it John always talked her around and promised to behave himself. As a matter of fact, he was behaving pretty well—for him, that is—when Betty suddenly ups and runs off with that awful old Homer." She paused for a moment, and added with less melancholy, "Mary was fit to be tied."

"But you don't think that she did run off with Homer?"

"No, I don't—it isn't reasonable, and I think it was just some sort of a blind."

I shook my head at her. "Every girl has her pride, and you can't convince me that anyone would admit to running off with Homer, unless it were sad fact."

Mrs. Budd sighed again and settled the amber beads at her neck. "Perhaps—I can't try to explain it—but I know that Betty never went away with Homer. Why, she used to say the most dreadful things about him behind his back—although he was always nice to her."

"Did Mary ever hear from Homer?" I asked curiously.

"Oh no—no indeed! Poor Homer! He'd be afraid even to send her a card." She laughed a little and then sobered up again. "I wish I could hear from Betty again—I've been simply frantic with worry. Of course John's been wonderful. He says I'm to stay on here, always, that I'm needed to take care of Eleanor and run the house, and he declares that he will never marry again, or even bother to divorce Betty."

A neatly uniformed young maid stuck her head through the glass doors and mentioned that lunch was ready, and Mrs. Budd nodded to me and bustled off.

I glanced at my watch and saw that it was only half past twelve, but decided that she probably had to get up early in the morning to get all her talking done.

I considered Homer with a certain amount of interest and reflected that when these absolutely faithful men did stray they usually went off the deep end for keeps—while a philanderer like John probably would never have left his wife. Not that I blamed Betty—I approved her conclusion that it was not worth while to keep a second-grade home together.

I shrugged it away, mentally cursed the architect who had embroidered double balconies onto the building, and picked up my book—but I hadn't even found my place before Lucy came flying out to interrupt me.

She and Smith were making out an invitation list for their party, but they were somewhat short of men—so many in the Army, Lucy apologized—and did I know any that I could get to come out from New York?

I didn't point out that her contemporaries were too old for active or any service; I merely said no, and that since I wouldn't be attending the party they needn't bother about a man for me.

"Don't be such an absolute sour lemon," Lucy shrilled. "You're living here, aren't you? And you'll have to be at the party—naturally. You must know tons of nice men in New York. My dear, if you're afraid of my poaching—"

"Look, Lucy," I said firmly. "I'm not asking any men to come and make free with Mary's apartment, so don't waste your breath over it. And incidentally, have you asked her if you can give a party here? You know how she is about cigarettes and coasters under drinks."

She evaded my eyes and became absorbed in one of her long, glittering nails. "Oh, Ken'll fix it with Mary. Heavens, she couldn't be unpatriotic enough to object to a soldier enjoying his furlough. In fact, Eugenia, I don't think you're showing the right spirit yourself. There isn't so much we women can do—but I'm helping Ken all I can, trying to cheer him up, not thinking of myself—"

"Take off the false face," I begged. "When are you having your party?"

She abandoned her nail and began to sparkle again. "Tonight. Ken says it has to be, because of that Alice. She has a date with a sailor tonight, and Ken says the sailor might be glad to save expenses, because he's been on leave since a week ago Friday, and he must be down to borrowing by this time. Do you suppose it's this Alice he's engaged to? Ken, I mean."

"No," I said, "it's probably a dark horse. But Alice—now there's a girl who could provide you with extra men."

"Why, didn't I *think* of that!" Lucy screamed. "Of course! She's the type that has the men lying up against her door, howling. I'll tell Ken."

She bounded off, and I took up my book. I figured I should have about an hour while Mrs. Budd had her lunch—more, if she were the type that took a nap afterward.

I didn't reckon with all the possibilities, though, because I had read only a page and a half when Ken came out and joined me.

"I've been looking everywhere for you," he said aggrievedly.

"Oh, I'm so sorry. I'll hang a bell around my neck so that you'll always know where I am."

He grinned at me. "Someday I'm going to smack you one, just for the fun of it."

"What did you do with Lucy?" I asked idly.

"I chained her to the telephone. She's rounding up the personnel for our party."

"Well, I hope you have a good time," I said. "But it seems like a lot of work and expense for nothing."

"The work and expense are my lookout," he said cheerfully. "The guests are bringing their own sandwiches and liquor, and I'll clean up after them. But Lucy says you're not coming."

"No."

"Well, look—as a matter of fact, I wish you would. I need you badly, because I want to have eyes only for you all night."

I laughed. "You mean you want to make Alice sit up and take notice. But you must have a bunch of other girls coming who could do the job for you."

He shook his head. "She knows all the others."

"And she knows you're not like that about any of them?"

He nodded, with a serious expression on his face.

"Why do you want to run after a girl that you have to get that way? If you get her."

"Listen," he said, "Alice's beauty may be only skin-deep, but it certainly looks good on the outside."

I considered it for a moment and asked, "Are you inviting the man next door—the brokenhearted Emerson?"

"Oh, there you go!" he groaned. "He has all the women swooning in the aisles. Of course he's invited. Lucy asked him first of all—phoned him at his office. He accepted, too. That guy loves parties—with all the dames casting themselves at his feet."

"Only I won't be able to, will I? Because I have to cast myself at your feet."

"That's the girl," he said, and gave my shoulder a pat that nearly dislocated it. "But don't look so bored about it—I'll keep you entertained."

"Are you going to do card tricks?"

Lucy came to the door behind us. "Here you are, children! Eugenia darling, Mary's on the phone and wants to talk to you."

I went along to the telephone, and Lucy followed and stood close beside me.

"Mary?"

"Eugenia, I hate to disturb you like this, when you're supposed to be getting a rest, but I'm simply out of my mind with worry, and I want some advice. I *know* Homer never ran off with Betty Emerson. In the first place, he'd never have dreamed of leaving me—and anyway, they weren't even slightly interested in each other—I'd have known if they were—I'd have sensed it. I think something has happened to him, and I must find out. Do you think I should call in the police?"

CHAPTER FIVE

I WAS SUDDENLY BORED and exasperated with Homer and his wild oat, and I wished to high heaven that I had never come to Mary's apartment. All I had wanted—and needed, too—was a little rest.

"Eugenia, please!" Mary was fussing in my ear. "You must help me. I'm asking for only a little clearheaded advice."

"But I hardly knew Homer," I protested. "I saw him only a few times when you brought him into New York. How could I possibly know what he'd do or wouldn't do? You ought to know whether he went off of his own accord or not. What about his clothes and luggage? Did he take them?"

"Well—but that's just it—I'm not *sure.* Homer had so much stuff— clothes and traveling bags and things. I did look once, but I couldn't tell whether anything was missing. Of course when they disappeared together we all assumed that they had gone away together—and then right away Mrs. Budd had that card from Betty, you see. But I never heard from Homer, and I've been thinking the whole thing over quietly here, and I *know* Homer wouldn't just run away with Betty, like that."

I drew a long breath and said patiently, "Yes—I see. Well, in that case I think perhaps you'd better call in the police. They'll find out where he really is, and at least you won't be fretting over that part of it any more."

"Yes—you're right!" Mary said with sudden decision. "Then I'll do that. My dear, you don't know the *relief*—to have decided on something definite! I shall have to come to town then. Tomorrow."

"Why don't you make it tonight? I'm told that we're having a party," I said, and felt like a tattletale. But I'd had an uneasy feeling that she ought to know.

However, it was wasted effort, for she said abstractedly, "I know—Lucy told me—it's nice for Ken. But, Eugenia, just see that there are ashtrays everywhere, will you? And coasters. The coasters are in the corner cupboard in the dining room, and there are a lot of extra ashtrays there too. And for a party like that I always use the cheap glasses in the kitchen. I keep my good ones in the dining room—so don't get them mixed, will you?"

"I'll take the utmost care," I told her. "I'll protect your things with my life."

"Well, it isn't that I mind, really, and I don't like to fuss or anything, but if you're a little careful ahead of time it saves so much."

"You're absolutely right," I agreed, shifting my weight from foot to foot. "Anyway, don't worry—I'll see to everything."

"Well, that's wonderful, dear, and I'll see you tomorrow."

I said good-by and hung up—and then bumped into Lucy, who had been standing directly behind me.

She asked immediately, "What did she say?"

"New recipe for baked spinach," I said, and wended my way. I went along to my bedroom and closed the door firmly after me, and then discovered that the book I had been reading was still out on the little balcony. I got another one out of my suitcase and stretched out on the bed with the pillows propped behind me. I was glad that the spread had been left off, so that I need not worry about messing it up.

I read over three chapters, this time, before Lucy interrupted me with a call to lunch.

"We've lost Ken," she said dolefully. "He got himself a date for lunch—but it wasn't with that Alice. Wouldn't you love to know who he's almost engaged to?"

I yawned and flung my book down to the bottom of the bed. "I do know."

"What! Who?" Lucy yelled.

"Nobody. He's working toward it, and when he says 'almost' he's giving himself encouragement."

"Oh." She considered it, and then the sun came out on her face. "I'll bet you're right, at that, and I'm glad. I hate to see the young men get hooked, don't you?"

I yawned again and dropped my feet to the floor. "No," I said, "it's the young girls I worry about. There they stand at the brink of life—sweet, shy, eager young creatures trying to see through the mists of the future all the lovely and exciting things that are going to happen to them—and when the mists clear away they find themselves surrounded by cooking, house cleaning, dirty dishes, and soiled diapers—all day and every day and half the night—"

"Listen, that lunch will be spoiled if you don't hurry," Lucy observed, poking at her hair in front of the mirror. "I made a sweet batch of hot biscuits. I thought Ken would be here."

"He should have told you," I said sympathetically as we went out into the hall. "Now we'll have to eat them ourselves."

She paused to finger a pair of small busts that adorned the top of the antique desk, and ended by turning them around to face each other.

"They look better that way—don't you think? More cheerful."

"Much more cheerful," I agreed. "At least they're staring at each other with their sightless eyes, and not at us."

"That's right." She surveyed them for a moment, gave a satisfied nod, and marched on into the dining room.

She had prepared a delicate little luncheon that would have been no more than an hors d'oeuvre to Ken, had he remained. We disposed of it promptly and then leaned back and lighted cigarettes.

"Now one of us has to go out and do the shopping," Lucy said busily, "and the other will have to stay and fix the place up all ready for the party."

I groaned aloud. "I came here for a rest—I didn't want this party in the first place—I didn't even want to come to it. I hate all the bustle of getting ready for a party."

"Eugenia, I think you're downright queer," Lucy said seriously. "Trying to crawl into a hole all the time and pull the dirt in after you. It isn't normal. Now all you have to do is go out and buy these things—I have the list all made out."

"You do the shopping, then," I sighed, "and I'll stay and hang the festoons."

But she looked so crestfallen that I gave up and went to get a hat. I showed her the coasters and extra ashtrays and the cheap glasses in the kitchen, and then took her list and departed.

I glanced at the thing when I got outside and found that nearly every item had a paragraph of explanation beneath it—and at the same time I realized that I had no money but my own with which to pay for everything. I felt that the situation needed reviewing, and after a moment's hesitation I turned into an air-cooled drugstore and sought a booth at the back. A waitress appeared and rattled off, with apparent relish, a string of things that they didn't have.

"It's all right," I said mildly. "I just wanted a vanilla soda, or anything else in that line that you happen to have."

She went off, looking disappointed, and I hauled out Lucy's list and started to go over it. However, I got stalled on the second item when a woman's clear carrying voice, in the booth behind me, said, "Darling, you do love me, don't you? You told me you did—and you know I love you. I want to hear you say it again—now."

There was a male laugh, and a familiar voice observed, "Don't get so serious, Dotty—you'll have lines between your eyebrows. Finish up your ice cream and let's get out of here."

I took a cautious glance at the mirror that lined the walls. John Emerson and a blonde—presumably one of the ladies at his feet.

"But, John," she was saying—and she had lowered her voice and put a throb into it. "You haven't told me you loved me since Betty left—not once since she left. And that makes me think—well, quite a few things."

"All of them right," I murmured, forgetting myself.

"Now look, darling—" he began, but she interrupted him fiercely.

"I want to know—I must know—are you going to divorce her and marry me?"

John's voice began to hint his exasperation. "Dotty, there is no point whatever in our discussing this now. I would have to wait some years before getting a divorce for desertion—and I can assure you that I will not divorce Eleanor's mother on any other grounds. Eleanor comes first with me, and you know it."

"But, John dear—of course. Please don't be angry with me—you know I understand all that. But it's only two years for desertion, and I'd wait—if only you'd tell me to. If I only *knew.*"

I wanted to urge her to shut up—but since I couldn't, I tried to close my ears and concentrate on the list. It turned out to be a collection of trifles—bits and pieces of decoration, and candies of various colors—all of it foolish and none of it necessary, as far as I could see.

My waitress returned and set a chocolate marshmallow sundae before me and departed again with a swish of her skirts.

I picked up my spoon and heard John Emerson say coldly, "I'm afraid that you took that black eye too seriously."

CHAPTER SIX

THEY HAD LEFT the booth, and I turned and quite frankly stared as they passed. John Emerson, with his eyes on his check, was fumbling in his pocket for change, while the blonde drooped along at his elbow. Neither of them noticed me.

I returned to my sundae, gave it a look of loathing because I never have liked chocolate, marshmallow, or sundaes, and decided that I was not going to eat it—war or no war. I got up and wondered whether it would be honest to walk out without paying, since I hadn't been satisfied, and the customer is always right—and then I realized that the customer wasn't half as right as he used to be, so I paid anyway.

I went out into hot, bright sunshine and walked along slowly, thinking about John Emerson and what seemed to be his stock phrase to his lady friends: "you took that black eye too seriously." I wondered idly what color his own eyes were, and decided to look and see the next time he crossed my path.

I got Lucy's gewgaws as cheaply as I could and wondered whether she'd forgotten about food and drinks, since her list was made up of such items as "four yellow candles—two yards exactly same color satin ribbon." Why satin ribbon? Was she going to tie bows on the candles? And if not, what was she going to use it for?

I shrugged it away and arrived back at the apartment at last with numerous little packages dribbling out of my arms. It seemed too hot to go inside, so I made for a group of chairs that were arranged under a tree on the lawn at the side of the building. It was cooler there, and I sat in one of the chairs, cast my hat and the packages onto the ground, and lit a cigarette.

I was getting comfortably drowsy when two men came and sat close by. They seemed to be arguing, and their voices were deadly serious.

One of them, pudgy and perspiring, said, "I don't care what you say—it was cold." He mopped at his forehead, and after a moment's pause added, "In fact you could have thrown them against the wall and made it. You ought to have your head examined."

I looked at the other's head. It was younger and more shapely, and the eyes were draped with sunglasses. He arranged his thin mouth in lines of satisfied superiority and then opened it to say with obviously false courtesy, "And what was I supposed to do with the spade?"

"What spade?"

"I suppose you've forgotten about the spade I had. Just tell me where I could have put the spade, and. I'll go and have my head examined this afternoon."

The pudgy individual was silent for a moment, and then he said flatly, "You didn't have a spade."

The younger one smiled—nastily. "No spade? Then perhaps you can tell me what I did have?"

There was another brief silence, and then, "Seven clubs, five diamonds—"

"Oh, God!" I said. "Bridge."

They both started, and turned to stare at me.

"Well, I'm sorry," I said defensively, "but I couldn't make out what you were talking about. I was puzzled, so I had to listen."

The younger man was clearly impatient of the interruption, but the other one laughed.

"Go ahead," I urged them. "I know you want to find that spade."

But the fat man wouldn't have it. He asked me if it were hot enough for me, made the usual comment on the humidity, and went on to say that he thought it might rain in a day or two. The younger one stood it for a while and then excused himself with brittle courtesy and left us to the weather.

It developed almost immediately that I was talking to J.X. Boxton, who admitted almost in the same breath that he was an undertaker. Since he was the first undertaker I had ever met, I looked him over curiously and found that he appeared to be somewhat like other people.

I was wondering whether he would talk shop or not when Lucy suddenly appeared in our midst.

"My dear!" she shrieked. "I've been calling you till my throat's ragged. Do you know what time it is? And all we have to do! I was up there on the balcony, simply yelling—I can't *imagine* why you didn't hear me—why, hello, Mr. Boxton."

Mr. Boxton, who had got to his feet, bowed gracefully and urged her to sit down.

"No, no—we have to get upstairs. We've a party on, and we'll have to work like fiends so much to do."

She began to gather up the packages, and then an idea hit her: "Mr. Boxton, you must come to our party—it's just spur-of-the-moment, you know. If you're not busy?"

His face lit up, and it appeared that he wasn't busy. He said he thought he'd drop around, and then gallantly carried all our packages up for us.

When we got inside Lucy confided to me that he was really an old bore but she'd had to ask him because of the shortage of men.

"Entirely illogical," I commented.

The apartment was transformed. Every piece of furniture in the living room and dining room had been moved, and while I eyed Mary's fancy glasses reposing on the table—instead of the cheap ones from the kitchen—Lucy bustled around and put the yellow candles into the candelabra. I waited to see what she was going to do with the ribbon, but she merely took it off to her room. I followed her, but it did me no good. She put the ribbon down on her dressing table and said, "We'll have some sandwiches—I have them all ready—and I'll make some coffee. We haven't time for anything else."

"All right," I agreed, and submitted to being pushed out of her room. "But listen—do you know anything about John Emerson's black eye?"

She said, "For heaven's sake! Some husband probably gave it to him."

"No—I don't mean that. Hasn't he any other kind of a black eye?"

"My dear, I don't know what you're talking about. Both his eyes are black—really, I've never seen such dark eyes. Fascinating. Now listen, when Ken comes in don't tell him about my inviting Mr. Boxton. Ken doesn't like him."

"Rubbish!" I said, feeling contrary. "I like Mr. Boxton—I think he's a lovely little man. And why should Smith have anything to say about the people I want at this party?"

"Don't be dumb, honey, you know we have to snake around the men a little, to get anywhere in this world. Shh—here he is."

He was, and he had the food and drink. He seemed to be in high good humor and said cheerfully, "Hello, girls. I couldn't get cakes with yellow icing, Lucy, but I got some very nice pink ones."

Lucy almost cried. "Pink is so naive," she wailed, "and it won't match anything—"

"Maybe I'd better run out and change the candles and ribbon," I suggested, grinning.

To my horror, she actually considered it for a moment; but then she shook her head regretfully. "No—it's too late. Come on—we'll have the sandwiches and coffee now."

Smith was horrified in turn and muttered, "No!" but Lucy swept us both into the kitchen and put the meal before us. She and I had to eat at top speed in order to get barely enough, for Smith ate the sandwiches whole, with his hand hovering over the plate and his eyes on the ceiling—pretending he didn't know what he was doing. In no time at all there was nothing but coffee left, and we were again free to converse.

Lucy put a cigarette into her long black holder and said thoughtfully, "That Budd woman seems possessed by an idea that her Betty could never have run away with Homer Fredon."

"She doesn't want to believe it," Ken said shrewdly. "But old Homer was pulling down plenty, in his job, and women like money."

"But since he's left the job he's no longer pulling down plenty," I pointed out. "I think it's odd, myself. He might have been piling it up in some other bank, I suppose—but Mary must have known what he was making, and I should think she'd have spotted it, if any sizable amount was being deflected."

"Something to that," Ken conceded.

"Maybe he piled it up in his own bank and drew it all out just before they skipped," Lucy said without much conviction.

I shook my head. "He and Mary had a joint account. If he'd drawn most of it out she'd have known about it and would have been satisfied that he did go off with this Betty. But she isn't satisfied, and that's why she's calling in the police."

They both yelled and began to clamor for more information, but I told them to ask Mary about it when she arrived in the morning. This diverted them and brought forth a good deal of groaning. If Mary was arriving in the morning they would have to set to and clean up the mess right after the party, instead of being able to sleep it off first.

"Well, anyway," Lucy said, "the Emerson maid—that little Suzy—is coming in to help, so it won't be so bad. She can clean up as she goes along, maybe."

Ken stood up, took a last wistful glance at the empty sandwich plate, and said he thought he'd better go and dress. He brushed some crumbs from his uniform and added that it was a pity he couldn't change his suit.

Lucy clicked her tongue in all seriousness and murmured that it was a shame, and Ken went on out into the foyer and snapped on the light. There was a moment's silence, and then he called back, "Mary's slipping. Homer's been gone at least a week, and his golf shoes are still slopping around under a chair here."

CHAPTER SEVEN

LUCY LAUGHED. "Probably poor Mary didn't feel like touching them with a ten-foot pole. If I were in her place I'd throw them in the garbage."

I got up and went out into the hall, feeling puzzled and a little queer. I had dusted out there in the morning, and I had seen no shoes of any sort.

Lucy followed me, saying, "Do let's get dressed—it's late."

I was examining the golf shoes, which stood side by side under a chair, and I said abstractedly, "But these were not here this morning, Lucy. Did you bring them out?"

She glanced down without interest. "Of course not. They must have been there—you just didn't notice them. I don't know what Mary thinks she's doing, anyway—leaving Homer's stuff around. His old pipe is lying beside his chair in the living room, too, and he never got away with anything like that when he was home. She wouldn't let him even leave a collar button lying around."

"But I'm telling you—these shoes were not here this morning "

"For Pete's sake!" said Lucy in utter exasperation. "Will you come and get dressed! People will be pouring in here at any minute!"

She swished off to her own room, and I went slowly to mine. I decided that it wouldn't take me long to dress—I had no formal clothes with me, and it was only a matter of a change, so I lay down on the bed for a while, with my arms folded behind my head.

As a matter of fact, I was seriously considering a return to New York. There was something queer about the situation at Mary's, when she and Mrs. Budd were both so convinced that Betty and Homer had not eloped together—and for no really valid reason. Then, why should Homer's shoes and pipe suddenly appear—to say nothing about John Emerson's damned black eye?

I crossed my legs, settled my head more comfortably, and wondered what excuse I could give for leaving so abruptly. I didn't want Mary to think me ungracious, and I was pretty sure she'd be upset about it—and of course Lucy would be disappointed. She was having a wonderful time.

Well, I thought, sighing, it's only Tuesday—I'll be seeing Mary in the morning, and perhaps I can think of a good excuse by then. I'd go back to my own apartment in New York—or even out to Aunt Martha's on Long Island—and hear about her operation again.

The first of the guests arrived, just then, and passed down the hall with a roar, and on into the living room. I swung my feet off the bed, reached for a cigarette, and sat there wondering whether I couldn't just forget the party.

There was the barest excuse for a knock at the door, and Sergeant Smith loomed into the room. He deposited his vast proportions on the bedspread—which still lay folded on a chair—and regarded me with a certain amount of sorrow.

"There's something wrong with you, though it doesn't show on the outside—or not much. You're young, and you seem to be healthy, and yet a party doesn't appeal to you. Now what is it? Some sort of a neurosis? Or are you in mourning for an absent boyfriend? And that's a dumb way to mourn, anyhow."

"What would a sergeant know about a neurosis?" I asked politely.

"Never mind that. Just tell me—is it a boyfriend or isn't it?"

"I'll tell you, if you tell me first to whom you're engaged. Not only is it necessary for Lucy to know, but I'm curious myself."

His eyes dropped, and he studied his knuckles with a very faint smile.

"You needn't have taken that quite so literally," he said after a moment. "I'm not actually engaged to anyone."

"But you hope to be soon?"

The smile became a little more definite, and he said, "Yes, that's it."

"Alice, I suppose."

"Good God, no!" he exploded. "I couldn't get Alice—too much competition."

"Such a pity!" I murmured. "Has she arrived yet?"

"Don't be naive." He got to his feet and explained, "She doesn't actually send a page boy with a trumpet on ahead of her, but she's waiting until the gang is all assembled before she makes her entrance. Like you. Now get ready, will you—and come on out."

"All right, Pop," I agreed, putting out my cigarette. "But listen—did you put Homer's shoes under that chair in the hall?"

He turned with his hand on the doorknob and said, "No, I didn't. Why?"

"Well, they weren't there this morning."

"Lucy must have done it—probably some sort of a joke, bless her little heart."

I shook my head. "She says not."

He considered it for a moment, with his eyes on the panels of the door, and then he shrugged. "Oh well, maybe they walked out by themselves," he said, and took himself off.

I went along to the bathroom and then had to stay there for quite some time, because a fresh batch of guests arrived, and some of them lingered in the hall, gossiping with Lucy. It was all about somebody's baby who had caused a great to-do by turning out to be a girl instead of a boy. It seemed the mother wanted to call it Paula, Jr., while the father wanted to try again and see if he couldn't get a Paul, Jr.

All this took considerable time, but they dispersed at last, and I was able to slip into my room, where I adorned myself in the most festive garments I had with me.

As it happened, my entrance, coincided with that of Alice—but I was mere stardust. She was accompanied by a sailor, two marines, and a thin civilian. The sailor looked sulky, but Alice was radiant—a nicely covered blonde, beautiful, well dressed, and with plenty of personality. I managed to stand at the entrance to the living room with her while she surveyed the throng—although she tried to push me out.

Ken made his way swiftly through the mob, cried, "Alice!" and held out both arms.

She caroled, "Darling! You look wonderful," threw her arms around his neck and kissed him, after which she swept on around the room with her entourage. Ken was left holding the bag with me.

"Something wrong with that," I said dubiously. "It looked more as though you were trying to make me jealous than her."

He said, "Ah, come and have a drink. You look very nice in your party burlap—I wish Lucy could have done me as much credit."

I looked around hastily, and found Lucy and the yellow satin ribbon at one and the same time. It was wound around her head, with the red curls sticking out here and there. Her dress appeared to be a white lace negligee.

"You're raving," I said. "She's very artistic. If I'd used my head I could have done as well myself. Only mine would be pale pink to match the cakes."

"I don't know what you're talking about," he muttered vaguely, and led me to a table on which reposed several of Mary's best glasses. He supplied me with a drink and then disappeared in the middle of a group who had walked into him and carried him off.

I found myself in the company of Mrs. Budd. We had reached chapter six of her appendectomy when John Emerson stepped in and delivered me.

"Mother, do see whether Suzy is attending to things properly in the kitchen. You know you are the only one who can manage her."

Mrs. Budd glowed, patted her silk bosom, and said, "All right, dear—of course."

She trotted off, and I glanced after her curiously, reflecting that tonight, at least, her grief for Betty seemed to be in abeyance. She appeared to think very highly of John, though.

He offered me a cigarette, and, looking him over, I decided that there was no doubt about his being smooth. I wondered idly if I were to be his next victim and, when he threw me over, if he would tell me that I had taken the damned black eye too seriously. I looked at his eyes and saw that they were very dark and were regarding me at the moment with a faint amusement.

"Worrying about what's going on at the office in your absence?"

"No," I said. "I put everything out of my mind."

"It's never a bad idea to relax once in a while." He was silent for a moment, and when he spoke again he had dropped the banter from his voice. "Is Mary coming back tomorrow?"

I nodded. "She's not satisfied about Homer, and she wants to go to the police with it."

"I know—Lucy was telling me." He frowned down at his cigarette and added, "I'm rather relieved, on the whole, because I'm not satisfied about Betty either. I'm convinced that she never went off with Homer—but I'd give a lot to know who it really was."

I shook my head. "I can't see why she'd write a card and say it was Homer."

The line of his jaw hardened, and he explained briefly. "To cover up the real culprit. I've an idea who it might be, too."

"Well, but she'd have to know that Homer was going away at the same time—and where did he go, anyhow?"

He shrugged it away indifferently. "Homer was a queer bird—no knowing what he had in his head. Anyway, I don't blame Mary for getting the police after him."

I was growing tired of the subject, and by way of a diversion I remarked, "You really have the blackest eyes I have ever seen."

To my astonishment, his face darkened to an angry red, and he said nastily, "The pupil of the eye is the only part that is actually black—the iris is never darker than a very dark brown."

CHAPTER EIGHT

I SHRUGGED and sipped at my drink, resisting a desire to beg him to keep his shirt on. He had turned slightly away from me and was staring across the room, looking thoroughly annoyed. I glanced at him once or twice, and was just about to remind him that he had twice referred to a black eye, himself, when Alice's sailor walked in on me.

The sailor wanted to dance. He swallowed my drink for me first and then steered me to one end of the living room, where a rug had been taken up to make a dance floor. The rest of the gang were already there, milling around, and there was not even elbow room, but the sailor nevertheless went through his extensive repertoire with ease. My part was not difficult—I could not have taken a wrong step if I would, because he firmly put me where I was supposed to go. There was only one place for my feet, and that was the spot that kept me from falling over.

The music stopped, and everybody left the dance floor for the open spaces of the carpet—except the sailor and myself. He merely called out to Joe to put on something else, and hummed his own music in the meantime, without relaxing the death grip on me. But his eyes were following Alice.

"Don't you think," I suggested breathlessly, "that she'd be more jealous if we were to sit on a couch while you tell me your life history?"

"What do you mean?" he demanded, and added almost immediately, "Oh, what the hell—okay."

He brought his routine to such an abrupt halt that I staggered, and then he led me to a small love seat. We sat down, and he draped his arm along the back and more or less loomed over me, while he endeavored to clarify his position.

"Listen, babe, I don't have to waste time on those methods—if I want them. I just go out and get them."

"My mistake, pal," I murmured. "I'm sorry."

He waved an arm. "That's all right. But just don't get ideas in your head."

"No, no—of course not."

"Look at poor old John," he said after a moment. "Can't get over it because Betty left him."

I took a look at poor old John, who was standing against the wall holding a drink and looking at nothing.

"I didn't think he cared so much about that," I said tentatively.

"Oh yes, he did," replied the sailor with a shade of reproof. "He cared a hell of a lot about Betty. He couldn't help playing around with other dames, but he never got tied up with them. I even told Betty once that she shouldn't pay attention to that stuff—but she told me to shut up."

"Did she play around with other men?"

"Well, I don't know, exactly," he said, squinting thoughtfully. "Betty was deep. But if she was—and she must have been—she clammed up about it."

"She must have played around with Homer."

He snarled disgustedly. "You or anybody can't get me to believe that."

"Well, why did she write and say she was with him—and where is he, anyhow?"

The sailor settled himself more comfortably and said in a voice of great earnestness, "Here's my theory. She was in up to her neck with somebody, and she found out Homer was going to skip—"

"Why?"

"Homer? Maybe he got sick of hanging his head out of the window every time he wanted to smoke his pipe." He interrupted himself to laugh uproariously and then went on, "I think Betty is living near some camp, pretending to be somebody's wife. She figured she might get the soldier into trouble—busted or something, if it got out—and yet they couldn't bear to be parted—so she used old Homer to cover up."

"It still doesn't explain why Homer left," I said, shaking my head.

The sailor ignored it. He had become very serious indeed. "Poor John, he really feels this. He loved that girl—loved her with all his heart—"

"Don't give me that stuff," I said inelegantly. "How could he love her with all his heart and then humiliate her by playing around with all sorts of other women?"

"They were just a series of beautiful friendships," said the sailor, and he didn't laugh, either.

I looked around the room and caught sight of the blonde who had been in the drugstore with John Emerson. She was talking to two other women with a certain amount of animation and sparkle. I dug the sailor in the ribs and asked him to identify her.

"Oh, her," he said without interest. "That's Mary's best friend—don't you know her? She's a widow. Nice gal."

"One of John's flames?"

"Yeah—sure. Only I think it's burned out."

"Who's the current flame, then?"

He thought it over for a while, and then shook his head. "Nope—nobody. Not for the last few months."

"How do you know?" I persisted.

"Poor old John's dames are always common gossip. My girlfriends always write me all the gossip, and John hasn't figured."

"Oh. Well, what's the name of the one who has just burned out?"

"Dotty, you mean—Dotty Manchester." He spared Dotty a glance and shook his head. "Poor old Bill Manchester—one of those eye doctors, y'know—swell practice. He got careless or something—got himself infected—up and died in a hurry."

I said I was sorry to hear it, and then found that he had more or less forgotten me. He was looking moodily across the room at Alice, who was having what appeared to be a very serious and intimate conversation with Ken.

"That girl, Alice," I said sorrowfully, "just doesn't care whose heart she breaks. Take any girl's sweetheart away "

The sailor snapped back to attention. "Ken your fella? Okay—we'll soon fix that."

He jumped up, pulled me to my feet, and began to drag me across the room. I yelled frantically, "Wait a minute—he isn't my fella!" but my voice was lost in the general uproar.

We brought up in front of Alice and Ken and the sailor went to the point with simple candor.

"Come on, Alice—ease off—you're breaking this little girl's heart. You come on along with me, honey."

Alice looked a little startled for a moment and then favored me with a contemptuous glance—as well she might. She gave Ken a mysterious smile that could have meant almost anything and moved off with her shining hair, her smooth silken draperies, and the sailor.

I searched for a cigarette and something to say to Ken, and found neither.

He looked me up and down and observed without venom, "You have a gall, lady, to be telling people that you've put a down payment on me."

"I didn't—" I began helplessly, but he waved a huge hand and interrupted me.

"Don't be adding more lies to all the rest. I'm nothing if not accommo-dating, and I'll *be* your boyfriend for a while. Will that make you happy?"

"No!" I bawled. "I don't want—"

"Tch, tch," said Ken. "Here, you come and have another drink, and you'll feel better."

He took me by the hand and dragged me to the dining room, where he poured a drink for me. Suzy was there, flushed and perspiring, and she looked up at us, opened her mouth as though she were about to speak, and then turned away and went off into the kitchen instead.

I sipped at my drink without enthusiasm, and then asked Ken if he knew what John Emerson meant by his "damned black eye."

Ken looked at me blankly. " 'Damned black eye'? That punk has two damned black eyes."

"You don't like him?"

"No, I don't," he said firmly. "I don't like his type—although I know the women lap it up."

"H'mm," I murmured absently, and considered approaching John Emer-son and asking him quite frankly to satisfy my curiosity. I decided against it, because I felt pretty sure that he'd merely lose his temper without telling me anything.

Instead I wandered away from Ken and sought Lucy out. I asked her, but she had no time or patience for me.

"I don't know," she said, brushing me aside. "Don't bother me. Can't you see I'm busy?"

She was, too—with Mr. Boxton, so I left her as requested.

I was feeling stubborn about the thing by that time, so I went in search of Mrs. Budd. I found her standing close to the foyer, beaming at the noisy crowd and fanning herself with a neat little handkerchief.

I dispensed with finesse and asked simply, "What does John mean when he talks about 'that damned black eye'?"

It was immediately apparent that she knew—and that she wasn't telling. She began to fan herself more violently and said in a flustered voice, "Why, I don't know, I'm sure. John's eyes are dark brown, anyway—people's eyes are never actually black, you know. When did John mention the black eye to you?"

"He didn't," I admitted. "I heard him say something about it to Mrs. Manchester, and I wondered what he meant."

"Oh," she said, and relaxed into a smile of relief. "It was nothing, I guess—just a figure of speech."

I felt that I'd been rude enough about something that was none of my business, and let it drop.

Mrs. Budd glanced out into the foyer and said in a bothered voice, "Now what in the world is the matter with Suzy?"

I looked and saw Suzy standing in the hall, with her head turned toward the front door. As we watched she turned and approached us in an uncertain fashion, and with another glance over her shoulder at the door.

"What is it, Suzy?" Mrs. Budd asked. "You know you have plenty to do. What are you standing about out here for?"

"Yes ma'am." Suzy cleared her throat and got her apron mixed in with her hands. "It's Mr. Homer. He's—in the kitchen."

CHAPTER NINE

MRS. BUDD AND I FLEW toward the kitchen and squeezed through the door together. Homer's old pipe lay on a table, still smoking, but he was not there.

Mrs. Budd turned to Suzy, who had followed us, and demanded excitedly, "Where is he?"

"I guess maybe in one of the bedrooms," Suzy said doubtfully. "I sort of watched the front door, in case he might slip out. See, he didn't want me to tell anyone he was here, and I said I wouldn't, but I kept thinking I ought to."

"Yes, quite right." Mrs. Budd hesitated and then started out of the kitchen with sudden decision. "I'm going to find him—I expect he's in his own bedroom."

I followed in her footsteps, and we went straight into Ken's bedroom. It was empty, and Mrs. Budd shook her head disappointedly. "He used to sleep here—it was his room."

She tried Lucy's room and mine, without result, and decided at last, with growing agitation, "Then he must be in Mary's room. Of course he never used to go there, much—she's so fussy about those worm-eaten old antiques of hers—but that's where he must be."

I was about to tell her that Mary's door was locked when she simply turned the knob and walked in. I supposed that Homer must have unlocked it—it seemed likely that he'd know where Mary was in the habit of keeping the key. Mrs. Budd and I gazed around the handsome apartment together—but there was no sign of Homer.

Suzy had followed us to the door and was still twisting at her limp apron. "Why don't you search the room?" she whispered. "He must be here."

Mrs. Budd said, "That will do, Suzy. You had better go and attend to your chores."

Suzy sighed, "Yes ma'am," and departed reluctantly, and Mrs. Budd went into the bathroom. She emerged again almost immediately with a worried frown between her brows.

"He's not there—he must have slipped out again—it's really very annoying." She looked helplessly around the room, tapping her foot nervously. "I must find him—he'll tell me where Betty is, so that I can get in touch with her."

I suggested that we look in the remaining bathroom, but when we got there we found that it was empty too.

"But he must have been here," I said. "Perhaps he slipped out when we went into Mary's room. I expect he'll be back—probably he doesn't want anyone to see him—wants to talk to Mary first."

She nodded. "But I want to talk to him too—I think he owes me that. I'm sure he could tell me where Betty is, and then I could tell John. Because John's wrong about Betty having gone off with some man—I think she's just hiding somewhere to teach him a lesson."

I couldn't agree with her, but as we turned back into the hall I reflected that it was a comforting theory for her to hold.

At the entrance to the living room we met Suzy again. She was mangling her apron more energetically than ever, and she suggested timidly but bravely, "You better search the whole place."

"We have just finished searching the place," said Mrs. Budd irritably. "Don't be silly."

"No," said Suzy, standing her ground. "I mean, look under things. You know."

"Get back to the kitchen," said Mrs. Budd, "and hurry. It's time to serve the supper."

Suzy departed, and Mrs. Budd began to elbow her way over to where John was standing. I watched her for a moment and then went back along the hall to the telephone.

Mary was both excited and angry. She held forth in a series of exclamations and eventually calmed to a point where she announced that she would come down first thing in the morning and told me to hold Homer in the apartment until she got there, if he turned up again.

I tried the door of Mary's bedroom again and found that it was still unlocked, but there was no key. I went to the desk and found that the key was where I had put it and after puzzling over it for a moment I came to the conclusion that it was Mary's regular habit to put the key of her room in the desk and that Homer knew it. I supposed that he must have been hiding in her room during the evening and had finally ventured out to smoke a pipe in the kitchen—because the poor old rabbit would hardly take such a liberty within the sacred walls of Mary's artistic bedroom.

I locked the bedroom again, replaced the key, and returned to the party. Suzy was trying to tell the multitude that a supper was laid out in the dining room, but her little pipe was completely lost in the general uproar. I turned and made for the dining room with all haste and found that only Mrs. Budd and John had managed to get in ahead of me. As a matter of fact, they seemed to be arguing and had paid no attention to the food, so I collected a tasty little meal for myself and sat down to eat it.

Mrs. Budd and John did not seem to notice me and went on with their argument.

" You should have *called* me," John was saying angrily. "I'd have gone after him and found him. Now it's too late—he's gone, and he may never come back."

"Now, dear, please don't get so excited—he'll come back, I feel quite sure of it. And Betty will too. I have such a strong feeling about it, John—I *know* she hasn't gone off with anyone. She's trying to show you how lonely your life is without her—and it is lonely, isn't it, dear?"

She looked up at him appealingly, and I coughed to let them know that I was there.

They turned around, and John came directly over to me. "I wish you had called me when Suzy told you about Homer. I feel sure that I could have found him."

"Oh well," I said easily, "I shouldn't worry about it—he's bound to turn up again. Apparently he doesn't like it, away from Mary."

John shrugged and turned to the table where the supper was laid out. I thought he looked worried and haggard, and Mrs. Budd, after watching him uneasily for a moment, went on into the kitchen, where I could hear her talking to Suzy.

John brought his supper over and sat down beside me. "Mary should know about this," he said, frowning down at his plate.

"I called her—she's coming down in the morning."

He looked up in some surprise. "In the morning? Not now—at once?"

"Well, no," I said. "She doesn't want to come rushing back the minute Homer shows his guilty face—he might get above himself."

The party came pouring into the dining room in a body at that point, and before long most of my coffee was in the saucer, while at least half of my salad lay around on the floor. John was completely surrounded, since, despite all Lucy's efforts, there was a shortage of men, so I was able to creep into the living room and finish what was left of my supper in peace.

Although I was tired of him, I found myself thinking of Homer again, probably because my mind would not accept him in his present situation. He had always seemed so contented! Of course I didn't actually know—I'd been going on what Mary had told me about him and my own impressions on the few occasions I had seen him in New York with Mary. He had seemed far more interested in his golf and their country place than in other women or cocktail parties. And he'd obviously taken pride in the good position he'd held in an insurance company.

The party began to drift back into the living room, and Ken appeared beside me, holding a cup of coffee and a doughnut.

"I've missed you," he said amiably.

"You've what?" I asked, astounded.

"Well—I looked for you a couple of times and couldn't find you."

"Perhaps if you had looked to right and left instead of just straight in front of you?" I suggested politely. "Have you heard about Homer?"

"Homer? No."

I told him what I knew, and he seemed surprised but not much interested. "Oh well—his whole interest has always been in the company where he worked and that summer place of theirs—and he depended on Mary—even if she did fuss him about ashtrays and bringing mud in on his shoes. I suppose freedom looked good to him until he kicked over and got it—and then he found himself going in circles without a rudder—so he came back."

He shrugged the subject away and began to tell me some of his Army experiences. My attention wandered, but I tried to keep my face interested and murmured, "Mmm," from time to time, until a couple of women flitted up and carried him off.

I wandered aimlessly out into the hall and then started back to the living room, but when I came abreast of my bedroom, something seemed to whisper "Why not?" so, with a quick glance up and down the hall I slipped in and closed the door after me. I figured happily that no one would be mean enough to call on me to help with the cleaning up if I were asleep when that dismal time arrived.

I turned toward the bed and then stopped short, because there was a girl lying on it. She did not open her eyes or move, and I realized that she had passed out. I stood there for a while, quietly cursing people who go around drinking too much, and then an idea came to me. Mary's room. I could get a night's sleep there and move out before Mary arrived in the morning. I grabbed a few things and hurried out into the hall, where I got the key from the desk and let myself in. I locked the door again on the inside and within a very few minutes was comfortably stretched out in the bed—which may have been an antique but unquestionably had a modern and expensive mattress and spring. I turned off the light and went to sleep almost immediately.

I was awake again after only a short time, and my drowsy comfort had gone. I was restless and even nervous, and I was haunted by a real or fancied odor—something like a hospital, and yet not quite like it, either.

I got up at last, turned on the light, and established myself on the chaise longue with a cigarette. But I had smoked too much; my mouth was dry and my throat rasped, and I put the cigarette out and went back to bed. I stayed there for about five minutes with my eyes firmly closed and then gave it up. I went to the door, unlocked it, and peered out, wondering if the party was over. An assortment of noises told me that it was not, and I decided to go across and see whether the girl in my room had recovered enough to depart.

In the hall I found myself mixed up with Lucy, Mrs. Budd, John Emerson, and Ken.

John seemed to be in a temper. "Of course you're going to cut your furlough short, Smith," he was saying angrily. "You needn't suppose that you have me fooled. You come up here on leave, have this party to show yourself to everyone, and think you've covered up the fact that Betty is living down near your camp with you."

CHAPTER TEN

FOR A WHILE Sergeant Smith was mute, his eyes fixed on John's face, while a dark red burned itself into his face and neck. When he did speak his voice was under control, but the effort was obvious.

"You've been under a strain, John, and I'm allowing for that—but I've no more idea of where Betty is than you have, and I don't want that lie repeated."

"You used to take her out before you went into the Army," John said hotly, "and since you've been in, you and she have written to each other regularly."

"Of course I went out with her," Ken admitted, the control slipping a little. "She was very pleasant company, and you were always busy going out with someone else. And as for writing—every soldier will write to anyone who's kind enough to send him letters."

Lucy put an oar in. "I think it's nice of the soldiers to correspond with us. I know I—"

John interrupted her without any consciousness of having done so. "I understand all that. But it's odd that Betty would never allow me to read either her letters or yours."

"There was no reason for that—at least none that I know of. Anyway, you'd better come down to the camp and prove it for yourself."

"Yes," said John nastily, "only don't forget to warn her in time, so that she can leave."

Ken tried to jam his hands into his pockets, but they wouldn't go, because his pants were too tight. "All right, think what you like," he said fiercely, "but you're barking up the wrong tree. I'm cutting my furlough short for reasons that are no damn business of yours—and you can rot before I'll explain them to you."

He turned and flung off—sideswiping me on the way so that I went spinning into Lucy. She gave me such a severe look that I felt obliged to apologize to her.

"John," Mrs. Budd quavered nervously, "I'm sure you're wrong, dear. Betty is only hiding, so that . . ." Her voice died away as John turned and walked toward the foyer.

I found Lucy regarding me intently and with narrowed eyes. "Why did you change your dress?" she asked sharply.

I glanced down at my prewar negligee, which was of pale pink chiffon. "I'm just undressed," I explained hastily. "This is my fire negligee, and I thought I might run into someone while I was crossing the hall."

Lucy, and Mrs. Budd as well, immediately wanted to know why I had undressed, and after only half listening to my halting explanation came to the simultaneous conclusion that I was feeling ill. They took me to my room and immediately set about removing the body. They did it so competently that I watched them with open admiration. The girl never stirred as they carried her out to the hall and arranged her on a long narrow antique settee—although she looked thoroughly uncomfortable and awkward.

That having been accomplished, Mrs. Budd and Lucy pushed me into my room, hoped I'd feel better in the morning, and somewhat insulted me by advising me to cut down on my drinking, since it affected me that way.

I climbed into bed, but it was no use trying to sleep, because the party had decided to sing. Instead I picked up my book and settled back to read. It was interesting, and I was comfortable, and I read through the breaking up of the party—which was a shrill babel of thanks and farewells—and the clearing up afterward—which was fairly quiet and sounded grim. There were two breakages, and each time I winced and hoped that Mary's good glasses had escaped.

At last everything was quiet, and I was surprised to find that it was only three o'clock—rather early for a party with the momentum that that one had seemed to have.

I yawned and put my book down and turned out the light—and at the same time someone opened the front door, closed it again, and switched on the hall light. I listened, not breathing much, but there was absolute silence—no footsteps advancing along the hall-nothing. I got out of bed, pulled on my negligee, and opened the door.

It was Mary. She was standing just inside the front door, staring along the hall with a look almost of horror on her face.

"Mary!" I exclaimed, startled. "What is it? What's the matter?"

She looked up. "Oh, Eugenia—it's you. But who's this? You know that settee is a valuable antique, but it isn't strong—I always avoid using it, even to sit on—that's why I have it out in the hall."

I walked forward and had to smother the grin that I felt coming on. The girl still lay where Lucy and Mrs. Budd had put her—apparently overlooked by the cleaning crew.

I murmured, "Tch, tch—give me a hand, Mary, and we'll put her somewhere else."

We started to raise the girl, but this time she woke up and announced that she wanted to go home.

Mary, who seemed to have recognized her, began to scold. "You know very well, Viola, that your father has forbidden you to drink again. I shall have to tell him."

Viola regarded her darkly for a moment and then delivered an opinion. "You are an abonimal ole tattletale—but definitely."

Mary took her around the shoulders and walked her out of the apartment and along the outside corridor to a door where she rang the bell—although the girl protested that she had a key. However, someone opened the door—presumably the father, since Mary did her tattling—the girl was pushed into her retribution, and Mary returned, brushing disgustedly at her neat linen suit.

"These young girls! I don't know what Lucy was thinking of—or Ken either—to invite her to a party of that sort."

"But, Mary—how did you happen to come down? I thought you were going to wait until the morning."

"Yes, I know—but I simply couldn't. As soon as I heard about Homer I was so restless and nervous that I couldn't sit still, so I simply got into the car and drove down."

She took off her hat and brushed the hair back from her forehead with a tired gesture. "It was a dreadful trip, though—misty up in the hills, and I had to crawl, in places. I must have wished a thousand times that I'd waited until the morning. Now tell me again about Homer."

I told her the whole story again and she became very agitated and not a little annoyed at our having allowed him to slip through our fingers. "I can't understand why you let him go, Eugenia—surely you could have held onto him until I came." She began to twist her hands together, and moaned, "What can be the matter with him—whatever is the matter? He must be ill."

"He'll come back, Mary," I soothed her. "He's bound to, and I'm sure he'll explain everything."

She turned away and went toward the kitchen. "I'll have to have some coffee. There's no use in my trying to sleep, anyway."

I followed and started to make the coffee for her, but things became complicated right away. She noticed that various utensils had either been put away in the wrong order or were hanging at the wrong angle—and as a matter of fact, it was pretty obvious, even to my eye, that the cleanup job had been a sloppy one. When I came to the coffee making, it immediately developed that there was only one way to make coffee—and I did not know it. All in all, it was fully half an hour before we sat down to drink the stuff.

I had to go over and over the story about Homer, and she seemed to find the parts that dealt with the golf shoes in the hall and the pipe in the living room almost beyond belief. Homer *never* left his shoes lying around anywhere—they were kept in a rack in his closet, or on his feet. And I gathered that he would as soon have thought of taking a bath in the living room as exposing his pipe there.

"Homer was always very cooperative about keeping the place nice. I know some people think I'm too fussy that way—John always says so. He told me once that I keep the place more like a museum than a home—but I have nice things, and I like to keep them nice." She stirred her coffee for a while in silence and asked doubtfully, "Do you think I'd better delay going to the police for a while? I mean Homer may come back—perhaps tomorrow."

"I'd wait," I agreed. "You'd look silly if he walked in while you were busy asking them to find him."

"Yes." She fidgeted with the coffee spoon and added in an annoyed voice, "It would be just like Homer, too. But what about Betty? Has she come home?"

I shook my head. "John was accusing Ken of having her living down near the camp with him."

Mary widened her eyes and looked thoroughly scandalized. "That's absurd! Perfect nonsense!" She thought it over for a while and added with less conviction, "Of course he went around with her—but he went around with so many girls." She gave it some more thought and ended by practically going over to the opposition. "I suppose that could have been just a blind, couldn't it? Anyway, I think John cheapens himself by making a scene about it. When a woman leaves her husband and child the husband should put her out of his mind entirely."

"Whom do you think she went off with?" I asked curiously.

"I don't know, and I don't care," Mary said crisply. "I'm as certain that it was some man as I am that it was not Homer."

"But you thought it was Homer at first."

"Well, of course when Mrs. Budd had that card from Betty—naturally. I was so angry and upset—and what else could I have thought? But when I had calmed down and been by myself for a while, I realized that it just was not possible. Homer would never have left me for Betty."

I nodded and refrained from adding that in my opinion Betty would never have left John for Homer either.

"Well . . ." Mary sighed, stood up, and started to clear away the coffee things. I picked up a dish towel and silently vowed to leave in the morning. I dried the delicate cups and saucers with care, and reflected that it must take Mary a long time to do her housework, and no wonder she could never keep a maid.

When we had finished, Mary said she'd just take a took at the living room, to see if they had left it in order.

I tried to get away. I said, "Good night, Mary, I'll see you in the morning," but she took my arm firmly and pulled me along with her.

She touched the wall switch in the living room, and in the sudden, soft glow of light we saw Suzy. She was sitting in an oddly awkward position in one of the chairs, and she was sound asleep.

CHAPTER ELEVEN

MARY HURRIED FORWARD and grasped the girl's shoulder. She shook it and demanded, "Where is he? Where is Mr. Homer?"

But Suzy's head had fallen forward onto her chest, and she didn't wake up.

"Stop it, Mary," I said sharply. "She's ill—we'll have to have a doctor. Is there one in the building?"

Mary shook the limp arm again and said excitedly, "Don't be silly—she's only drunk," but I pulled her away and urged her toward the front door.

"I tell you the girl's ill. Go and wake the Emersons: "

She went reluctantly, and I stood and watched her ring the Emersons' bell. After some little time John appeared, wrapped in an elaborate silk robe.

He said, "Oh. Hello, Mary—you're back. What is it? Have you found Homer?"

"No, no—it's Suzy. She's in my living room, and Eugenia thinks she's ill. I wish you'd come."

"Suzy?" repeated John vaguely, and brushed back the lock of dark hair that had been hanging rather becomingly over his forehead. "But she came in with us—she's in bed."

"John, please! She's in my living room, and I think she's drunk. You must come and see to her."

John belted his robe more firmly and stepped out into the hall, as Mrs. Budd appeared, behind him attired in a flowered wrapper.

"She's not drunk," he said with a touch of impatience. "Suzy never drinks."

Mrs. Budd followed and whispered to me anxiously, "What is it? What has Suzy been doing?"

I explained as we made our way down Mary's hall, and Mrs. Budd said, "Tch, tch," several times.

In the living room John was bending over Suzy. Her head was hanging sideways now, and her eyes, blank and expressionless, were only half closed. I drew in my breath sharply.

"We should get a doctor at once."

John straightened slowly, his eyes still on Suzy's face. "Yes, we must certainly have one. But I'm afraid it's no use—I think she's dead."

Mrs. Budd gave a little scream, and Mary gasped, "Oh no, John! She—she can't be."

John turned away and without comment went along to the telephone at the end of the hall.

"Oh, poor Suzy—poor girl!" Mrs. Budd cried hysterically. "What could have happened—whatever could have happened? She was perfectly all right all the evening—except that once she told me she felt a little sleepy. After she told us about Homer being here, that was."

Sergeant Smith appeared in a bright green robe and asked, "What's all the activity? Emerson's hanging onto the phone out there in the hall." His eye fell on Suzy, and he added, "What's the matter with her?"

"Hello, Ken," Mary said wanly.

"Mary! When did you blow in?"

"I came tonight. But oh, Ken, we're so worried. John says she's dead."

Ken came closer and peered at Suzy's face. "The poor kid," he said soberly. "John's getting a doctor, isn't he?"

Mrs. Budd began to cry. "I wish I hadn't been so cross with her all day—but I was bothered about the party, and Lucy leaving all of the arrangements to me. It's just like Lucy. I wish—"

"What's just like me?" Lucy asked from the door. "What's going on anyway? Why—er—Mary."

"Lucy!" said Mary. "Did you give this girl anything to drink?"

"Certainly not," Lucy snapped, looking thoroughly offended. "I don't drink much myself, and I don't go around trying to get other people drunk. She didn't even ask me if she could have any."

Mary wrung her hands, and I could see the expensive glitter of her rings. She said distractedly, "I wish the doctor would come. Where's John?"

"I got hold of Sand, from upstairs," John said from the foyer. "He'll be down in a minute—he's throwing a few clothes on."

Ken began to talk soothingly to Mary, and Mrs. Budd, after mopping her eyes and blowing her nose, looked Lucy over and asked her why she had not undressed yet.

"Why, I have," Lucy said loudly, and then remembered and glanced down at the white negligee, which she now wore over her nightgown, and without the yellow ribbon in her hair. She gave Mrs. Budd a suspicious look and apparently decided that silence was the best course.

The doctor came and was taken to the chair where Suzy lay. He made a brief examination in a dead silence that took on a stunned quality when he announced curtly, "She's dead."

Presently Mrs. Budd began to cry again, and the rest of us stirred. Ken asked, "But what was it, Doctor? It must have been very sudden, because she was quite all right during the evening."

The doctor nodded. He would not commit himself, but admitted that he was inclined to think she had been poisoned. There would have to be an autopsy, and the police must be notified.

"Oh no!" Mary gasped. "Not here, surely. How did she get here anyway?"

"That's what I'd like to know," John muttered. "Smith told her to go, after things had been cleared up, and she came back with us."

"She could have come over the balcony," I suggested, "unless she had a key for the front door."

Mrs. Budd, mopping up with a very damp handkerchief, said vehemently, "She didn't have a key—why on earth would she? And why would she come over the balcony? Someone must have told her to come back, and let her in."

"Talk sense, Mother," John said shortly. "Why would anyone call her back here? The work was done."

Mary and the doctor had gone out to the telephone, and it was just before they reappeared again that Lucy decided to have hysterics. She was no amateur, and she put on a very fine exhibition indeed. We were all fully occupied with her—except the doctor, who seemed to feel that in these busy times this was one job that might safely be left to the first-aid corps.

I was in the thick of the fray, and only dimly aware that some strange men had appeared in the living room, and that first Mary and then John stepped over to speak to them. I saw nothing of the actual removal of Suzy, for Lucy caught a glimpse of it and began to go off like a series of skyrockets.

After it was over Dr. Sand had a few words with Mary and John, and then prepared to depart himself. On his way out he stepped over and looked at Lucy for the first time. "Just wondering what she eats for breakfast," he said mildly as I wiped the sweat from my brow and looked up at him. "All I'd ever ask for in this world would be half that energy—only half of it."

He went off, and Lucy calmed down to the point of being coherent.

"It was Homer," she sobbed. "He's gone mad. Poor Suzy told everyone he was here, so he silenced her forever."

Mary walked over and gave her a ringing slap in the face. "That's enough, Lucy. I won't have you talking scandalous nonsense about Homer—you know he wouldn't hurt a fly."

Mrs. Budd collapsed into a chair and said indignantly, "She deserved that, Mary—I'm glad you did it. These people who go around spreading tales! It certainly looks as though poor Homer had become a bit touched in the head—bringing Suzy back here and poisoning her—but Lucy has no right to mention it."

Mary's jaw dropped, and I said hastily, "If the poor girl has been poisoned, surely it was suicide."

John and Ken both said, "No," and then appeared to be disgusted at finding themselves agreeing with each other.

Lucy had been stretched out full length on a couch, but she sat up now and pushed her wildly disordered red curls back from her face.

"Why, that's an idea," she said quite calmly. "Maybe the poor thing had an unhappy love affair."

"Suzy had no boyfriends," said Mrs. Budd firmly.

"Oh." Lucy was still working on her hair. "Well, I suppose that's why she wanted to die. That gets a girl down, too."

Mary was twisting her hands again. She said desperately, "Oh, stop—stop! This is dreadful—what am I going to do? If Homer would only come—he'd be able to help me."

"It's all right, Mary," John soothed her. "We'll all help you—and probably Homer will come back in the morning."

Ken took over at that point. He marched Mary off to her room and forced her to take some sort of a sleeping pill. He said good night to Mrs. Budd and John and saw them to the door, and then came back and told Lucy and me that if we didn't get to bed and get some sleep all the bags around here wouldn't be in closets.

Lucy was afraid to go to her own room, so she trailed after me into mine. She settled down in a chair and began to talk, but I went straight to bed and closed my eyes. I heard her puzzling for a while over Ken's remark and wondering audibly whether he had meant us as a whole or just the spaces under our eyes. She left it unsolved, and the last thing I heard her say before she went to sleep was that Mary had put the two busts on the antique desk in the hall straight again.

I woke up at eight o'clock, to the persistent sound of the front doorbell. I opened my eyes blearily and saw Lucy stretched out in the chair, with her feet propped on my suitcase. She looked awkward and uncomfortable, but the bell had not roused her, and after waiting for a moment I dragged myself out of bed and made my way into the hall.

I glanced at the antique desk—and then looked again. Lucy must have been mistaken about Mary having straightened those busts, I thought—for certainly they were facing each other now.

CHAPTER TWELVE

AS I WENT ON to the front door I wondered whether Lucy had taken the trouble to turn those two busts, during the night, so that they faced each other once more.

If she had, she was playing a losing game, because if Mary wanted them facing outward they would face outward as long as Mary lived and could move.

The doorbell rang again, and as I opened up I saw Lucy come yawning out of my room and disappear into her own.

Three men advanced around and past me into the hall, and one of them mentioned that his name was Bartholomew Egbert.

I closed the door, since they seemed to have come to stay, and said, "I don't believe it."

The articulate one swung around and barked, "How's that?"

"No one ever had a name like that," I said, and realized that I was still only half awake.

He looked me over and then announced rather stiffly, "I wish to speak to Mrs. Fredon."

I shook my head in an effort to clear it. "You could speak to her, all right, only she wouldn't answer, because she's had a sleeping pill, and she's still out."

"Who are you?" he asked abruptly.

"I'm a guest."

"Do you have a name?"

I nodded. "It's just nothing, though—just a name. I'd hate even to mention it, after hearing yours."

He looked me over again—thoroughly—and then suggested smoothly, "Suppose you mention it anyway."

"First I'd like to know the names of your two silent partners, and what your business is here."

The silent partners grinned fleetingly and looked down at Egbert, who was almost a head shorter than either of them. Egbert himself removed his glasses and began to polish them with an immaculate handkerchief.

"We are policemen," he said after a moment.

"In that case, shouldn't you be able to flash a badge?"

The other two did so immediately, but Egbert merely finished polishing his glasses and perched them on his nose. "It shouldn't be necessary," he said equably. "I am almost famous. You should know me."

"There are a lot of things I don't know. I never finished college."

"No. Well, perhaps you can lead us to an assortment of chairs, so that we may ask you a few questions."

I started for the living room, but Egbert caught sight of the dining room on the way and decided to use it.

We all sat down around the table, and I heard Lucy go into the kitchen and start banging pots around. After a while she opened the swinging door and peered out at us, and her eyebrows shot up into her hair. I grinned at her, and Egbert turned around.

"Come in, if you please—I'd like to talk to you."

Lucy stared at him, and her hand went automatically to straighten her hair. "Why, I can't," she said, looking a bit fussed. "I'm in the middle of breakfast. I'll have it ready in a minute—only I'm afraid I—er—didn't plan for so many."

"Quite all right—we have breakfasted. But please go on with your preparations, and perhaps we can talk while you're having yours."

Lucy gave me a baffled look and then disappeared, and he turned to me.

"You are Miss Gates? Miss Eugenia Gates?"

I admitted it.

"And in the kitchen—Mrs. Lucy Davis?"

I nodded.

"Where is Sergeant Smith?"

"I suppose he's around somewhere," I said vaguely.

Egbert turned to one of the silent stalwarts and snapped, "Find him."

The man disappeared, and I was again in the line of fire.

"Now, when and where did you first see this girl Suzy?"

It was simple enough to tell him what I knew of Suzy, but it was so very brief that he seemed to disbelieve it. He kept interrupting, and seemed to be inferring that I had known Suzy as of yore and had had a score to settle with her.

When I had hotly denied it for the third time I asked, "Does all this mean that she was deliberately murdered?"

Egbert took off his glasses and started to polish them again.

"Don't do that," I said crossly, "you just did it. Anyway, I can't see why you insist that she was murdered. She might have taken whatever it was by accident."

Egbert said, "No. She took too much to have taken it accidentally. Murder or suicide."

Stated unemotionally, in Egbert's precise voice, the words gave me a feeling of blank, cold fear. I realized fully, for the first time, that either poor little Suzy had been so desperate that she wanted to die or someone had been so desperate as to kill her. And here—right in this apartment, with all those people milling around. I closed my eyes and felt a shudder pass through me from head to toe.

The man who had gone to look for Ken came back, apparently without having found him, and at the same time Lucy pushed through the door from the kitchen carrying a tray loaded with fine delicate little plates. On each plate lay a dainty square of toast, with about a spoonful of scrambled egg on the top. Lucy distributed the plates—one in front of each of us and one at her own place—and disappeared into the kitchen again.

The silent chorus looked hopefully at Egbert, who was regarding his own portion in some perplexity. He picked up the toast at last and, being careful of the mound of egg on top, pushed the whole thing into his mouth. The other two followed suit at once, and when Lucy presently came in again with some cutlery I shook my head at her. "Places for two, only. The gentlemen are taking theirs home with them."

Lucy looked at the empty plates in astonishment. "Well, forever! What did they wrap it in? Do they want some waxed paper?"

Egbert cleared his throat, and I said hastily, "It's all right. Have you any coffee out there?"

"Of course." She disposed of the cutlery and returned to the kitchen, where I could hear her whispering. I knew Ken was out there, and I wondered whether he was planning to skip back to camp and avoid the trouble that seemed to be brewing—since the Army was such an unreasonable outfit at times.

I said nothing, but Egbert had heard the whispering, too, and motioned to his pals, who got up and went into the kitchen. The whispering stopped, there was a word or two, and then the two men returned with Ken, Lucy, and the coffee.

"Ah, Sergeant Smith," said Egbert, beaming through his glasses. "I am investigating the death of Suzy Howland, and I'm sure you'll cooperate by giving me any information that you can." He added with a slight bow, "Bartholomew Egbert."

Ken looked a bit stunned, but pulled himself together and said, "Good morning, Mr. Bartholomew. Anything I can do, of course."

"You don't know him well enough to use his first name," I interposed, hungrily watching the coffeepot.

They both ignored me, but Egbert repeated his name, and added that it was a cross he'd born all his life because his aunt had been given the honor of naming him—and only because his parents owed her money and hoped she'd be pleased enough to forget it for a while longer. He said he'd thought of shortening it to Bart, but Bart Egbert wasn't quite right either, somehow.

"You can't build any sort of a decent house on a faulty foundation," I said, still watching the coffee. "Your aunt had to end up with Egbert, no matter how she started."

Egbert didn't even turn his head, but he observed to Ken that I was without doubt the rudest young lady he had ever met. Ken agreed heartily, and Egbert went on smoothly to suggest that I had probably crossed swords, in my usual crude fashion, with Suzy.

Ken wiped the smile from his face and frowned, and Lucy, busy pouring the coffee, looked up and said loudly, "Nonsense! Eugenia has better manners than a lot of people I know. At least she wouldn't take the food right off the serving plates and wrap it up to take home."

The two men dropped their eyes to the empty plates and broke into grins, and Egbert, in a sudden fit of temper, ordered them out into the hall to wait.

"That's rude, if you like," Lucy said indignantly. "You could have let them have their coffee."

"We are policemen, madam," said Egbert, still annoyed, "and we did not come here to drink coffee."

"Now, Sergeant Smith, I understand that Mr. Homer Fredon recently eloped with Mrs. Emerson from the next apartment—as far as can be learned. However, several people seem to think that the lady did not go away with Mr. Fredon, and have, in fact, hinted that you know where she is."

Ken lost his temper and practically bellowed. He denied everything at least six times, and talked at some length about how it had been only a beautiful friendship.

Egbert calmly wrote something down in a notebook, read it over, and looked up again.

"I believe Mr. Fredon turned up here last night?"

"Yes, he did," said Lucy. "Suzy was the only one who saw him. But he came back again—he spent the night on the living-room couch."

CHAPTER THIRTEEN

EGBERT SWUNG AROUND on Lucy and asked, "What do you mean, Mrs. Davis?" and at the same time I said, "I don't see how that's possible. The party was going on in there first, and then later poor Suzy was there."

Egbert transferred his attention to me and requested, as a favor to him— or else—that I remain quiet for a few consecutive minutes.

"Now go on, Mrs. Davis. How do you know that Mr. Fredon spent the night on a couch in the living room?"

"Why don't you go and look?" Lucy said impatiently. "He left a light blanket on the couch, and a pair of his pajamas. *Somebody* certainly was lying there, because it's a soft couch, and it's all squashed in. You know the one, Eugenia—that large thing over by the piano. Mary always starts to squirm if anybody sits on it, because she has to fluff up the pillows again when they get up."

Egbert decided to investigate, and we all trailed after him. The couch was a bit out of the way of general traffic—probably so it wouldn't be sat on too often—and was as Lucy described it. A light summer blanket lay across it, with one corner trailing on the floor, and a pair of crumpled pajamas with quiet striping in subdued colors.

We gazed for a while, Egbert tapping his teeth with a pencil, until I said thoughtfully, "He couldn't have been here long, anyway."

Egbert stopped tapping and asked, "Why?"

"Well, I heard the party leave, and then after a little while I heard Mary come in. If Homer had come in before Mary, I'd have heard him too."

"You might have been sleeping," Egbert suggested. "He was trying not to be seen or heard, anyway, as far as I can gather."

I shook my head. "I didn't sleep—I was reading. If he came in first, then he knows how to open and close the front door without making any sound."

This caused a major spurt of activity. Egbert, Ken, and the male chorus pounded along to the front door to see whether it could be opened without noise, and Lucy and I retired to the dining room to drink some more coffee.

"Such a commotion!" Lucy sighed. "And all over nothing. Just imagine anyone murdering that poor little inoffensive thing! Perfect nonsense!"

"Do you think she killed herself?"

"For heaven's sake, no. Suzy was quite happy and contented."

"You can't be sure of that," I said slowly. "She was only a young girl, and doing housework for Mrs. Budd couldn't have been much of a life. I mean, would you like to be a domestic employed by Mrs. Budd?"

Lucy almost shuddered. "Of course not—but you're forgetting that if Suzy didn't like it she could have had dozens of other jobs for the asking. You know what it's like these days. So what's the use of saying that she committed suicide because she couldn't stand working for Sarah Budd? Even though I don't know how she *did* stand it. Sarah is one of my oldest friends, and I'm devoted to her, but she's an aggravating fusspot, and—"

"How do you think Suzy came to be poisoned then?" I interrupted hastily.

"Oh, it was some sort of an accident—and if they weren't all crazy they'd see it. Fussing around and carrying on. Why don't they let the poor child rest in peace?"

They all came back from the front door at that point, and Egbert asked me to go to my room, leave my door as it had been last night, and see whether I could hear them opening and closing the front door. I did as I was asked, and took the opportunity to get dressed—but although I listened carefully, I heard no sound from the front door.

So Homer could have come back after the last of the guests had left and before Mary arrived. Apparently he had got his blanket and pajamas and gone to bed on the couch. It seemed probable that Suzy had come in while Mary and I were having coffee in the kitchen, and she must have seen Homer. My presence in the kitchen probably deterred him from having it out with Mary—and so he had gone on down the hall and out again. Poor Homer—unable to find a place to lay his head in all his vast apartment.

When I had finished dressing I wandered out into the hall and, glancing at the two busts on the antique desk, decided that it was Homer who had rearranged them. Probably, in his homesickness, he'd wanted to see things the way they'd always been.

The doorbell rang, and I went along to answer it—deadheating with one of Egbert's men.

We opened the door to John Emerson and Mrs. Budd, who passed me with a couple of brief words and walked in silently.

"Lovely day," I said politely. "This is the police—outer fringe. The nucleus is in the dining room."

John glanced at the stooge and away again, but Mrs. Budd went pale to the lips and repeated in a hoarse whisper, "Police!"

"Will you come into the dining room?" said the spider politely.

Mrs. Budd and John followed him—Mrs. Budd looking scared and John grim. I wandered along behind but continued into the living room and then out onto the balcony. The sun was bright and warm, and I tried to enjoy it, but my thoughts kept turning to Suzy, and I couldn't shake off a feeling of depression. I could not imagine her committing suicide but it seemed even more impossible that anyone would murder her.

I glanced at the silly partition that divided the balcony, and the next instant I had climbed across and slipped into the Emerson apartment. I did not know what I intended to do, exactly, and I felt scared and guilty, but for some reason I kept on.

The layout was identical with Mary's apartment, and I made straight for the smallest bedroom—the one Lucy had been forced to use, at Mary's. It had been Suzy's room, all right. I stood with my back against the door and my two hands behind me on the knob, and looked. Everything very neat and tidy and simple—appropriate and in quiet taste. I took a long breath and moved forward to the closet. Neat and clean inside, with a few modest clothes on hangers. I closed the door, crept over to the bureau, and went rapidly through the drawers. Neatness and order again—nicely laundered underwear, gloves, handkerchiefs, a few cosmetics in one of the top drawers, and a small blue leather appointment book.

I hesitated over the little book and then opened it, wondering what earthly excuse I had for doing such a thing.

There were a few dates scattered through it things like "visit Aunt Agnes" and "dinner and movies with Emily"—these always on a Thursday or a Sunday. But the last entry had been written on a Monday, only two days previously. It said: "Must go in there today."

I had a combined attack of nerves and conscience, at that point, and got myself out of Suzy's room a good deal more quickly than I had gone in. I was barely in time, for I had only just made the living room when I heard someone open the front door. I flew back to Mary's apartment, wondering all the way what had possessed me to be such a fool—and then I discovered that I still had the little appointment book clutched in my hand. I stood and looked at it, feeling guilty and annoyed with myself. There was no way of getting it back now—and although it didn't seem important, I felt that Egbert had a right to play with his own toys.

Ken walked into the living room and raised his eyebrows at me. "So you've been over in the Emersons' apartment?"

I said, "What do you mean?" but I could feel myself blushing.

"We looked everywhere for you, until some bright soul concluded that you'd gone in to look after Mary. The cops departed, but they'll be back, because they want to see Mary, and they want to talk to you again. So what were you doing in the Emerson apartment?"

I sat down and pulled out a cigarette. "Well—as a matter of fact, I just wanted to see Suzy's room."

He regarded me in silence for a moment and then asked, "Did they catch you?"

I slouched down in my chair and grinned at him. "It was touch and go, but I made it. That poor kid's room is neat as a pin."

"You'd better sit tight and behave yourself," he said ominously. "This thing is serious—probably murder."

"I know B. Egbert wants to think so," I admitted. "But after all, poison is mostly taken by accident."

Ken shook his head with a bothered look. "There's something going on, though. Homer and his game of hide-and-seek, and all that. I wish he'd show up again."

"How long had Suzy been with the Emersons?" I asked presently.

He said, "About two years," as Lucy walked in and demanded, "What are you two talking about?"

"About Suzy—how long she'd been with the Emersons."

"Suzy," said Lucy emphatically, "was a jewel—an absolute jewel. I often wonder what Betty was thinking of to go off and leave her. She'll never get another like that."

"She probably didn't stop to think," Ken said, and Lucy bridled.

"You can be sarcastic, but most women spend the best years of their lives with the responsibility for a lot of stupid housework dumped in their laps."

"No system," said Ken absently. "The housework should be off anybody's mind by 9 a.m." He turned to me and added, "You'd better go and get Mary up. They want to ask her some questions."

"Certainly not. She's sleeping, and they can wait."

But Mary walked in while I was still speaking. She was dressed, but not quite her usual tidy and immaculate self..

"I can't sleep in there," she said querulously. "I haven't been able to sleep there since Homer left. I believe the room is haunted."

CHAPTER FOURTEEN

LUCY BUSTLED OVER, put her arm around Mary, and led her to a chair. "My dear, you're just nervous and tired out. I knew of a house once that was haunted—but apartments never are—I mean there just isn't the right *atmosphere.*"

"That room is," Mary said tiredly. "I can't sleep there any more—and I need sleep badly."

"Come oh, then, and have a snooze in one of the other rooms," Ken suggested. "You can have mine."

Mary sighed and shook her head. "No, no—I'm dressed now, and besides, I have things to do. But I'd like some breakfast."

Lucy explained that breakfast was over, but said that she'd fix something and went off to the kitchen, and I turned to Mary and suggested that perhaps it would be better if I left and went back to New York. "You're having trouble," I added, "and I'm only in the way."

Mary looked doubtful and undecided, but Ken walked over and stuck his face almost into mine.

"Oh no, you don't!" he said softly. "In the first place the police wouldn't like it, and we need you. You can't just go flitting off at the first sign of trouble."

That seemed to decide Mary, and she said definitely, "No, don't go, Eugenia—I'm going to need all the help that I know you'll be kind enough to give me."

"Eugenia," said Ken idly. "It's a moniker with a bit too much starch in it, as far as I'm concerned. To myself, I have always called you Gussie."

I ignored him, and Mary broke in fretfully, "Ken, the furniture is all out of place here—we'd better set it right again."

But Ken negatived the idea, either because he didn't want to be bothered or in all sincerity. "We can't change anything just now. The police have only looked around in here, and they'll almost certainly want to go over it more thoroughly. I know they wouldn't want anything touched."

Mary fussed and fretted a bit until Lucy appeared with coffee and various fancy little bits and pieces of food. Ken brought a small table to Mary's chair, and we all gathered around.

He ate his share of the food in three bites and then told Lucy that she was peerless in the flavor field, but if she didn't stop teasing him by serving a mouthful at a time he'd bite a piece out of Mary's best Chippendale. Lucy let out a yell of laughter, but Mary wanted to know which piece of Chippendale he meant. I started to laugh, and choked over my coffee, and Ken gave it as his opinion that we were all about ripe for the wagon.

Mary set down her cup, glanced about the room, and observed, "The dust around here is frightful."

"We dusted yesterday morning," Lucy said coldly.

"Yes, my dear, I know—I didn't mean that. You must not be offended— it's just that I'm upset—that poor child dying right in this room—and Homer behaving so oddly—"

I took a last swallow of coffee, sighed deeply, and stood up.

"Come on, Mary—we'll clean the place up from end to end—the way it should be done."

The lost, helpless look she'd had disappeared at once, and her eyes sparkled with eagerness. She dusted her hands a little with her napkin, dropped it onto the table, and stood up.

Lucy and Ken thought we were crazy, and said so quite frankly. Ken added that we'd better not clean up the living room or Egbert would be mad. But Mary was already forging ahead to the broom closet, so I followed her and called back to Ken to be sure and let me know when Eggy had his tantrum, because I wanted to see it.

We started with the hall, and I asked Mary which way she liked the busts on the antique desk to face. She glanced at them, and then to my surprise said, "That's the way I like them—half facing each other—I fixed them last night. Homer must have turned them to face outward—I know that's the way he liked them. In fact he used to change them on me all the time—it was the only way he ever interfered. He must have been here if they were straight."

I nodded. "Since Monday, I guess, because Lucy turned them around on Monday night."

Mary's eyes welled with slow tears, and I said hastily, "Look at the dust under that couch! Awful!"

She blinked, and we both stooped down. The floor under the couch seemed shining and spotless to me, but she said, "Oh dear! Hand me that mop, will you? I've never seen the place in such a state."

We worked on that clean and polished hall for fully half an hour before it was finished to Mary's satisfaction. When at last we stood and surveyed it, mops and dusters in hand, and wiping our brows, I suggested that we could save dishwashing by having our dinner on the floor there.

Mary was not amused. She merely said, "What in the world are you talking about, my dear? There'd be crumbs all over the place."

"Let's get on to the next room," I said hastily.

The next room was the one occupied by Ken, and Mary sighed. "This is Homer's room. I'd like to get it all clean and ready for him. Ken can go in where Lucy is, and I'll send Lucy home. After all, we don't need her now."

"Well, no," I said doubtfully, "but I don't think she'll want to go."

Mary looked thoroughly cross and said, "She'll *have* to go, if there's no place for her to sleep."

"She does all the cooking," I pointed out, "and while you're so upset like this, she'll save you a lot of work. Why don't you let me go instead—and she can have my room?"

"No, no, Eugenia, I want you here—you must not leave. I shall need you."

It didn't seem to me that I knew her well enough to be one of these pals who rally around in time of trouble, but I resigned myself. However, I didn't intend to let Lucy and her exquisite cooking go without a struggle, so I said earnestly, "I'll stay if you want me, of course—but I think we should keep Lucy—she's more of a help than you realize. Haven't you a cot or a couch or something that you could put in my room—and she can sleep in with me?"

Mary considered it for a moment with drawn brows and then suddenly brightened.

"All right—yes—I'll get Ken to help. There's that studio couch in the living room—I never liked it there anyway. We can bring that into your room. It's a good arrangement, actually, because it will make a double guest room, and then, too, the guest can lie on the couch, during the daytime, for a nap, or anything, without messing up the bedspread the way they always do."

Ken walked in on us, and his face assumed a look of outrage.

"What are you doing, Mary? Are you trying to *make* work for yourself? I keep this room clean myself—and I mean *clean*—" He turned to me and let out a yell. "Hey, you! What's that you're using for a duster?"

I looked down in some confusion and stammered, "Why, I—I don't know. It's just an old piece of cloth I picked off the floor."

He came over and snatched the thing out of my hand. "Old piece of cloth," he said bitterly. "That's my pajama, and it's almost brand-new."

"Do stop fussing, Ken," Mary broke in crossly. She was busy getting dust out of the carving on one of the chairs and added abstractedly, "We're fixing this room up so that it will be ready for Homer, and we're moving you in with Lucy."

Ken, who had opened his mouth for further belligerence, left it hanging open, but was stricken speechless.

"We've been told to make the soldier's furlough as pleasant as possible," I explained.

He looked from one to the other of us and then asked mildly, "Has Lucy been consulted?"

Mary still had most of her mind on her work, and she said in an absorbed voice, "Oh no—but she won't raise any objection. Lucy's obliging about little things like that."

"She writes to ten soldiers, and does canteen work, and things like that," I explained.

Lucy came snooping to the doorway, stuck her head in, and asked, "What's going on here?"

"It's nothing," Ken said, waving a huge hand. "Nothing at all. They're just going to move me in with you."

"What!" Lucy shrieked.

"I'm a gentleman," he assured her. "I know there's only one bed in there, but we can take turns."

Mary turned away from the carved chair with a little sigh of satisfaction and said, "Ken, get Lucy to help you bring that green studio couch from the living room and put it in Eugenia's room."

"They've changed their minds," Ken said to Lucy. "They're putting me in with Eugenia."

Mary blinked at him. "I don't think that's very nice, Ken, even as a joke. Lucy will sleep in with Eugenia, of course, and you'll take Lucy's room."

"All right," Ken said resignedly. "Come on, Lucy."

When we had finished fixing Ken's room for Homer, Mary decided that we'd do hers next.

"I think if I give it a thorough cleaning," she explained, "I might feel comfortable in it, the way I used to."

As we crossed the hall I remembered how I had felt in that room of Mary's—nervous and uncomfortable for no reason on which I could put my finger. In the end I had put it down to sleeping in Mary's sacred bedroom behind her back, as it were.

We went furiously to work and sweated up and down and back and forth across that room, until I was ready to drop. Finally, when Mary's back was turned for a moment, I crept away and sought out Lucy.

"For Pete's sake," I said desperately, "make some afternoon tea so that I can have a recess."

Lucy giggled, said, "I know what you mean," and obligingly headed toward the kitchen—where I was embarrassed to find Ken hanging up his newly washed sleeping garment.

I went back to Mary's room, and on with the grind.

"This is a lovely bed," I said, hoping to slow her up.

"Yes, it is—but it's not really appropriate, you know—too cottage. I'm going to have it taken up to the country—it'll be entirely suitable there. I've already bought another one for here—but I have to wait until the moving company is taking a load up that way before they'll take this bed."

"I like this big drawer underneath," I said. "Handy for storing blankets and things."

Mary glanced around. "Oh, that drawer! It's no use to me at all—I've never even been able to open it."

CHAPTER FIFTEEN

I LOOKED at the drawer again and remembered releasing the corner of the bedspread that had been caught in it. The drawer had moved smoothly and easily.

"Mary, I mean this drawer under the bed. It opens quite easily."

She turned around, impatient at being interrupted in her work, and brushed her hair back with her elbow.

"My dear, that drawer has never been opened—I ought to know. Homer and I both worked on it when I first got the bed. We had to leave it in the end, because we didn't want to force it for fear of breaking something. It's quite valuable, you know."

I lifted the spread and started to pull on the thing, but this time it would not budge, although I tried for some time.

"But; Mary, it *did* open," I persisted. "When you told me to lock your room I came in here and looked at the bed, and a corner of the spread was stuck in the drawer. I pulled it out and then pushed the drawer in again without any trouble."

"Oh, you must have been mistaken. Here, take these china figures into the bathroom and wash them, will you? And be very careful—they break so easily.'"

I said, "Just put them down there, and I'll do them in a minute," and slipped out of the room.

Out in the hall I leaned up against the antique desk, feeling slightly dizzy. Somebody had deliberately jammed that drawer, I thought—and why? Something must be hidden in it—it was big enough. Suzy had been poisoned, Betty gone off nobody knew where, and Homer was sneaking in and out of the place for reasons best known to himself. Homer must be found at once, I thought rather wildly, and I must get that drawer open—or somebody must.

Ken emerged from the kitchen and called to me, "Hey, what are you loafing around like that for, when you should be washing the ceilings and getting dust out of the cracks in the floor?"

"You probably think you're kidding," I said bitterly. "Listen, Ken, something peculiar has happened. There's a drawer stuck—will you come and open it for us?"

"Lead the way," he said cheerfully. "Only I don't know what you consider peculiar about a stuck drawer. It happens all the time."

We went into the bedroom, and Mary looked up and said, "Ken, it's a perfectly beautiful day—why don't you take a walk?"

"Don't you worry about my getting in the way of your house cleaning," he laughed. "If I do, just brush me along with the rest of the dirt."

"Why, I never meant anything of the sort," she protested. "I just thought—"

"Here's the drawer," I said. "You pull one end, and I'll pull the other."

Mary came over immediately and began to fuss, but we ignored her and concentrated on pulling. It was no use, though, for it would not move, and presently Ken told me to stop and began carefully to examine the bed and its drawer.

"Do be careful," Mary fretted. "You're soiling the spread."

Ken glanced up at her. "I'll have to get some tools to open this."

"I will not allow you to start chiseling and hammering on that bed," Mary said, putting her foot down. "That drawer has been stuck forever, anyway, and there's no need to start trying to open it now."

"But, Mary, it was open," I said seriously, "and now somebody has jammed it. After all that has been happening, I think we ought to open that drawer and make sure that it's—well, empty."

She flung around on me, completely exasperated. "Eugenia, really! This trouble over Suzy has made you hysterical. I will not have my valuable antique bed destroyed just because we are all upset. You were mistaken about the drawer—it never has opened, and I don't intend to have it opened now. And you're not to tell the police about it. I won't have them coming in here with hatchets and wrecking all my nice things."

"Whoa, Mary, back up," Ken said easily. "We'll let the drawer blow, if you say so. Anyway, Lucy has tea ready, and she said we were to hurry or the biscuits would be cold."

"Now why in the world did Lucy want to bother with afternoon tea?" said Mary, who had suffered too many interruptions already. "And butter so scarce, too."

"Well, I'm used to my tea," Ken said, his eyes still on the drawer. "We always have it in the afternoon, at four o'clock, in the Army. The corporals bring it around, you know—and to see those men serving tea under fire is an inspiration."

Mary looked at him for a moment with her forehead puckered and then said vaguely, "Oh, I see—it's a joke."

Ken sighed. "If you'll excuse me, I'll go and join the tea party."

"I'm coming too," I said firmly, although I knew Mary had an eye on the china figures which had not yet been washed.

She called after us, "You two go ahead, and I'll come in a minute."

Lucy had the tea spread out in the living room, and the three of us fell on it and had to use stern control to leave a biscuit or two for Mary. By the time she had torn herself away from the work and joined us, the tea had cooled and the biscuits were cold—but she didn't seem to notice it. Her eye fell on the green studio couch, which had not yet been moved, and she wanted to know, more or less politely, when Lucy and Ken were going to get around to it.

"Don't give it another thought," Lucy said airily. "We'll carry it out as soon as we've finished tea."

There was a light tap on the french doors that opened on to the balcony, and Egbert stuck his head into the room.

"You must forgive this rather informal entrance," he observed, settling his pince-nez, "but we were doing a little investigating on the balcony and heard your voices."

He stepped in, followed by his two men, and Ken remarked, "I had a feeling that we should have muzzled Lucy."

"Me!" Lucy shrieked. "Why, every time you open your mouth I think it's a thunderstorm blowing up!"

Mary tried to make a quiet getaway back to her beloved housework, but Egbert pinned her down neatly.

"Mrs. Fredon, I believe I have news of your husband."

Mary stopped on a dime and swung around to face him. "What is it? Where is he?"

Egbert's eyes shifted behind the glasses, and I could have sworn that his mind was, humming busily, trying to think up what to say next. He moved forward and after only a brief hesitation said smoothly, "If you'll just sit down and answer a few questions for me I'll be glad to tell you what I can."

Mary registered annoyance and sat down reluctantly, but before Egbert had time to start on her she started on Lucy, Ken, and me about getting the studio couch into my room.

"Come on, girls," said Ken, "we'll each take a cushion to start with."

"No, no," Lucy demurred, "I'll tell you how we'll do it. Put the cushions and the mattress on the floor, and we'll carry the bottom in first. I like to get the worst part over with."

Egbert said, "Now, Mrs. Fredon "

"No, you can't do it that way!" Mary exclaimed. "Take the cushions and mattress into the hall first, and go over them with the hand vacuum, and then put them on the bed. After that, you can carry out the bottom parts—go over it with the vacuum—and put it right under the window in Eugenia's room. I'll come as soon as I can."

Egbert cleared his throat and put a little more firmness into his voice. "Now, Mrs. Fredon, I'd like you to tell me if your husband has had any business worries of late."

Mary gave him her rather abstracted attention, while we started to take the parts of the studio couch out into the hall, and I heard her say, "No," decisively, as I went into the hall with a couple of pillows perched on my head.

When we had the pillows and mattress piled up in the hall Ken dropped his voice and said, "Lucy, remember when you gave an imitation of a vacuum cleaner at the country club that time? Do it again, will you, and put everything you've got into it, while Gene and I get the other part of this thing."

Lucy giggled happily and then sent her voice soaring into a steady drone. It was without doubt the best imitation of a vacuum cleaner I had ever heard if I had ever heard any.

Ken and I carried out the bottom section without accident, and to the accompaniment of only three apprehensive shrieks from Mary. In the bedroom we had to move a small table and a chair from under the window, but as soon as we had placed the couch there Ken put the table and chair on top of it. He said he wouldn't be responsible for moving one stick of furniture in Mary's apartment, and that the table and chair were now back in their original places, although a little closer to the ceiling.

Lucy stuck her head in the door and asked if she had done enough vacuuming, but Ken said no, Mary might think we had not been thorough enough and would make us do it over again.

"But my throat's sore," Lucy said huskily.

Ken eased her out into the hall, whispered, "Just a minute or so more," and closed the door on her.

He came back to me and handed me a cigarette. "Now we're alone, and I'll have to work fast."

"What at?"

"You. Now look here—you can see the sort of furlough I have—no one to take me in and love and care for me. I'm an orphan, and nobody cares. Mary is a good soul, and generous, but my cigarette ash and the soles of my shoes trouble her very dreams. In fact next furlough I'd like to come and visit you."

I laughed. "I live in a one-room apartment."

"Don't quibble—and why do you turn me down so promptly anyway? I know you have no steady in the Army."

"You don't say."

"If you did," he went on, "you'd be writing letters all the time, and going around asking for stamps and things."

"I don't think Egbert could have done better than that," I said admiringly.

"Never mind Egbert—I want you to write to me and let me take you out when I can get off."

"Dropping all other dates when you appear?"

"Yes." He caught my arm and swung me around. "We could have a lot of fun, and you know it—if only we didn't have all these people milling around."

"But what about the girl to whom you're practically engaged?"

"I found out that she's just been married."

"Oh dear," I said, "that's a pity."

"No, it isn't—I like you better—and if you're not tied up in any way I don't see why you won't give me the opportunity to—er—"

"To see whether you like me or not?" I supplied courteously.

"All right—if you want to put it that way. And at the same time you can be finding out whether you like me or not."

"Nothing could be fairer than that," I agreed.

"Good," he said, and enfolded me in a huge embrace with a kiss attached to it.

I disentangled myself and explained, "The kissing part comes later—it's illogical to put it in here."

"Listen, shut up, will you." He gave my head a playful push that practically dislocated my neck. "Now I want to make a date with you for about two o'clock tonight in Mary's ex-bedroom."

"I—what?" I said feebly.

"It's that drawer under the bed. Somebody has been busy with his little hammer—quite recently—and nailed the thing shut."

CHAPTER SIXTEEN

"I'M GOING to open that drawer," Ken said, "and if there's nothing in it, all right. Mary needn't know about it because there won't be a mark on her precious antique. I'm a smooth workman."

"I think it should be opened," I agreed uneasily, "but it seems to me the police should do it."

"No," said Ken. "Egbert's heart would be broken if he got all steamed up and then found the drawer empty."

Lucy pushed the door open and came in.

"I'm through," she croaked. "I suppose Mary will say we didn't clean the thing thoroughly—but I have my vocal chords to think of. Listen, we have to market for tonight's dinner."

"We'd better get going then," Ken said, instantly serious. "Let's see—what do we need?"

"Why don't we just go out for dinner?" I suggested, and was ignored by both of them.

They went along to the kitchen, discussing the fascinating subject, and I moved to a point just outside the living room and listened.

"I assure you," Mary was saying indignantly, "that my husband had no interest in other women. He barely noticed Mrs. Emerson, and I doubt that he was even aware of Suzy's existence."

"And yet he poisoned her," said Egbert delicately, "and very probably did away with Mrs. Emerson as well."

Mary gave off sounds of pure fury and could be heard getting to her feet, so I backed up and went to my room.

So that's the way Egbert figured it, I thought—and it sounded reasonable to me. Something had happened to Homer's mind, and he was sneaking around killing young women. He was hiding somewhere close by, too—perhaps right in the apartment—and I was a young woman.

I shuddered and, looking at the studio couch, felt a surge of thankfulness that Lucy was sleeping in with me. I tried to think of something else and immediately pictured the drawer under the antique bed—and Betty's dead body nailed into it.

My teeth were chattering by that time, so I clenched them together and went over to look out of the window. It gave on to a closed court, and there was nothing to see but the Emerson windows directly opposite. They were neatly draped with glass curtains, so that it was impossible to do any snooping.

I turned away and thought about Betty again. She couldn't be lying dead in that drawer, my reason protested feverishly—the weather was warm, and there would be an odor—there *had* to be an odor. I was conscious of a feeling of nausea, and when it had passed I went quickly out of the room.

Mary was in the hall, frowning and looking thoroughly annoyed. She did not see me, and went on into her own room, closing the door firmly behind her. It occurred to me suddenly that Ken was laboring under a misapprehension. Mary had complained of her room being haunted and had cleaned out Ken's room and had the studio couch moved. She had told him that she was fixing it up for Homer, and he had evidently assumed she was moving in there herself—and that the coast would be clear for him to open up the drawer.

But I knew that Mary had cleaned her own room with an idea of sweeping out the haunts along with the dust. I'd have to tell Ken, and perhaps we could persuade Mary to use Homer's room.

I turned toward the kitchen and met the intelligent shine of Egbert's pince-nez.

"Hello there," I said casually.

"Would you care to tell me just one thing—truthfully?" he asked with deceptive mildness. "Why are you here?"

"I embezzled some money belonging to my boss, and I'm hiding out until it blows over."

Egbert sighed and murmured, "You are most difficult."

"Well, it's no wonder," I said crossly. "I come here for a vacation, expecting peace and quiet, and the place might as well be a lunatic asylum. How would you like it?"

"I could not say," he replied equably. "I don't take vacations—I don't care for them."

I said, "Pardon me."

The doorbell rang, and he went along and opened up to Mrs. Budd, who was waving a card in the air.

"Here it is, Mr. Egbert—but you musn't pay too much attention to what she says. Betty was only trying to scare John a little."

Egbert took the card and studied it carefully, and I moved up behind him and peered over his shoulder.

It was a plain penny postal, and the writing said simply:

DEAR MOTHER,
   Have eloped with Homer. Don't worry about me. Feeling fine.
                                          Love,
                                          BETTY

Egbert turned it over, and I saw that it was postmarked Binghamton, New York.

"Is this your daughter's handwriting?" Egbert asked.

Mrs. Budd widened her eyes in surprise. "Why, of course."

"Are you sure?" Egbert persisted gravely. "Look again."

Mrs. Budd wrinkled her forehead, searched Egbert's face in a perplexed manner, and then looked down at the card with the first faint shadows of doubt in her troubled eyes. "Why, I—I never thought of anything else. It must be her writing—she'd never go off without a word and leave me worrying."

"You are prepared to swear that that is your daughter's handwriting?" Egbert asked.

Mrs. Budd blinked over sudden tears and stammered, "Of course I'm sure—but what do you mean anyway? If you think my Betty didn't write this, then where is she?"

Egbert shrugged. "Don't worry about it, in any case. We'll find her in a day or so."

Mrs. Budd brightened and said eagerly, "Oh, I wish you would"

Egbert patted her shoulder and suggested that she get a little rest and leave everything to him. They had a slight tussle over the card, since each wanted to keep it, but Egbert won. He tucked it into an inside pocket ushered Mrs. Budd out the front door, and then turned and made purposefully for the kitchen.

There followed a considerable uproar. I gathered that Egbert wanted Ken, Lucy, and myself in the living room for what he called further questioning, while Ken and Lucy wanted to do their marketing for the evening meal. Egbert finally bullied us all into the living room, but Ken and Lucy were so unruly that he couldn't get his questioning done at all. Ken had been begging one of Egbert's two stooges to go and do the marketing—nd in the end Egbert, in his exasperation, commanded the stooge to gather up the list and the ten-dollar bill that Lucy had been waving around and be on his way.

The stooge was humiliated, and Egbert felt called upon to explain.

"We should all be willing to step out of line a bit when it's a question of our armed forces. The sergeant naturally wants a home-cooked meal when he is on furlough."

The stooge seemed more or less satisfied and biffed off.

Egbert started on us in earnest then. In the first place he wanted a list of the guests who had been at the party, and it took Lucy and Ken a long time to remember everyone. While they labored over it I tried once or twice to steal away, but was nabbed by Egbert each time.

When the list of guests had been completed we had each, in turn, to give a personal history of ourselves. Lucy rather enjoyed that part of it, and spent a lot of time telling about all her beaux. She mentioned Ken as being one of them, and he immediately spoke up and denied it. Lucy attempted to argue the point, but gave up cheerfully enough when Ken remained obdurate.

Egbert flashed him a glance through the piece-nez and said crisply, "But you were Betty Emerson's beau."

"I was *not* her beau!" Ken shouted. "I merely took her out once or twice."

"Well, whose beau are you?" Egbert asked.

"This one's," said Ken, indicating me.

Lucy gave a little shriek, and Egbert snapped, "You only met her on Monday. Whose beau were you then?"

"I was not a beau at that time," said Ken with dignity.

Egbert rubbed his chin thoughtfully for a while and then stood up.

"I'm going now," he announced in ringing tones, after which he gestured toward the remaining stooge and lowered his voice. "I'm leaving Mac here—he has his instructions. But I want to warn you people about Mr. Fredon—only you must not tell Mrs. Fredon, because she will undoubtedly try to hide him if she knows what we think."

"But what *do* you think?" Lucy whined, looking scared.

"We think he's a dangerous lunatic," said Egbert.

CHAPTER SEVENTEEN

EGBERT'S ASSISTANT created a diversion by coming in with the groceries. He was red in the face and loaded to the chin with packages. Egbert—rather unfairly, it seemed to me—gave him a cold stare, brushed past him, and left the apartment. The fellow spilled the packages onto a table, dropped some change down amongst them, and fled after his boss. Mac was left standing rather forlornly in the hall.

Ken approached him and with a suspiciously friendly air invited him into the living room for a smoke. Mac started to refuse, but Ken took him by the arm and pushed him along. He established him in the living room with a cigarette and a drink of some kind at his elbow, and then gave Lucy and me a significant look.

"Now you girls run along and cook the dinner. Mac and I will take care of the dishes."

Mac looked somewhat astonished, and Lucy and I were stared out of the room by Ken, who was saying volumes without opening his mouth.

In the kitchen Lucy went briskly to work, and I hung around waiting for orders. Apparently she had none for me; however, as she began to move swiftly back and forth across the room, she bumped into me, no matter how small I made myself. I decided to remove the hazard and, murmuring something about setting the table, I eased out and crept along to the living-room entrance.

Ken was doing the talking, as usual.

"Yes—Mr. Egbert told me before, about Mr. Fredon. It began at his office, I believe—he was behaving oddly, and the officers of the company went into conference about him."

Mac's voice sounded eager and interested. "I'll just make a note of that, Sergeant—Mr. Egbert will want to hear it, because he contacted the office, and they all clammed up—said he had been behaving as usual."

"Don't bother making any notes," Ken said hastily. "I'll tell him when I see him again. But about the people who live in the other apartment here—I heard there'd been some talk among them about Mr. Fredon."

"People never want to tell the police anything," Mac said, sounding disgusted. "Mr. Egbert took a lot of trouble to inquire all around, and everybody seemed to think there hadn't been any change in Mr. Fredon in twenty years—right up to the time he disappeared. And this Mrs. Emerson, too—nobody noticed anything different about her. Maybe we better phone Mr. Egbert—he ought to have this information."

"I'll do it," Ken said quickly. "Just give me his phone number—or a number where you think I can reach him—and I'll contact him."

Mac handed out a couple of phone numbers, and Ken put them carefully in his pocket to be thrown into the wastebasket later. He took another swallow of his drink and said without a blush, "If there was no suggestion from anyone that Mr. Fredon was unbalanced, I don't see why Mr. Egbert came to the conclusion that he is a dangerous lunatic."

Mac set his glass down and said judicially, "What else can we think? He seems to have spirited this Mrs. Emerson away, and you know what he did to the girl Suzy."

"You can't be absolutely sure that he had a hand in either one of those things," Ken pointed out.

"Well . . ." Mac shrugged. "Mr. Egbert has to have some angle to work from—and that's the one he's taking."

Ken nodded gravely and murmured, "H'mm—yes, I see—yes, of course. And—er—are you a fisherman, Mac? Speaking of 'angle,' reminds me—"

I turned and left. The job of pumping Mac seemed to be over, and I had no wish to listen to Ken telling lies about his prowess as a fisherman.

I went into the dining room and threw a cloth over the table—and then wondered whether I ought to set a place for Mac. He was not supposed to have his meals with us, I thought, and I was quite sure that Mary would be annoyed if he did. On the other hand, Ken would almost certainly bring him in and sit him down, so I arranged a place for him, and when I had finished with the table I made off to my room.

Mary was there, stretched out on the studio couch, sleeping. The table and chair were now properly on the floor, and artistically arranged against the wall.

I tried to be quiet, but Mary stirred almost immediately and turned her head.

"I've been having a little nap," she explained, blinking. "I didn't want to crumple any of the bedspreads, so I came in here."

I nodded and said, "See if you can get off again—you need some sleep."

But she moved her head restlessly and began to talk instead. She had some bitter things to say about Egbert, because of his insinuations regarding Homer.

"Homer isn't like that," she insisted. "And even if he had had a mental breakdown—as that man seems to think—it wouldn't affect him like that. I know it wouldn't, Eugenia—I know Homer too well. Oh, if he'd only come back and I could talk to him."

"You'll want to talk to him before the police get to him, won't you?" I said thoughtfully.

"Oh yes—yes indeed. It would be terrible if they started pounding at him before I could warn him."

"Well then, why don't you sleep in Homer's room tonight, and when this Mac settles down somewhere—"

"What Mac?" she interrupted excitedly.

I had to explain about Mac, and she didn't take it very well; in fact, she was furious. She wanted to get up then and there and order him from the house, and it took a lot of soothing and explaining on my part to balk her.

"It will be all right," I said finally. "We'll get a shabby chair that's fairly comfortable and put Mac in it. He's bound to go to sleep."

"I have no shabby chair," said Mary coldly.

"As soon as Mac is soundly asleep we can stick a note in the front door telling Homer to go to his own room, and that you will be waiting for him there."

She thought it over and then not only gave her approval but seemed to be quite pleased. The only thing that troubled her was finding a suitable chair for Mac's slumbers, since she seemed convinced that he was certain to soil or damage anything with which he came in contact.

I told her to think it over carefully, warned her that dinner would be ready soon, and left her mumbling something about an old slipcover that she might bring out.

I headed for the kitchen, figuring that I ought to pretend to help Lucy again, but I ran into Ken in the hall. I told him that I had arranged for Mary to be out of her room during the night, but my voice trailed off at the end when I noticed that Mac had seated himself in the hall near the front door. He had helped himself to a chair from the living room—a delicate thing of curved, softly glowing old mahogany, upholstered in pale rose brocade.

I flew to him and told him that he'd have to take it back and then wait until the missus appeared to tell him what chair he might use.

He did as he was told, and after he had sweated off to the living room Ken dropped the grin with which he had watched the performance and asked me, "How the devil can we get into Mary's room tonight with the gendarme sitting in the hall?"

"If we can get him to face the front door we might be able to sneak in behind his back," I suggested.

"Maybe," Ken said dubiously. "Anyway, if he catches us we'll just have to take him along."

Lucy let out a trilling call that dinner was ready, so we collected Mary and went along. We tried to collect Mac, too, but he insisted stubbornly that it was not his place to eat with us, and asked if he could phone out for a sandwich. In the end he ate in the hall, in the nearest approach to a shabby chair that Mary could find, and from a tray that Lucy insisted on preparing for him. He sat with his back to the hall, directly facing the front door.

The dinner was delicious in every detail, but Mary dominated and dampened the conversation by wondering over and over again how she could get Mac away from the door, so that Homer could get in unobserved. Ken finally told her to go to bed in peace and leave it all to him. He'd think of some way to entice Mac from the line of his duty.

The evening was tiresome. Mary would not go to bed, and spent her time fretting about Homer, Suzy, and the condition of her chair when she should finally get it back from Mac.

Our combined efforts did get her off to bed at last, and when we had settled her the three of us retired to the kitchen for a drink. Lucy wanted to go on drinking and kick her heels up a bit, but after we had finished one round Ken hustled us both off to bed. It was eleven-thirty, and he said to me out of the corner of his mouth, "One hour from now—exactly."

But he was badly off schedule if he expected Lucy to be in bed and asleep within an hour. At twelve-thirty she was patting cream into her face and still had a few exercises to do. Even when she slid in between the sheets on the studio couch and stretched out with a sigh, she was not ready to go to sleep. She talked at some length on a variety of subjects, and when she unexpectedly fell asleep in the middle of a sentence I waited five minutes before I dared to leave.

Mac was still in his chair, but I decided that he had gone to sleep, since he made no move when. I crept across the hall behind him.

Ken was working on the bed with a flashlight held under his chin. He hissed, "Over half an hour late!" and then had to grab for the flashlight, which tumbled down his chest.

"Shut up!" I hissed back. "Why don't you turn on a light?"

"You want to bring everybody in here to find out what's going on?" he asked disgustedly. "Here, hold the damn flash while I work on these nails."

I took the flashlight and watched him for a while in silence.

"I suppose the drawer will be empty," I said after a while, trying to make my voice casual.

He said nothing for a moment, and then straightened suddenly and announced, "Now she ought to work."

I wanted to run away, and the flashlight drooped in my cold hands.

Ken said sharply, "Hold the light up," and I raised it as he rolled the drawer smoothly out from the bed.

There was a blue blanket covering something that lay beneath, and Ken snatched it away. I had only a glimpse of the thing before the flashlight fell from my numb fingers and hit the floor with a dull thud.

It looked like an Egyptian mummy.

CHAPTER EIGHTEEN

I HEARD KEN MURMUR, "Steady!" and felt his hand on my arm. My one thought was to get out of the room, but when I tried to move away Ken's hand tightened and held me.

"Stay where you are," he whispered. "You mustn't go rushing out there— what's the matter with you? Hold still while I pick up the flashlight."

He stooped over and groped around on the floor but contrived to hang onto me at the same time. I hoped hysterically that he would not find the flashlight, but after a moment he murmured, "Here it is—now don't scream," and threw the beam of light directly into the drawer.

It was a body, swathed from head to foot in bands of yellowish material—something that might have come from a museum. I began to tremble and Ken jerked at my arm warningly,

"I'm going to turn on a light," he announced, suddenly brisk. "We'll have to get hold of Egbert at once."

He began to grope around the walls, and I presently shook off the numb feeling that had held me silent, and whispered loudly, "Ken, don't be a fool—look for a lamp. This is not an ordinary room with a common wall switch—it's like a museum—mummies and all—"

I began to giggle shrilly, and he was back at my side in an instant.

"For God's sake, don't get hysterical—leave it to Lucy. She does a better job anyway."

This brought me around at once, and I helped him to look for a lamp. When we had found one and lighted it, its small glow was so eerie in the large, dim room that I flew around and switched on all the others, including even the delicate crystal pair on Mary's dressing table. Ken removed the shades from two that were close to the bed and stooped to examine the swathed body more closely. I gave it a quick glance and saw that the windings, in this brighter light, seemed pinkish rather than yellow.

But I could not look at the thing, and I turned away until Ken had finished.

He presently joined me and said, "Come along, we'll get in touch with Egbert."

I went into the hall without a backward glance, feeling intensely relieved to be out of that dreadful room.

Mac jumped about a foot when Ken tapped him on the shoulder, and I slipped into my room and left them to handle the matter. I got into bed and lit a cigarette, while Lucy continued to sleep peacefully through the sounds coming from the hall.

Mac was phoning, and Ken pacing up and down, and after a while I heard Mary's voice. Ken talked to her, but she seemed to be arguing, and I knew that she was trying to get them out of the hall so that Homer could come in.

Ken apparently urged her back to bed eventually. I could not hear what he said to her, but I knew he had not told her about our discovery, or there would certainly have been a rumpus.

I put out my cigarette and immediately lit another one. Lucy continued to slumber, and I thought—with a giggle that stemmed from my controlled excitement—that she would soon be out in the kitchen again, making coffee and dainty tidbits to keep our spirits up. And then, although I tried not to, I thought of Homer. A dangerous lunatic—he must be—he must have stolen that mummy from somewhere. Or perhaps he made it himself—wrapped it up. He *had* wrapped it up himself—of course he had—it was not a real mummy, I was sure of it, somehow—even though I had had only brief glimpses of the thing.

I flung out of bed and took two aspirins, and then I caught sight of my face in the mirror. It looked so ghastly that I put on some powder and lipstick—and then I wiped it all off again, because I thought it looked even worse.

I heard Egbert come in, and at the same time Lucy gave a prolonged snore and woke up.

"What on earth are you doing?" she asked, blinking at me.

"Preparing for the fray," I said, and sounded a bit feverish. "You'd better get up and make some coffee—we're going to need it."

I left her gaping at me and went out into the hall in time to follow Egbert, Ken, and Mac into Mary's bedroom.

Egbert peered into the drawer and then nodded five times. "This bears me out, you see—mad as a hatter."

"We'd better find out who it is," Ken suggested. "Shall we unwind it?"

"Yes, of course," said Egbert. "Here, give me a hand—we'll lift it onto the bed."

I had presence of mind enough to snatch Mary's spread off the bed as Ken and Mac leaned over the drawer. Egbert glanced at me, and I thought he was going to order me from the room, but instead he turned back to help the other two. As they raised the thing I thought I heard something drop from it back into the drawer, but no one else seemed to notice it. They lowered the wrapped figure onto the bed, and Egbert closed the drawer with an impatient foot. As the three of them bent over the bed I moved around to the other side—and this time Egbert spoke his mind.

"Miss Gates, I think you should go out while we do this."

I said, "No," and stood my ground, feeling like a naughty child, and Egbert shrugged.

They were searching for the end of the binding, so that they could start to unwind, but before they could find it Lucy burst in with Mary following her. Egbert and Mac turned together and tried to hustle them out, but Mary's quick eye had caught the outline on her bed.

"What is it? Oh, please—what is it?" she cried feverishly.

Since the attention was thus diverted from Lucy, she was able to make her way to the bed and have a good look. Her mouth opened, and she took on breath for a magnificent scream—and then no sound at all came out, and I knew that she was really scared.

I stepped over to her and gave her arm a little shake. "You're wonderful not to lose control, Lucy. You're going to make us some coffee, aren't you? We'll need it."

She swallowed a couple of times and whispered, "But what is it?"

Mary was getting unruly, so they let her come and take a look, and she screamed and hung onto Lucy.

"Oh, Homer! Oh, poor Homer! My God! Who did it?"

Egbert had been perspiring for some time; he now began frankly to sweat.

"It's not Mr. Fredon," he said irritably. "Mac, will you unwind the goddam thing—or do you want to stand there all night and play with it?"

Ken and Mac began to unwind in a silence broken only by Mary's sobs— but when the feet were free she blew her nose and dried up a bit. They were obviously the feet of a woman. From time to time, after that, Mary mopped at her eyes and murmured, "Oh, poor Betty!"

The girl's underwear was still on her body, and the rest of her clothes had been wrapped in with her. I caught a glimpse of tousled golden-brown hair, but Lucy and I turned away when the face was exposed.

Mary began to get noisy again, and Egbert snapped, "Look at her, Mrs. Fredon, and see if you can identify her."

"It's Betty Emerson," Mary moaned. "Oh, the poor thing—"

Egbert turned to Ken, who nodded, and then to Lucy, who snatched a quick look and muttered, "Yes—yes, it's Betty."

Ken moved away from the bed and touched my arm. "Come on—Lucy, Mary—you'd better go."

The four of us went out and along to the living room, where we sat down. Mary was crying into a damp ball of handkerchief, but Lucy was quiet, and looked shocked and scared. Ken was swearing softly.

"They'll think Homer did it," Mary wailed. "In fact they've told me . . . It's not fair—just because he isn't here . . . Homer would never do a dreadful thing like that. I tell you I know him, and he never would—but they won't listen to me—"

Lucy said slowly, "Poor John—this is going to be terrible for him."

"Oh, John!" Mary exclaimed, diverted. "What did he care for her, anyway—always running around with other women?"

"I'm sure John loved Betty," Lucy said conventionally, "but I was thinking of the money. He only makes peanuts, you know—they all lived on Betty's money."

"Well, one of them will surely get it now," I said, surprised.

"Oh no," Lucy replied with an emphatic shake of her head. "When Mr. Budd died he left Betty an annuity, and that's all. She wasn't married then, and she was supposed to look after her mother. But the money stops at her death, and the others haven't a dime."

CHAPTER NINETEEN

"I THOUGHT John Emerson must be a big executive somewhere," I said in some surprise. "He has that air about him."

"He's an insurance salesman," Ken explained. "Occasionally he sells something, but more often he just goes around with the girls and boys."

"I suppose that's partly why he was so upset when Betty left," I said thoughtfully. "No money and no prospects."

"You're wrong about the prospects," Lucy objected. "That what'saname—the oculist's widow—is simply rolling in the stuff, and she's been standing on tiptoe, holding her breath for months, waiting for him to say the word. And with all that, he's busy casting her off like an old glove right now."

"John is not a money snatcher," Mary said soberly.

Ken backed her up. "No, he isn't. Since Betty had it, they lived comfortably and he didn't bother much—but he'll buckle down now and make a decent living."

"He'll have to buckle to some tune," Lucy sniffed, "to make as much as Betty had."

Mary lost interest and began to agonize over Homer again, and after a while we heard Egbert in the hall, and then the voices of Mrs. Budd and John Emerson. We waited in dead silence, and I was conscious that my hands had balled into fists and I was hardly breathing.

When Mrs. Budd's scream came it seemed to release the tension and we all stood up. Mary said, "I must go to her," and hurried into the hall, and the rest of us followed slowly.

We came face to face with John Emerson, who looked at us rather wildly, without really seeing us. A strand of his dark hair lay across his forehead, and his face was livid. He was muttering, "Who did it? Who did it? I'll find out—"

Lucy and Mary began to speak soothingly to him, and Ken went off, with his jaw set, to get him a drink.

I went into the bedroom to see whether I could help Mrs. Budd. She was on her knees beside the bed, crying quietly, and as I approached, Egbert stepped away from her.

"What's the matter with Emerson?" he asked in a low voice. "He's taking it very hard, and I understood they were not a very happy couple."

"He was supposed to be fond of her," I said inadequately, but Egbert shook his head and looked vaguely dissatisfied.

A group of men pushed into the room, one of them carrying a camera, and I helped Mrs. Budd to her feet and urged her along to the living room with my arm around her. Mary and John were sitting on a couch, John holding a drink, and Ken, with another drink, was in a chair close to them. Lucy had disappeared, and I supposed that she had gone to the kitchen to make coffee.

John's face was pallid, and he stared straight in front of him and seemed to have no interest in the drink, which was tipped at a dangerous angle. Mary was talking to him quietly—mostly sympathy, with an occasional plug for Homer. John suddenly interrupted her in mid-sentence. He downed the drink at one gulp and stood up. "I've got to get to my little girl—I'll have to think of something to say to her—and I don't want anyone with me when I tell her!" He glared around at us wildly and then plunged out of the room.

Mrs. Budd broke away from me and hurried after him, pushing aside Mary, who tried to stop her, and calling hysterically, "John! Wait for me."

Into the uneasy silence that they left behind I asked, "Where is the child?"

"She's at camp," Mary sighed. "Poor little thing."

She began to cry again, and I was vastly relieved when Lucy, cheerful as ever, came in with a loaded tray.

Ken went to help her, and she said, "Pull those portieres—the place is full of weird men. We all ought to have our pocketbooks with us—even if they are the police."

Ken pulled the portieres with a heave of his arm, which brought Mary out of her sorrow at once and set her to worrying about whether he had done any damage.

We gathered around the tray, and Ken said restlessly, "I don't know what Egbert's doing, but I should think this problem ought to be easily solved now. Those two girls killed . . ." He drank coffee, squinting into space. "Betty wrapped up, like that . . . what was that stuff that was wound around her?"

"I bought it some time ago," Mary said dully. "Wanted it for ruffles for the curtains at the country house."

"Why, I remember that," Lucy exclaimed, round-eyed. "But I didn't realize that it was that ruffle stuff. Don't you know, I told you it was a too yellowy pink—only you wouldn't have it. I suppose you found out—that I was right."

"I did not," Mary said indignantly. "I just hadn't got around to taking it up there yet. I'm sure it would have matched perfectly."

Lucy sniffed and passed the remark that she had a very exact eye for color.

I said to Ken, "I don't know why you think the problem should be easy to solve now. It seems to me to be all snarled up—"

I stopped abruptly, because I remembered the theory regarding Homer. I hadn't been much impressed with it before but now it seemed very logical.

Surely anyone would have to be insane to wrap a body in that senseless fashion.

"It seems pretty clear to me," Ken said reasonably. "There was no reason for Betty's death. Nobody wanted her dead—and the same goes for Suzy—" He stopped as he became conscious that Mary's eye was fixed upon him.

"Now look, Mary," he added a bit lamely, "I didn't say it was Homer—but I do say that it's someone who's gone off his rocker."

Mary gave him a bleak look, but she said nothing, and I wandered over to the drawn portieres and peered through.

The police were still milling around, and I thought suddenly of the little book I had picked up in Suzy's room. I had left it somewhere in my room, and I reflected uneasily that if it were found there I might have trouble explaining it. I worried quietly for a moment and then slipped into the hall and across to my room. No one seemed to notice me, and I drew a little breath of relief as I closed the door behind me—and then turned around and came face to face with Egbert.

To my surprise, there was a faintly guilty flash from the pince-nez, and all he said was, "Er . . ."

I gazed at him and saw the return of complete aplomb. "I've mislaid something," he explained smoothly. "I was taking a look in here. You don't object?"

"Not at all," I said feebly, and supposed that the apology was the result of an obscure length of red tape that put my room out of bounds for him. "If you don't mind leaving for a few minutes?" I went on, recovering myself. "I wish to do something of a personal nature."

"Certainly, certainly," said Egbert, and made for the door.

I found the little book in a drawer of the dressing table and then stood for a while holding it and wondering what I could do with it. In the end I decided to stuff it down behind the cushion on the chair in which Suzy had been found.

I had been nervously turning the pages of the book, and, having made my decision, I glanced down at it—and then became interested—Suzy had had a love affair.

She had written: "Oh, lovely Thursday—I'm going to see him."

She saw him for three Thursdays after that, but when the fourth was in prospect she carefully explained to herself that he couldn't make it because of a business appointment. She was unhappy about it, and finally, humbly suspicious that he might be out with another woman. However, she saw him once more—apparently for the last time, because her next free Thursday bore the notation, "Saw them today—I just couldn't believe it. My world has tumbled down like a pack of cards." Poor Suzy—her big moment had evidently taken to beauing another woman around.

She saw "them" frequently after that—not only on Thursdays, but on other days as well.

There was only about a week more of writing in the book, but before I could finish it I heard Egbert's voice giving directions to someone in the hall. What a nose he had, I thought with reluctant admiration—trust him to search my room when I really had something hot in it.

I stuck the book down the neck of my dress and then went along to the bathroom, where I figured I could read it in peace while Egbert finished searching my room. There were several men in the hall, but I walked through with my head up and without being molested.

I locked the door, fished the book from the neck of my dress, and quickly read through that last recorded week. It was quite trivial but on the last page Suzy had written, "I threw that needle in the garbage."

CHAPTER TWENTY

I LEANED against the washbasin and thought that Suzy sounded a bit lunatic now—maybe it was catching and she had caught it from Homer.

I left the bathroom and went along to the living room, where I quietly dropped into the chair in which Suzy had died. I slipped her little book down behind the cushion and was busy lighting a cigarette when Lucy let out an agitated cry.

"Gene! Get up for heaven's sake! Don't you realize that that's the chair—"

I got up hastily, and Mary looked around and frowned. "Lucy, please don't be so silly. I can't just give that chair away."

"Where's Ken?" I asked, trying to break it up.

"He's trailing around after the police," Lucy said, yawning. "Trying to find out what they know." She yawned again. "I'm so tired I could die—but I think I'm too excited to sleep."

I was tired too, so tired that I was dropping, and I suggested, "Let's go to bed anyway. Egbert's so busy that he won't miss us, and he can always ask his little questions in the morning."

Mary and Lucy could not make up their minds about it, so I went off alone, undressed in the space of about two minutes, and crawled into bed. I was restless for a while, but I had begun to simmer down nicely and was getting drowsy when Lucy came in and woke me up again.

"That man Egbert told us to go to bed," she explained, "so Mary and I thought we might as well. There's nothing that puts lines in your face like lack of sleep."

I watched her as she started to pat cream into her face all over again, but this time it did not take so long, and I decided that she was slopping it a bit. She flopped onto the studio couch with a sigh and switched off the light.

"This is an exciting week, isn't it?" she asked happily from the darkness.

"Yes."

"Of course it's obvious to everybody but Mary that poor old Homer has gone crazy, but she's acting like an ostrich and simply won't face it."

"What is she living on?" I asked. "Has Homer's salary stopped?"

"Either stopped or stopping—but Mary's closemouthed and won't say anything. Only as far as I know she won't have anything until Homer's dead—he has a simply huge amount of insurance for her. But of course if they simply stick him in the asylum she won't even be able to pay the premiums. Too bad."

"What happens if they never find him?"

"Oh well," said Lucy indifferently, "I think you have to wait seven years or something, in a case like that, and then they declare him legally dead whether he is or not."

"So Mary will have to pull her horns in, financially, like the Emerson clan."

"A bit, maybe," Lucy agreed, "although I think they had a basketful of bonds somewhere—but not John Emerson. He can find himself a nice rich wife any afternoon in the week. He's slick."

Silence fell, and I took the opportunity to go off to sleep. I woke up once to find that Lucy was snoring like a trumpet, but I just said, "Hush!" and she shut up.

In the morning I was awakened by a tapping on the door and opened my eyes to see Lucy already on her way to answer it. It was Mac, with a message that Egbert had phoned and would arrive in about an hour. He wanted a general interview, and Mac thought we'd like to dress and have some breakfast first.

Lucy beamed at him and said, "Yes indeed—thank you. Will you wake up Mrs. Fredon and the sergeant too? I'll be right out."

Mac departed, and Lucy closed the door and went to work on her face without delay. I went yawning to the bathroom and took a shower, and was mildly surprised, on my return, to find Lucy still busy with her face.

"Nearly done," she announced cheerfully.

In another minute or so her face was its usual self, and she hurried into her clothes in no time at all. I was still dressing after she had left the room and was banging pots in the kitchen.

I got out in time to set the table and had just finished when Mary appeared and began to set it all over again, because I had not done it properly. The result was that when Lucy pushed through the swinging door with a tray loaded with food and coffee all the silver was in a heap in the middle of the table.

Lucy lowered the tray, yelled for Ken, and sat down.

"Pass me a knife and fork, Mary," she said. "I'm so hungry that I won't care if they don't match."

"You shouldn't have brought the breakfast in yet," Mary fussed. "I haven't finished setting the table."

Lucy reached over for a knife and fork and started to eat, while Mary, with three spoons in her hand, eyed her resentfully. When I helped myself to some cutlery and followed Lucy's lead, Mary gave up and tackled her own breakfast.

Ken came in shortly and ate up everything that was left, after complaining that we hadn't saved enough for him.

We hadn't quite finished when Egbert arrived and sat down in our midst. Lucy offered him coffee, but he refused almost impatiently and turned his pince-nez on Mary.

"Mrs. Fredon, you insist that your husband is sane?"

"Most certainly I do," Mary snapped.

"We have not been able to find him," said Egbert.'

"Maybe you haven't looked."

"We have made a thorough search," said Egbert severely.

"If he can elude the police so successfully he must have his wits about him," Mary pointed out.

Egbert said, "I agree," and everybody looked at him in surprise. We all waited breathlessly for his next words, but he merely lit a cigarette instead.

Mary looked somewhat cheered and said with quiet triumph, "I told you that Homer was not doing these terrible things."

Egbert smoked for a while and then observed, "I understand that the material that was wound around Mrs. Emerson's body was intended for trimming on some curtains."

"Drapes," said Mary, "yes. But I was so upset when Homer left that I was not able to do the work."

"Where was the material kept?" Egbert asked.

Mary looked into space and thought it over for a while. "Oh—I remember, now. I bought all they had, you know, because I thought it would match all the curtains, and I intended to gather it and make ruffles—it would be very suitable for the type of house I have, and it would have a uniform look from the outside. I think I bought too much of the stuff, as a matter of fact, although of course you need plenty when you're going to ruffle it. I brought it home in the car and put it in my room, and later I opened the package and showed the material to Homer. He liked it very much and thoroughly agreed with me that it was the right color—even though Lucy didn't think so "

"I still don't," Lucy interposed firmly.

"And so?" Egbert prodded.

"Well, then I couldn't find a place to put it—so annoying—it was such a large package. I left it on a chair in my room. When I went up to the cottage for the first weekend this summer, to open up and clean the place out, I forgot to take the package, and I was furious with myself. Homer didn't come with me—he had a bad headache and wanted to stay in bed. It was very upsetting, because I needed him—there are so many things for him to do when we open up. He wanted me to wait for another weekend, but I had everything planned, so I went up alone—except that I had a woman with me to help with the cleaning. We managed all right, although I missed the help that Homer could have given me. And then, when I got back on Sunday night, Homer was not here. When he didn't come home all night I supposed he had gone on a business trip—and forgotten to leave me a note—although I was worried and uneasy. I was just going to phone his office, on Monday morning, when Mrs. Budd came in with that card from Betty. I was very much upset—naturally—and so I can't remember whether that material was still on the chair in my room or not. I didn't notice it, one way or the other."

Egbert, who doubtless had heard the story of Homer's flight before, and merely wanted details about the ruffle material, nevertheless sat through Mary's recital with resigned patience. He sighed when she had finished, and then swept a look around the table that warned of a change of subject.

"Anybody here ever been in the undertaking business?" he asked mildly.

Lucy choked on her coffee, and after Ken had nearly floored her with a gentle tap on the back she sat mopping at her eyes and asked feebly if these quizzes couldn't be held between meals.

Egbert ignored the suggestion and sternly put the question to each one of us—but nobody had been in the undertaking business. Lucy offered Mr. Boxton, who lived in the building and had freely talked shop on several occasions. "Perfectly ghastly, too," Lucy said cheerfully. "You've no idea how callous they get."

Egbert nodded. "I know about Mr. Boxton. But it seems hardly likely that he embalmed Mrs. Emerson."

"Embalmed?" I echoed hollowly.

"Yes, certainly—how did you think she lasted? But in spite of the wrapping, which gives the idea of a mummy, the embalming was up to date. Injection of a drug."

"Listen, wait a minute," Lucy exclaimed suddenly. "Homer had some of that stuff—whatever it is—that drug. Don't you remember, Mary? Mr. Boxton gave it to him."

CHAPTER TWENTY-ONE

MARY FLEW INTO A TEMPER and declared that we were all against her. She admitted that Mr. Boxton had given Homer the drug, but declared defensively that Homer liked to dabble in chemistry and had wanted it only for scientific purposes.

"But your husband had never studied medicine or chemistry?" Egbert asked.

"He had—he did," Mary fumed. "He studied medicine by himself, because he was very interested in it."

Egbert seemed unimpressed. "Where did he do his dabbling in chemistry? Here—or at the cottage?"

"Mostly at the cottage. But sometimes he'd bring something back here with him, when he was very interested and wanted to go on with it. But I'm sure he never brought that stuff down—that Mr. Boxton gave him. You can look around and see."

Egbert cleared his throat, and I swallowed a laugh at Mary giving him permission to look around, when he'd already been into every nook and cranny—in his quiet way.

"He had that stuff up in the country, then?"

But Mary lost her assurance and began to look doubtful. "Why—I suppose so. I mean, he always took that kind of thing up there. Of course I didn't exactly see him do it, but—"

"He couldn't have taken it up to the cottage, Mary," Lucy broke in. "Don't you remember, Mr. Boxton gave him that stuff on the Thursday before he disappeared. Anyway, Mr. Boxton didn't actually give it to him for nothing, did he? Seems to me Homer paid for it."

Mary, dispensing with all subtlety and finesse, turned to Lucy and told her, in a ladylike voice, to pack up and go home.

Ken smoothed it over. "Look, Mary, Lucy's right and you're wrong. We all want to clear Homer, and the only way to do it is to tell the truth and get to the bottom of what has happened. Lucy's your friend, and she's trying to help you and Homer. You ought to apologize and ask her to stay."

"You really should," I murmured, thinking of all the meals Lucy whipped together without help from anyone.

Egbert held his peace and waited, with a gleam of hope in his eye. Mary, tracing a pattern on the arm of her chair, stewed in silence for a moment and then said fretfully, "Well—but Lucy is supposed to answer questions, and I don't see why she volunteers information that will only confuse Mr. Egbert."

Egbert assured her, with a certain amount of severity, that nothing ever confused him, and went on to say that the drug was not in the apartment, so where was it?

"How can you possibly know whether it's in the apartment when you haven't looked?" Mary asked reasonably. "I know he must have got it up to the country, where he keeps all those things. Anyway, I give you leave to search the entire apartment—and I'm sure you won't find it."

Egbert looked a bit gloomy, and I didn't blame him, since he now had to go and pretend to search the apartment. Especially when I thought of Suzy's needle that she threw in the garbage—that must have been it, and Suzy knew all about it.

But worse was yet to come. The only thing that could have kept Mary from supervising a search of her apartment was a broken leg, and she went hurrying off after Egbert, with a grim look on her face, to make sure that there would be no mayhem. Lucy, Ken, and I exchanged happy smiles as we heard her instructions about where the search was to start, how it was to be done, and the amount of care that was to be shown when breakables were involved.

I presently glanced out of the window and got to my feet. "It's a lovely day—I think I'll go for a walk."

"Oh no, you don't," Ken said lazily. "I tried it this morning. We're besieged."

"What do you mean?"

Lucy, who was fussing with her hair and had a bobby pin in her mouth, said in a muffled voice, "Reporters. They've been trying to get up here all morning. You'd have to walk in the center of a mob with questions bouncing off your head."

I took another look at the weather and sighed. It would have been a relief to get out of the place and away from it all for a while—but I gave up the idea and went out onto the balcony and looked down. Certainly there seemed to be a lot of people milling around on the lawn.

"Sit down," Ken said behind me, "and they may not notice you. If you stand there they'll spot you and throw up a ladder or something."

I sat down, while Lucy edged out and took the other chair, and Ken sat on the floor with his back against the doors.

"You know, Homer asked for that drug," Lucy said in a low voice and with a glance in the direction of the living room. "Boxton is a funny one, anyway. He shouldn't talk shop at social gatherings, but he always does—he practically boasts about it—tells the most ghastly stories—you've no idea."

"Who was around," Ken asked, "when Boxton gave Homer the drug?"

"Well, he didn't give it to him then," Lucy explained. "He just promised it for Thursday. He was going to have it all fixed in a hypo, I think, so that Homer could try it out on an animal or something."

"Do you think he actually gave it to Homer?"

"Why, I suppose so," Lucy said, widening her eyes. "I mean he must have."

"Who else was listening to that conversation?" I asked.

"Mary was there," Lucy remembered, squinting thoughtfully, "and both the Emersons—they were together for a change—and Mrs. Budd, and John's girlfriend was there—Dotty—and myself. It was in May, but it was a hot night and we were sitting on the lawn down there. I'd had dinner with Mary and Homer."

"And it was the following weekend that Betty and Homer disappeared?" Lucy nodded. "Saturday."

"But wasn't she missed Saturday night?" I asked.

"No," Lucy said, "she was going up to stay with a friend in New York and was not expected back until Monday morning—and that's when the card came saying she'd eloped with Homer." She thought it over for a moment and shook her head. "Whoever sent that card must have been cracked—imagine Betty eloping with Homer!"

"It does seem like Homer's work," Ken admitted. "Only Homer—and I think he'd have to be loony at that—could think that Betty would elope with him."

"He knew that Mary was going to take that bed up to the country, you see," Lucy explained eagerly, "and he figured he could get rid of the body in his own good time once it was up there."

Ken shook his head. "He must have been nuts—because they'd certainly have to take that bed apart before they could move it."

"No, you're wrong. That bottom part with the drawer was all in one piece when it came—it was only the posts and the canopy that were taken down. Mary tried to open the drawer and couldn't, so she said it probably had been stuck for generations and gave up trying."

"My guess is that it was nailed up by the moving men who brought it," Ken said.

"I suppose she was poisoned like Suzy," I suggested, breaking the silence.

Ken shrugged and said the autopsy would show what was what.

"What kind of poison was it?" I asked. "With Suzy, I mean."

But they didn't know, and we fell silent again until Lucy began to worry about the marketing. I said that surely Mary's grocer would be willing to send an order if it were telephoned, and the other two agreed without enthusiasm. It seemed that in order to get decent food you had to go around to the shop yourself and poke the stuff with your finger before buying it.

For some time I had been vaguely aware of sounds from the Emerson living room, and now I began consciously to listen. It was as though furniture were being moved around, and there was an accompaniment of muffled voices. The voices were raised occasionally and became sharp enough to be identified as belonging to Mrs. Budd and John. Once Mrs. Budd came near the french doors, and we heard her say, "If you had only put it where I told you to in the first place, you wouldn't have lost it. Anyway, I don't see that it matters so much."

There was a short, angry reply of some sort from John, and then silence. Ken stirred and said, "I wonder what the devil he's looking for?"

Lucy, who didn't want to miss anything, whispered, "Shh!" and then John's voice came, shrill and quite clear.

"It's just that it annoys me—losing that damned black eye!"

CHAPTER TWENTY-TWO

KEN'S FOREHEAD was wrinkled in a puzzled frown, and Lucy's mouth had dropped open a little.

I looked at them for a moment and then burst out in exasperation, "You two must know something about that black eye he's always cussing out—I don't know how many times I've heard him swearing at it, but I still haven't found out what he's talking about."

Ken shrugged and muttered, "Darned if I know," but Lucy was silent, her eyes half closed and thoughtful.

I prodded her, after a while, and asked urgently, "What is it, Lucy? What does he mean by his 'black eye'?"

She looked at me vaguely and said, "I don't know, he's always talking over people's heads. I think I'll go in for a moment. I've just thought of something new."

Ken tried to catch her skirt as she passed him, but he missed, and it flapped into his face instead. He swore under his breath and then asked aggrievedly, "Isn't that just like Lucy?"

"What did she mean—new recipe?"

But he shrugged and said that Lucy was often incoherent and there was no use in trying to straighten her out, and he added that as long as we were more or less prisoners doing time together we might as well sit and enjoy our little patch of blue sky. He suggested courteously that I tell him all about myself—and without giving me a chance to open my mouth, plunged into his own life history.

He had reached the age of ten—a fine, sturdy, manly little boy—when John Emerson interrupted by appearing on his balcony and making a slow tour with his eyes on the ground.

"Have you lost something, Mr. Emerson?" I asked.

He started and swung around on us, but as soon as he had recovered himself he said shortly, "Nothing. That is, nothing of any consequence."

Well, I thought, he hasn't lost either of his own dark brown eyes—and probably the thing wasn't an eye at all—maybe it was the title of a book. Perhaps he wrote poetry for his girlfriends and called it *The Black Eye*.

"Mr. Emerson, do you write poetry?" I asked.

The two of them stared at me as though I were a lunatic, and John said briefly, "Never wrote a line of anything in my life."

I subsided.

John glanced at Ken and said, "I apologize for having accused you of going away with Betty—it was stupid, but I really believed it:"

"Quite all right," Ken replied amiably. "I understand how you must have felt—don't give it another thought. If there's anything I can do, please let me know."

John turned away and muttered, "No, thanks, there's nothing."

Some sort of a commotion started in the living room behind us just then, and Ken and I went on in to see what was happening.

Mary was complaining about the carelessness of people who dropped things down behind chair cushions, while Egbert stood beside the chair in which Suzy had died, with her little book in his hand. Lucy, apparently with some idea that Mary's remarks were being thrown obliquely at her, had her head well in the air. I tried to drape myself with an air of innocence.

Egbert presently cleared his throat and shut Mary up by informing her that Suzy had undoubtedly dropped the little book into the chair, since it was Suzy's little book, after which he walked out of the room. I watched him go and wondered why he had bothered to lie about it. I knew he must have searched that chair as soon as Suzy had been removed from it—and nobody knew better than I that the book had not been there then. Egbert, I thought, was full of devious purposes and little white lies. He had us boxed up in an apartment, confusing and trapping us, and biding his time before he pounced.

"Isn't there a roof garden on top of this building?" Ken asked Mary.

"Yes," she said abstractedly, "yes, of course—only there's so much to do here. The whole place upset, you know. The floors need waxing—"

"Mary!" I interrupted sharply. "For heaven's sake, relax. What on earth is the use of cleaning the place and waxing the floors just so that Egbert and his men can tramp through and mess everything up again? You'll be ill if you don't have some rest. If there is a roof garden, let's go up and sit there and forget about Egbert—and your floors too."

But I might as well have saved my breath, because Mary had wandered off and, by the time I had finished, was already wiping down the legs of the piano. Ken watched her gloomily, and I felt a sudden pity for him—spending a furlough like this.

"Haven't you a date for today with any of your girlfriends?" I asked.

He shook his head. "I was all fixed up with Alice, but she phoned and put it off. I suspect Egbert of having had a hand in it, because he's made it pretty obvious that he'll feel much happier if we all stay penned up together where he can keep an eye on us."

"Egbert can go and fly his kite," I said firmly. "I'm going out today, and he and the reporters can do what they like about it. And right now I'm going up on the roof."

Ken followed me out into the hall and passed the remark that I probably hadn't made my bed yet.

"No," I said, "I haven't, but since I'm going to get back into it tonight, it would only be wasted energy."

"Suppose there's a fire, and the neighbors all come running in? Mary could never hold up her head again."

I ignored him, and Lucy stuck her head out of the kitchen. "Where are you going? Lunch will be ready in about half an hour."

"We'll be back," Ken promised her, and joined me at the front door where a man, apparently belonging to Egbert, was unhappily but courteously trying to explain that everyone would be happier if I stayed inside.

Ken brushed him aside, and he bleated, "Just a moment, please—if you will wait just a moment till I get Mr. Egbert. I believe he wants to speak to you before you go."

"Nothing doing," said Ken. "If he wants us we'll be up on the roof."

The man looked nonplused, and seemed, somehow, to be half rushing away to get Egbert and half staying to try and hold us. He lost out completely, and Ken and I went outside and closed the door firmly in his face.

Ken said, "We won't wait for the elevator—it might bring on another emergency—and anyway, it's only four flights up."

The four flights left me completely breathless, but Ken seemed to take it in his stride. When we emerged onto the roof he took a deep breath and said, "Ahh! This is more like it."

We wandered around for a while, and then I caught sight of a man, standing on the far side of the roof, apparently admiring a pot of geraniums. A second look identified him as Mr. Boxton, and I thought idiotically, I suppose he never sees geraniums at his funerals—they wouldn't be appropriate.

He raised his head and saw us, and then came bustling over.

"Frightful business, this," he said energetically. "Terrible. And I'm supposed to be on vacation and can't get off as I'd planned. That man Egbert actually threatens to hold me as a material witness or some such thing, if I try to go. Scandalous thing!"

"We're worse off than you are," Ken said without sympathy. "Take my girlfriend here—we're forced to keep steady company. No choice."

Mr. Boxton gaped at us, and Ken added, "I suppose they're on your neck because of that stuff you gave to Homer?"

Mr. Boxton sighed. "I never should have done it—never—but he was always such a steady, reliable sort of man. Never any foolishness, you know—you could trust him—and he was so absorbed in his little experiments." He sighed again and finished dolefully, "And then he runs away with another man's wife and kills her."

"But he couldn't have run away with her if he killed her here," I protested.

"Oh yes, he did," said Mr. Boxton wrathfully. "Mrs. Fredon goes up to the country, and she's no sooner left than Homer and Mrs. Emerson come out and get into his car—the small car. Mrs. Fredon had the big one—"

"When did they come back?" I asked breathlessly.

"They came back Sunday afternoon," said Mr. Boxton.

CHAPTER TWENTY-THREE

I DREW IN MY BREATH, but Ken gave me a warning look and then asked casually, "Why, did you see them come back?"

"Yes, I did," Mr. Boxton declared emphatically, "and they were laughing and joking. They'd had a high old time, wherever they'd been."

Ken shook his head. "Just because you saw them go out together one day and come back together the next doesn't prove it was one trip."

"Yes, it does. They wore the same clothes, only a bit dusty, and the car was dusty, and anyway, I saw him pull a couple of overnight cases out of the car. They didn't see me—I was coming home after a morning of golf—I'd been in good form, too, and I hurried along to tell them about it, but they got in ahead of me, and I never caught up with them."

"Where were you when you saw them go out the day before?" Ken asked.

"I was sitting on my balcony, and I happened to notice them—she had on a red suit, and you couldn't miss it—but they just got in and drove off, and I didn't pay much attention."

"You're on the eighth floor," Ken said, considering. "You wouldn't be able to see much of them from there, I suppose."

"Well no," Mr. Boxton admitted. "But I could see enough to know who it was."

"Have you told the cop Egbert about this?"

Mr. Boxton frowned. "No, I haven't. He annoys me—and anyway, he can find out by asking."

He seemed a bit upset at Egbert having been introduced into the conversation, so I said soothingly, "He is a bit of a pest, isn't he?"

There followed a fairly comprehensive description of Egbert's bad points, delivered by Mr. Boxton with a certain amount of vigor, and then I asked, "Did you think Homer and Betty were eloping when you saw them go away together like that?"

"Oh no," said Mr. Boxton, calming down. "Who'd be apt to think a thing like that? Betty was a gay, pretty young creature."

"I wonder you didn't tell someone you'd seen them come back on Sunday," Ken said after a moment. "I mean, when it came out that they were supposed to have eloped."

"It wasn't any of my business," Mr. Boxton declared petulantly. "John Emerson and I don't have much to say to one another—he once called me a nosy old—well, anyway, it was an opprobrious term—so I steer clear of anything that concerns him."

"But why didn't you tell Mrs. Fredon?" I asked.

"There's no use in my trying to be civil to Mrs. Fredon," Mr. Boxton said bitterly. "Just because I once spilled a little coffee on that fancy couch of her—such a commotion—and ever since, she barely nods to me. Homer and I have always been on very good terms, though—and personally, I don't believe that man Egbert's insinuations about him."

"What insinuations?"

"That Homer is crazy and is doing all this murdering. As a matter of fact he's quite sane—you get to know something about that sort of thing in my business—and I can tell you that Homer is as sane as you and I."

"I suppose you do acquire a certain amount of medical knowledge," Ken conceded admiringly. "Have you any idea what sort of poison was used? Something quick?"

Mr. Boxton looked serious and a trifle disappointed, and it was obvious that he didn't know. Apparently his knowledge of poisons was not specific, for he didn't even try to guess. "I've been thinking about it," he said weightily, "but I haven't come to any conclusion as yet."

We were interrupted by Egbert himself, who came snaking across the roof and greeted us with a brief flash of his teeth and the observation that it was a nice day, wasn't it?

Mr. Boxton glowered at him and suggested that if he were to look at the sky he might change his mind. We all looked up and discovered that we were surrounded and hemmed in by heavy black clouds. Ken said philosophically, "Well, anyway, it doesn't matter much to us prisoners."

Egbert ignored it and merely said mildly, "I think you two are wanted downstairs. Mrs. Davis said something about setting the table."

"Mrs. Fredon sets the table," I told him. "She's the only one who can do it to suit her. We wash the dishes."

"Do you, indeed?" murmured Egbert. "But perhaps you have a system of your own. I noticed this morning that the kitchen was piled high with dirty dishes."

"Damn it all," Ken muttered, "I forgot. I told Lucy we'd do them if she'd attend to the cooking. I hope Mary stays out of the kitchen—she'll have a heart attack."

Egbert cleared his throat and prepared to hold forth, but Ken got in ahead of him.

"Have you found out who sent that card to Mrs. Budd from Binghamton?" he asked.

Egbert cleared his throat again and said briefly, "No."

"Do you know who was up in Binghamton that weekend?"

Egbert shrugged.

"I suppose that means you don't," Ken went on in what was fast becoming his sergeant's voice. "You should have checked the hotels to see whether Homer and Betty were there."

Egbert adjusted his pince-nez and said coldly, "I did. Naturally."

Ken looked a bit disappointed. "Oh. Well—were they?"

"Yes." Egbert replied, still chilly. "Checked in under their own names, in different rooms."

"Did you find out what they did up there?" I asked after a moment.

Egbert nodded. "They arrived in time for a late lunch at the hotel, after which they went out—but just where has not been ascertained. They returned for a late dinner at the hotel, talked for a while in the lobby, and retired. The following morning they had a late breakfast—at the hotel—and left. That's all."

"They must have come straight back," Ken said thoughtfully, "because they arrived here in the afternoon. And almost immediately Betty was murdered and Homer disappeared."

Egbert added, "And a few hours later—at around nine—Mrs. Fredon returned to find the apartment in the same spotless order in which she had left it."

But how could anyone, I thought, restore Mary's apartment to its usual exquisite, neat, and cleanly order—after killing a person there? It seemed impossible.

Egbert was eying us, and I gave him an innocent little smile. I felt pretty sure that there was a purpose behind anything he told us; probably this was an inducement to us to blurt out various pertinent things that we were keeping under our hats. However, the results were negative, for the three of us stood before him in wide-eyed silence, and he presently told us, rather irritably, that we'd better go down for lunch.

We were back inside the apartment, with the door dosed, before we noticed that Mr. Boxton was still with us. I think he did it on purpose, because as soon as he was safely in he said in a loud, carrying voice, "What am I doing? I'm getting so absentminded these days," and of course Lucy heard him and immediately came bustling out to invite him to lunch. He accepted gaily and accompanied her back to the kitchen.

I hurried along to the dining room, where I found the table neatly arranged for lunch. I knew that Mary would have Lucy in the doghouse for inviting Mr. Boxton, and with a vague idea of making things easier for her I inserted another place—complete with cutlery and napkin—and then went along to my room to wash up a bit.

I could hear Lucy and Mr. Boxton laughing and joking in the kitchen, and I presently went out there, but they paid no attention to me. Lucy was showing Mr. Boxton a new dance step, and I retired into a corner to be out of the way.

It was a large kitchen—modernized and gleaming—and had every imaginable convenience, from an intricate electric mixer right up to a fancy dishwashing machine and a huge bin which held frozen vegetables and fruits, so that Mary could have an out-of-season meal whenever she happened to want it. The stove had two ovens and eight burners, and I was admiring it idly when Lucy suddenly yelled, "Oh, my God!" and rushed over to it. She wrenched open one of the ovens, gave a gusty sigh of relief, and then called shrilly, "Lunch, everybody! All ready!"

Mr. Boxton and I helped to carry the stuff into the dining room, and there followed a short, silent struggle during which Mr. Boxton stood up manfully under Mary's glacial stare—and then we all sat down and began to eat.

Ken sent a calculating glance at Lucy and Mary and then asked casually, "Did you know that Betty actually sent that card to Mrs. Budd saying that she and Homer had eloped?"

Their heads jerked up together, and Ken, having got his effect, immediately supplied a theory. "I think she was joking. It seems obvious to me that Betty and Homer had some private business in Binghamton. I don't believe it was a secret—I think they were going to tell about it—and Betty sent the card off to her mother for a laugh."

Mary said intensely, "I don't believe it," and Lucy protested, "But I thought they didn't go to Binghamton at all?"

"Betty may have," Mary said quietly, "but Homer was here all the weekend."

CHAPTER TWENTY-FOUR

LUCY REACHED for a piece of bread and said, "Mary, do be reasonable. How could you possibly know whether Homer was here when you were away yourself?"

Mary ignored her and spoke to the rest of us. "I know it quite well, because that's the weekend I had all the winter rugs off the floors, and the summer rugs didn't go down until Monday. That Mrs. Brindle, who lives underneath, put in a complaint—she's always complaining, anyway—and she said that the noise had been very disturbing—that she could hear every step on the bare floors. She declared that it was going on late Saturday night and started again on Sunday morning at ten o'clock."

"Oh, Mary!" Lucy protested. "Don't be so silly. That Brindle does complaining in her spare time for relaxation—she has to sit and think up things to complain about. There's no use trying to make sense out of anything *she* says."

"Well—but I told her there was no one at home that weekend, and she declared that I ought to call in the police. She *insisted* that someone was walking around."

"I think it's easily explained," Ken interposed. "She heard Betty and Homer when they came home, and in her complaint she stretched the time of the nuisance back to ten o'clock—and even to the night before. That's more or less typical of chronic complainers. Suppose we forget the whole thing."

"Certainly," said Mr. Boxton. "That Brindle woman is right out beyond the pale. I had it from the superintendent that she lodged a complaint when I moved in here—strictly on the basis of my profession, you understand. Seemed to think I might meet her in the lobby with a corpse tucked under each arm." He paused to laugh heartily, and then switched to a more serious subject. "Did I ever tell you about the time I won the state team of four? Bridge, you know."

No one gave him any encouragement, but he told it anyway. It was a long story, and he referred to himself, throughout, as the winner—although there seemed to be three other people who won the thing along with him. However, it developed that these three other people might have done reasonably well in a game of old maid, but Mr. Boxton had had to carry them to victory in the state team of four on his own shoulders. He did all his own laughing at the humorous parts in the story, and when he paused for breath, at the end, Mary heaved a delicate little sigh and then announced flatly: "I intend to clean the kitchen thoroughly this afternoon."

Lucy protested instantly and vigorously. She had everything arranged now so that she could lay her hand on whatever she wanted. She didn't mind cooking for everybody, but it made everything ten times harder when you didn't know where anything was. She ended up on a passionate plea. "Can't you just leave it until I go—and then clean up my dirt once and for all?"

"Not another minute," said Mary firmly. "I took a look at the kitchen a while ago, and it's in a frightful state. If that sort of thing goes on we shall have cockroaches."

Lucy sent an agonized look at Ken, and he tried amiably to help. "That mess you saw," he told Mary, "was there because Gene led me astray and diverted me from my duties. If you'll just have a little patience you'll find the kitchen bright and shining again—directly after this meal, in fact."

Mary shook her head obstinately. "No man can do a proper cleaning job. I shall do it myself."

Her eyes wandered around to me, and I immediately claimed a headache—but Lucy went at it in a more direct fashion.

"Don't expect any help from me, then. There's no need for you to touch the kitchen—but if you insist, you'll do it alone. I have enough to do with the cooking."

"I didn't ask you for help," said Mary coldly, "and I don't want any. I shall do it alone."

Ken and I washed the rather formidable collection of dishes, but though we invited Mr. Boxton to help he remembered that he had an engagement and departed hastily.

Lucy put the food away to a running accompaniment of grumbling.

"Some women make a god out of their homes—fire, famine, or flood—Sister comes down with scarlet fever or Junior breaks his leg—it doesn't matter—the dust has to be removed from the corners. They don't care how many lives they make miserable—waxing the floors comes first. When you go into their houses you're afraid to use the ashtrays and you feel all the time as though you should have left your shoes on the mat outside. You meet women like that at parties and all over—and they're so dull it makes you want to scream. The only time they come to life is when somebody asks about the best way to clean up white woodwork or something. Then listen to them go!"

"All right, pal," Ken said finally. He removed his dishwashing apron and wrung it out. "You've relieved your feelings. Now you can relax and let Mary relieve hers by laundering the kitchen."

"It's easy for you to talk," Lucy said gloomily.

We left her there with her brow furrowed, and Ken steered me along to the front door.

"Where are we going?" I asked, pulling back. "It's time for my nap."

"I always insist on the boys having a nap after lunch back at camp," he said, giving me a cold eye, "but you're only a lousy civilian, and we have work to do. We're going to call on that pearl among women—Mrs. Brindle."

"My dear Holmes!" I began, but he slapped a hand over my mouth and pushed me through the door.

He was all purposeful energy until we got to Mrs. Brindle's door, when he seemed to suffer a relapse.

"What's the matter now?"

"I—er—don't know how to open the proceedings."

"Just step to one side and watch," I said, and rang the bell firmly.

The door was opened by a young maid—which immediately placed Mrs. Brindle as one apart and distinct from the common people, who were all fresh out of maids.

"We wish to speak to Mrs. Brindle," I said. "It's very important."

The maid admitted us to the foyer and disappeared, and I ran my eye over the furniture. There were no antiques—solid stuff, and completely mongrel—just the sort of thing to cause Mary to raise an eyebrow.

Mrs. Brindle swept into the foyer, and her assurance was so aggressive that the furniture immediately appeared to be quite all right. She was a medium heavyweight, with a gray, upswept coiffure and a cold, fishy gray eye. I could see that she was preparing to ask brusquely what she could do for us, so I got in ahead of her.

"Mrs. Brindle, we're staying in Mrs. Fredon's apartment—upstairs, you know—and we want to apologize for that terribly noisy party we gave. I *know* it must have kept you awake all night—and we had no idea of it turning out like that. It was to have been just a few friends in for a little bridge—but I'm afraid they were not the right kind of people. They brought liquor with them, and other people whom we didn't know—and they pulled the rug up and danced. Why, there was a girl named Alice—"

Ken kicked my ankle, and Mrs. Brindle said grimly, "They danced—all right—fearful racket. Couldn't you make them stop after I'd sent up the complaint?"

It was the first I'd heard of a complaint, but Ken seemed to know all about it. He coughed gently and explained, "I'm afraid it was ignored by the person who answered the door—a marine—and he said, 'Tell her to—er—well, these marines get the polish scraped off them a bit—but anyway, the trouble with these floors is that they're not properly soundproofed."

Mrs. Brindle suddenly beamed on him and decided to let us into the living room. When we were settled into an odd assortment of chairs she said to Ken, "You are quite right about the floors. I have often said so. And of course when there are no carpets it's really dreadful—every sound pounding into your head."

Ken nodded sympathetically. "Mary was telling us that you were bothered by the noise that weekend she took her winter rugs up."

The Brindle eye glittered. "It was outrageous. I don't know what Mary was doing—she practically bit my ear off when I mentioned it—but she started Saturday night and kept it up all day Sunday, banging around on those bare floors—"

"But Mary wasn't here that weekend, you know," Ken said.

Mrs. Brindle gave him an alert glance. "So she told me. Anyway, someone was there."

"Did it sound like a man or a woman?" I asked, and felt a bit like Egbert.

Mrs. Brindle began to enjoy herself. She gathered that there was something sinister about the footsteps, and she went into a deep huddle with herself. However, when she rose to the surface again, all she could say was, "Well, really—I'm not sure. But I'll tell you one thing—I believe whoever it was was looking for something. At the time I just assumed it was Mary doing her endless housework—spends her life, you know, chasing the dirt around up there. Never stops to think how a vacuum cleaner or a waxing machine sounds to someone sitting right under it but what I mean is, those footsteps were simply incessant."

"Where were they, for the most part?" Ken asked.

"I should say more in Mary's bedroom—but they were all over the place." She coughed and leaned a little toward Ken, with her chilly gray eyes on his face. "Tell me—you ought to know—what really happened up there? It's most peculiar and unpleasant, living in a place where murder has been done. I've put in a complaint to the management."

Ken murmured that we didn't really know anything and that anyway it was all in the papers.

Mrs. Brindle snorted. "That's simply an evasion, young man. After all, you were right there—you could tell me some of the details."

I spoke up then and told her some of the details in a low, confidential tone, while Ken squirmed uncomfortably in his chair.

In no time at all we were gossiping about the Emersons, the Fredons, Lucy and Mr. Boxton, and Mary's occasional maid who came in for cleaning when she felt like it—the only one Mary would tolerate, and the only one who tolerated Mary.

Mrs. Brindle had something to say about them all—Lucy, who was always running after the men, John, who was always running after the women, Betty, who had had a secret boyfriend—Mrs. Brindle shot a significant glance at Ken—Mrs. Budd, who was slightly common, didn't I think? Homer was a fine man, but dull—always talking about dull things—and Betty was certainly not the type to run away with a dull man—although, come to think of it, there was one subject they both seemed interested in and had discussed together quite frequently—very odd, too, because it was Egyptian mummies.

CHAPTER TWENTY-FIVE

I COULD SEE that Mrs. Brindle felt no significance in what she had just said, and I realized that Egbert must have kept quiet about the mummified condition of Betty's body. Ken and I did not exclaim or comment, but there must have been something electric in our silence, for Mrs. Brindle stopped abruptly in mid-sentence, looked from one face to the other, and asked, "What's the matter?"

"Nothing," Ken said, too airily. "Nothing. Nothing at all."

It seemed clumsy to me, and I added hastily, "We mustn't impose on you any longer, Mrs. Brindle. We came down only to apologize, but it's been so pleasant . . . Mr. Egbert will be sending out an alarm for us."

Ken rose at once, and Mrs. Brindle reluctantly accompanied us back to the foyer. She asked in a ghoulish whisper, "Do they keep you *prisoners* up there?"

"It's just that they like us to be around within call," Ken explained. "Help them out when they get stuck."

She gave him a half-doubtful look and then made us promise to return at the earliest opportunity and tell her the latest developments.

Out in the hall, with the Brindle door closed behind us, Ken grinned at me and announced, "This is where I leave you. I'm going to run the blockade and try to get in some supplies—a few delicacies to tempt your appetite."

I nodded. "Go ahead. My appetite can always be tempted by a steak, and I could use some candy, and—"

But he was already sneaking quietly down the stairs, so I went on up by myself. The door was locked, and I had to ring, and Mary answered, with a strand of hair hanging across her forehead and her hands red and still wet.

"Where have you been?" she asked crossly. "Ken has disappeared, and Lucy went out and left me. Said she wanted to get some supplies. She deliberately insulted me, too. She wore a hat and dress of mine and then told me she wanted to look dowdy so that the reporters wouldn't recognize her."

"Oh, don't let Lucy bother you," I said, swallowing a grin. "She was just talking."

Mary mopped at her wet hands with her apron. "Well, I should hope my clothes are in quiet taste anyway. Lucy's things were always a bit gaudy."

I gave a conservative nod to keep her quiet, but spoke no words that she could repeat to Lucy.

I discovered that I was being maneuvered toward the kitchen so I stopped dead and said firmly, "I'm going to take a nap."

"Why on earth?" Mary asked, looking exasperated. "You slept all right last night, didn't you?"

"Yes, but I'm going to take a nap anyway."

She followed me into my room and said fretfully, "If you'd help me in the kitchen it would be done so much sooner."

"Now look, Mary, you need rest yourself, and if you'd go in now and take a nap—and let the kitchen blow—you'd feel a hundred percent better."

To my utter surprise, she showed signs of indecision and finally admitted weakly, "I am dreadfully tired; perhaps I'd better rest. It's all been so upsetting and frightening—and Lucy nagging at me all the time, as though I hadn't enough . . ."

I untied her apron and steered her along to Homer's room. "You just forget Lucy and everything else. You need to relax."

I removed the spread from the bed and held it out of her reach so that she couldn't refold it the right way, and after fussing a bit she presently lay down and heaved a deep sigh.

"I expect you're right—I feel as though I might sleep a little. Close the door after you, please—I don't want Lucy banging in and disturbing me."

I closed her in and went back to my own room, which was in a mess because neither Lucy nor I had touched it since we got out of bed in the morning. I yawned and, wandering over to the window, had a look at the Emersons' apartment across the way. I backed up immediately and hid behind the drape, because Mrs. Budd was standing at one of the open windows and appeared to be washing the surrounding woodwork. As I watched her she stopped suddenly and, laying the back of her wrist across her eyes, began to cry with the easy abandon of a child. I swallowed uncomfortably and was about to turn away when John appeared behind her. He put an arm across her shoulders and spoke soothingly to her. After a minute or two his voice became clearer, and I heard him say, "Go and powder your nose, now, and get your hat, and I'll take you for a drive. You need some air."

"But we can't, John—you haven't enough gasoline."

"Yes, I have. Come on." He urged her away from the window, but the last I saw of her she was still shaking her head.

I yawned again and, stretched out on the bed, and immediately my mind became a beehive of thought and speculation. That small object, for instance, that had dropped back into the drawer when Betty was lifted out—I had heard it distinctly, although I had not seen it. But surely Egbert had found it; he must have searched the drawer.

Perhaps he hadn't found it, and it was still there. I considered this for a while and then got up off the bed and went out into the hall, determined to have a look myself.

But the door to Mary's room was locked, and I returned to my bed, wondering who had locked it and why. Surely they couldn't lock Mary out of her own room—with all her things in there? And if they had, did she know about it?

I went off to sleep after a while and must have slept for some time. I woke up perspiring, heavy-eyed, and cross. The telephone was ringing persistently. I lay there for a while, frowning and wondering why nobody answered, and at last dragged myself off the bed and stumbled across the room.

The bedroom door was locked, and there was no key. I rattled the knob, unbelieving, for some time, and at last knelt down and peered into the keyhole. The key was in the lock—on the outside—and there could no longer be any doubt that someone had deliberately locked me in. I made a quick, feverish search of the room while the phone petered out, but there was no other key, and at last I went slowly back to the door and knocked tentatively. There was no response and no sound of any sort, and after knocking and calling for a while I went over to the window. The Emerson curtains were stirring in a light breeze that had sprung up, but there was no sign of anyone. I leaned out and called Mrs. Budd's name, and then John's, but the curtains continued to flutter lazily, and no face appeared behind them. I was pulling myself together for one last yell when I heard Mary's voice and turned to see her head bobbing out of Homer's window.

"Eugenia! For heaven's sake! Are you locked in too?"

"Yes!" I bawled. "What's going on anyway?"

"I don't know—it must have been that man Egbert. Listen, don't rouse the whole neighborhood. Can't you make the fire escape, there?"

I turned my head and saw that the rear living-room window, next to me, opened on to a fire escape. The iron railing was only a few inches from my own sill, and after eying it dubiously for a moment I called to Mary, bravely, that I'd try.

I eased out onto the sill, gingerly, and clutched the railing with sweating hands. I had climbed over it and was in the living-room window in a matter of seconds—but my legs were trembling as I made my way to the hall, although I felt brave and dashing at the same time.

The apartment was very still, and it was a relief to hear Mary's voice calling that her key was lying on the floor, outside. I found it and opened the door for her.

She was more annoyed than anything else. She had a crooked hairpin in her hand, and she explained, "I got the key out, all right, but these hairpins aren't strong enough to turn the lock. When that policeman comes around here again I shall have it out with him. I'll go to somebody higher up, if necessary, but I will not submit to being locked into my room like a rat in a trap."

"When did he lock us in?"

"If I'd known *when* he did it," Mary said impatiently, "I'd have protested—naturally. But I was asleep, and he must have been very cautious about it, because I'm a light sleeper and the least thing wakes me."

"Well, don't worry about it now," I soothed her. "Did he lock the other doors?"

She went over and tried Ken's, but it was open. "No—you see—but of course Ken was not in his room. My own room was already locked—I did it myself to keep Lucy out. She simply lives on other people's affairs."

I looked at my watch and found that it was nearly eight o'clock.

"Why—our two supply merchants have never come back," I said in some surprise. "We've been left to shift for ourselves. I suppose they met up with each other and decided to go to a movie or something. Probably that was one of them on the phone a while ago."

Mary was not interested. She was still plotting vengeance on Egbert, who, she decided, had gone off and forgotten to unlock our doors after completing whatever shady business he had been up to.

I doubted that Egbert had had any hand in it at all, but I could see no value in further discussion, so I suggested that we get something to eat and led the way to the kitchen.

We had a meal that was sufficient—if not up to Lucy's standard—and after we had cleared up, and Mary had toured the kitchen looking for the last crumb so that she could sweep it away, I told her that I had a headache and thought I'd go straight to bed. I merely wanted to get away from her fussing, but she brought me an aspirin and stood over me until I had swallowed it. However, she presently retired to Homer's room, and I settled myself comfortably in bed with a book—having made sure, first, that the key was on my side of the door.

For a while I read in peace, and then I began to think again of the small object that had dropped back into the drawer when Betty was lifted out. I tried to tell myself that Egbert would certainly have searched the drawer, but I couldn't get it out of my mind, and after a while I got up and went out into the hall. I took the key to Mary's bedroom from the desk where she kept it and quietly unlocked the door. No sense in letting Mary hear me, I thought nervously—she'd think I was snooping, like Lucy. And maybe I was, too.

Once inside the room, I almost turned back, but curiosity was a bit stronger than fear and I switched on a small lamp and hurried over to the drawer. It was heavy and stiff, and after a lot of tugging I was able to get it only part way out. It was in shadow, and I could not see much, so I stretched an exploring hand. My fingers touched something marble cold, and I drew them back as though they had been stung. In fascinated horror I peered more closely into the drawer—and recoiled, gasping and sweating. Betty seemed to be lying in there, wrapped up as a mummy again.

CHAPTER TWENTY-SIX

I HAVE NO RECOLLECTION of what happened immediately following my gruesome discovery. My next sensation was a sort of gasping surprise because someone seemed to have thrown a bucket of cold water over my face— and then I saw that Lucy and Ken were looking down at me anxiously. I tried to say something and Ken said, "Shh!" rather sternly. "Don't shh her," Lucy shrilled. "Gene, for heaven's sake, what happened to you?"

"Can't you at least wait until I get her onto her bed?" Ken protested. He leaned over, raised me with the utmost ease, and slung me over his shoulder. He walked out into the hall, and I caught sight of Mary at the door of Homer's room. She called out, "What is it? Ken! What has happened?" Almost immediately she let out a shriek, and I thought she had discovered the body, but it wasn't that. I heard Lucy say, "All right, Mary—don't have hysterics. A little cold water won't hurt the carpet. Keeps the moths out."

"But what has happened?" Mary asked agitatedly. "What was she doing in there?"

Ken turned into my room and deposited me on the bed, after which he sat down beside me and held my hand.

"Now keep quiet. Lucy is going to fix some brew that will calm you down—or give you a lift—I forget which."

"Did you see it?" I whispered feverishly. "How could Egbert have left that body there—it's dreadful! And cold—so terribly cold. How does he keep it as cold as that?"

Ken looked at me oddly and asked, "Where did you see the body?"

"In the drawer, of course—in that drawer under the bed. But I don't know why I fainted. I never have before."

He stood up abruptly. "The drawer was closed when we came in. Just a moment—I'll take a look."

He went off to Mary's room, and I gathered that Mary was there, presumably mopping up the water, for I heard her voice raised in protest and accusation. She said something like, "If you people would leave that drawer alone you wouldn't always be finding things in it," and then for a while there was silence.

Presently Ken came back and sat down beside me again with a serious look on his face. "Just close your eyes and try to be quiet. Lucy is getting a doctor, and you'll soon be all right again."

"But did you see it? In the drawer?" I asked impatiently. "Why do you suppose he keeps it there?"

"Listen, Gene," he said soothingly. "There was nothing in that drawer—it was quite empty. The excitement has been too much for you."

"Do you mean it's gone?" I gasped. "But it can't be—it was there."

Ken said, "Shh."

I dropped my head back onto the pillow and thought about it. Someone had removed the body—and there had been only Mary in the apartment with me. But if Mary had done it, surely she would never have left me lying on her precious carpet. I smiled, and Ken stirred and said, "That's better."

I turned my head on the pillow and looked at him. "Go and search for it, Ken. It can't be far away. Somebody moved it when I passed out. But you ought to look now. Please—don't waste time. It must be around somewhere."

He looked at me with pity, and after a moment Lucy appeared with a cup of broth. I decided languidly that I should try to keep my strength up, so I started to sip the broth—and ended by drinking it in great gulps and wishing I had more.

"The doctor will be here in just a little while, dear," Lucy said in her bedside voice.

"He can give you a going over, Lucy," I said, slipping my legs over the edge of the bed. "You're looking a bit seedy. I have to go and find that thing."

They both pushed me back, and while we were fighting it out Mary came in.

"Eugenia, what on *earth* were you doing in there? Why couldn't you have stayed in your room, instead of prowling around like that?"

I figured that I was being scolded for having brought a wetting upon the carpet. I shrugged and said, "I had to go in—and I found something, too."

"Were you and Mary alone in the apartment?" Ken interposed. "I thought Egbert was keeping a man here?"

"I expect he had to go off," Mary suggested a bit vaguely. "He locked us in, you know, before he went. Surely the police have no right to do a thing like that."

This had to be explained to Lucy and Ken—for which they swapped an outline of their own movements. They had met in the local market, and after prodding and sniffing at the meats, vegetables, and fruits, they made their selections. Ken ran across Alice at that point, and she indicated that she would be free for afternoon tea, if Ken cared.

Ken cared, and Lucy departed in a slight huff and established herself in a cocktail lounge. She met several people that she knew and had eventually had dinner there. Ken had parted from Alice at about seven and had run across a pal of his who had taken him to a tavern for a couple of drinks. In the end he and Lucy had met in front of the apartment and had come in together. They had found the door to Mary's bedroom open, the small lamp still burning, and I was stretched out on the floor.

"It was horrible!" Lucy shuddered. "We thought you had been killed—like the others."

Egbert and the doctor arrived together, and both came in to see me without delay. The doctor was a venerable old soul with white hair, who explained that he had been retired for years, but since he lived in the building, he'd stretch a point and take care of me. Ken and Lucy gave him my symptoms, and I was unable to get in a word of any sort.

Apparently my case presented no baffling problem. The prescription called for a little bromide, and the orders were for absolute rest and quiet and plenty of good food.

Egbert gave me a look that placed me—in his opinion, at least—as a sissy of the first water, but he was hustled out of the room by Lucy, Ken, and the doctor. They closed the door gently behind them, and I was left there—getting quiet and rest.

I took up a book, but I couldn't read. I was scared, all right—but I knew that I was not having hysterics or hallucinations or anything of the sort. I still shuddered at the memory of that ice-cold body. Egbert seemed all-powerful in his own little world, I mused, and yet surely even he would not have the authority to keep the body lying around in a drawer.

I heard him, then, talking out in the hall to Ken. "It's the manpower shortage," he was saying fretfully. "I could not spare a man to stay here this afternoon. But it is utterly absurd, for Mrs. Fredon to accuse me or any of my men of locking her into that bedroom."

"I suppose so," Ken said abstractedly. "Well—I have to go and get this prescription filled. The doctor says it won't do her any harm."

"These women who go into hysterics!" Egbert muttered gloomily. "It holds my work up. I could clear these things up in half the time if they'd only behave themselves."

They moved off and were out of the front door before I could rise from my bed and throw something at Egbert.

I settled back and began to think about the body again. It was its dreadful coldness that I remembered best—too cold, even for dead flesh, for anything that had been lying long in that drawer. It must have been put there, I thought uneasily, while Mary and I were locked into our rooms. But where had it been brought from—and how could it be that cold?

I had a dizzy spell at that point, so I stopped thinking and watched the ceiling spin around for a while, but as soon as my head had cleared, my mind became active again at once.

Mary and I had been locked into our rooms while Egbert—for reasons of his own—had brought the body through the streets in an ice wagon, carried it up to the apartment, and placed it in the drawer. But I had found it and fainted, so he had to remove it again—only just what he'd done with it I did not know. I burst out laughing at the absurdity of it. And yet Egbert had the body, so how could anyone else have put it in the drawer?

A cold doubt as to my own sanity assailed me momentarily, but I brushed it aside. Whatever the explanation, the body had been there.

The body. Not Betty's . . . someone else . . . wrapped in the same way, and frozen in some fashion. Homer, of course—poor old Homer. That's why the police, had been unable to find him. He was dead, and his body had been hidden in somebody's ice chest. No, that was wrong. He couldn't have been in an ice chest . . . . And then I got it. The cold-storage vegetable bin in Mary's kitchen. It was a huge thing and was not used in the summer–and Homer's body had had to be removed because of Mary's announced intention of doing a thorough cleaning in the kitchen. For some reason it yeas important to keep him from being discovered.

I had to look in that vegetable bin at once—I felt so sure that I was right about the whole thing. I threw back the covers and got out of bed, but I had to get right back in again, because Lucy and Mary came into the room with a tray.

"We've brought you a little snack," Lucy said brightly. "The doctor said you must have plenty of good, nourishing food."

I accepted the tray with thanks and invited them to sit down. Lucy found a chair at once, but Mary hesitated.

"Do you think we ought to let her talk? You know what the doctor said."

"He was talking through his hat," Lucy declared. "Eugenia's no more mentally disturbed than she's always been."

Mary made a sound of shocked protest, and I said grimly, "So that's it— he thinks I'm loopy. Well, you two wait a minute until I finish this snack, and I'll show you something. I'll prove to you that I have my wits about me . . . ."

My voice trailed off, and I suddenly devoted myself exclusively to the tray. I felt quite sure that Homer's body was back in the vegetable bin, but I had been forgetting that Mary still expected him to return home at any time, and the thing would have to be broken gently to her.

I ran a restless hand through my hair and winced at a sudden sharp pain as my fingers encountered a rough spot in the scalp. I pulled my hand away gingerly and saw that my fingers seemed to have specks of dried blood on them.

CHAPTER TWENTY-SEVEN

"WHAT IS IT—what's the matter?" Mary asked.

"Snappy diagnosis," I murmured, feeling around my scalp gingerly. "He says I'm mentally disturbed—or temporary insanity or something—and here I have a head wound. I knew I wouldn't have fainted—I never faint. Somebody tried to brain me."

"My dear! How awful!" Lucy screamed.

Mary said, "Let me see," and took a look at my head. She drew in her breath sharply and added, "This is bad, Eugenia—we'd better get that doctor back here."

"I won't have Grandpa again," I said firmly. "Get someone else."

Lucy shook her head. "Doctors are scarce and hard to get, unless you're a regular customer. I had a hard time getting him."

"Wasted effort," I muttered, still exploring my battered head.

Ken came back, and Lucy excitedly told him the tale. He examined my head, declared that the wound was a minor one and that he would attend to it himself.

I lodged an immediate protest, and he begged me not to be ridiculous. "When I first went into the Army I was with a medical unit, and we were given a very complete and thorough three-month course. Those medical corpsmen—"

"I suppose you know everything it takes a doctor six or eight years to learn?"

"The Army has to cut corners," Ken explained simply.

He sent Mary and Lucy off to collect supplies and then tried to get me to take a dose of Grandpa's prescription, which he had just brought back from the drugstore.

I balked and told him to drink it himself.

"Come on," he insisted impatiently. "It's only a mild bromide, and you need it—even if you're not temporarily insane. Anybody would need a bromide after living in this apartment for the last few days."

Mary and Lucy came back with various articles, including a pair of scissors and a razor—and we were immediately plunged into another hot argument. That one I won—Ken agreeing finally and reluctantly not to shave my head around the wound. He grumbled constantly, while he bathed it, and declared that the hair kept getting in his way. In the end he contrived some sort of an awkward bandage, and Lucy, after looking it over silently, went and fetched the yellow satin ribbon, which she tied around my head in such a way as to hide Ken's fearful handiwork. I thanked her quite humbly until I remembered that I had paid for the ribbon and had never been reimbursed.

I wanted desperately to go to the kitchen and look into the vegetable bin, but I knew that Mary would be at my heels, and so of course I couldn't. I lit a cigarette and watched her and Lucy clean up the mess that Ken had flung around during his fancy surgical dressing. He was too busy admiring the results of his skill to help them, and he paced up and down the room explaining in detail how a dressing of that sort should be applied.

Lucy stopped once or twice to listen to him, and observed finally, "I think that's right interesting—I always like to learn things. Only why didn't you do it that way?"

"What the hell do you mean?" Ken roared. "I did."

Lucy looked both astonished and offended, and he had to apologize, and then immediately asked her if she would prepare a little supper before we all went to bed.

"I'm not going to bed," Lucy declared, "unless Egbert sends a man to guard us. If people are going around hitting people on the head it's time we had some protection."

"Oh, don't be so hysterical," Ken said disgustedly. "Gene probably stumbled and hit her head on something—and had a few hallucinations."

Mary backed him up. "I think that's exactly what happened," she agreed comfortably.

Lucy departed to prepare the supper, and Mary went off to clean up the bathroom, which she described as a "mess."

"I've just eaten," I said, "and I don't want to eat again."

"All right, all right," Ken agreed, "nobody's going to force it down your throat. But the rest of us could do with some nourishment—we've merely been working over you for a couple of hours or so."

I got off the bed and, when he protested, told him I was going to the bathroom, which shut him up. I went straight to the kitchen, where Lucy greeted me with a shocked cry.

"My dear—you ought to be in bed!"

I went over to the vegetable bin and asked, "How do you open this thing?"

Lucy joined me. "Here—like this." We raised the lid together, but the bin was empty. I looked at it for a moment, decided that it was quite large enough to hold a human body, and then slowly closed the lid again.

"I could have told you there was nothing in it," Lucy said, mildly interested. "Mary and I cleared out all the radishes tonight. What did you want out of it anyway?"

"Oh, nothing much," I replied vaguely. "I wanted a—I just wanted to gnaw on a carrot."

To my dismay, she provided me with a carrot at once, and I muttered, "Thank you," and backed out of the kitchen.

I went along the hall, hid the carrot in Mary's antique desk, and then slipped into Mary's bedroom.

I sent a frightened glance around but the room appeared to be empty, and after a moment or two of working my courage up I moved forward and hastily searched the closet and the bathroom. Nothing.

Back in the middle of the room, I hesitated, finger tapping at my teeth—and then I went over to the bed and pulled out the drawer beneath it. It was empty, as I had expected, and before I had time to close it again Egbert's voice spoke smoothly behind me.

"What are you looking for, Miss Eugenia?"

When I got my breath back I told him, through gritted teeth, that I was searching for the body that had been in the drawer only a short while ago.

Egbert's eyebrows crept up, and he pursed his lips—but forbore to comment.

"If you take my supposed mental derangement too seriously," I warned him, "you'll be making the mistake of your life."

"I have already searched for that body of yours," he said mildly. "Not a sign of it."

"Well, it has to be somewhere," I insisted. "Do you know that I was hit on the head?"

He didn't know—and he subjected me to such a painstaking questionnaire that I began to wish I hadn't mentioned any of it. My head started to spin after a while, so I told him to desist and staggered off to my room. He followed right after me—probably to his regret, because Ken was still there and lit into him at once. Ken wanted to know when the thing would be cleared up—declared that the solution was considerably overdue, and complained that the women of the household were not being adequately protected.

I slipped onto the bed and lay there, listening, and after a while, Egbert managed to edge a few words in.

"Passing over the fact that two women have lost their lives," he said with chilly scorn, "I suppose you mean that the situation is spoiling your furlough."

"Yes, it is!" Ken bellowed defiantly. "I've only a few more days, and I want this thing out of the way so that I can enjoy them."

"Those are the wrong tactics to use on Mr. Egbert," I suggested, from the bed—and was instantly quelled by two furious looks from the pair of them. I hastily picked up a book and pretended to read it.

Having ganged up on me, they immediately became more amiable with each other. Ken sat on the foot of my bed, and Egbert perched himself on the edge of the studio couch.

"I have a real problem," Egbert said seriously. "It is possible, of course, for Mr. Homer Fredon to have committed these crimes—but everyone else in the vicinity had ample opportunity as well. And there seems to be no motive—none whatever. We thought, at first, that Mr. Fredon had done it in a fit of insanity, but his friends and business acquaintances are definitely against the idea that there was anything wrong with him. Then, too, he could hardly have hidden himself so effectively if he had been demented. However, that is still the best theory for motive—the only other one being that Mrs. Fredon and Mr. Emerson wished to marry and so disposed of the encumbrances—and Mr. Fredon's body has been hidden somewhere."

The idea of Mary and John sending each other lace-edged valentines was so absurd that I laughed heartily.

Egbert gave me a cold stare and then returned his attention to Ken. "We have searched the Fredons' cottage thoroughly—but Mr. Fredon is not there."

I put down my book and said, "Now listen. When you searched this apartment, did you look in that freezing bin in the kitchen?"

"Certainly," said Egbert, addressing the ceiling.

"What was in it?"

"It was full of radishes."

"Did you stir the vegetables around and look under them?"

"No," said Egbert, abandoning the ceiling and looking at me with frank dislike. "They appeared to be solid."

"Was the freezing unit on?"

"Yes."

"All right," I said, "now listen to this. That thing is not used in summer—it's kept empty and turned off. Mary stocks it in the fall with harvest delicacies, which are gradually used up through the winter."

Egbert shifted his position on the couch and asked uncomfortably, "Is that contraption usual in a private home?"

I shook my head. "I think they use them on ranches, and fancy farms, and things like that. Mary bought it for the cottage, but she found it so useful for storing summer fruits and vegetables that she brought it down and had it installed here."

"And it should not be in use at this season of the year?" Egbert murmured.

"It isn't usual."

"Your idea, then, is that there was a body concealed under the vegetables which was moved to the drawer under the bed, just before you discovered it?"

"It sounds pretty involved, the way you put it—but that's just what I mean. If you prefer to think that I've been having hallucinations that's your privilege."

"What do you suggest as a course of action?" he asked politely.

"I think if you search this apartment you'll find the body. "

"Whose body?"

"I think it's Homer—I'm almost sure of it."

Egbert stood up, said lightly, "I'll have another look around now," and sauntered out.

Ken turned on me and sent a pointed look at my head. "You ought to be in some kind of a home. You know Homer was playing hide-and-seek with us a couple of days ago—we even found his pipe still smoking after he'd left it in the kitchen."

"That was a couple of days ago—and besides, we never actually saw him."

My voice trailed off and I forgot Ken for a moment. I was reminded that I had never actually looked in that drawer for the small object that had fallen back into it. I got off the bed, determined to look at once, although I was nearly convinced that anything the drawer might have contained was surely in Egbert's pocket by this time.

Ken trailed after me, asking irritably, "What the devil are you up to now?" but I ignored him and hurried along to Mary's room. He helped me to open the drawer, at the same time calling me a careless fool for getting out of bed with a fractured skull complicated by mental derangement.

The drawer seemed to be quite empty, but I carefully felt around in the corners—and after a moment my fingers touched something small and smooth and hard. I thought at first that it was a marble—and then I took it to the light and gave a little gasp of horror. It was an artificial eye—a black eye that stared up at me with cold, expressionless opacity.

CHAPTER TWENTY-EIGHT

KEN WHISTLED SOFTLY and took the thing out of my hand. "False eye," he murmured. "That's what it looks like."

"John Emerson," I whispered. "Remember, he was looking for a black eye."

Ken nodded. "I'd better phone him and tell him it's been found."

"But what is it? I mean, what does he use it for? He has both his eyes."

"I don't know," Ken said slowly. "We'd better try to find out."

"We ought to tell Egbert about it. Where is he?"

"I'm here," Egbert's voice replied from behind us. "What do you want to tell me?"

I jumped, and wondered—as I had wondered before—how the man could move around so quietly, and I released some of my nervous irritation by asking nastily, "What sort of sleuthing lessons do they give you people anyway? I just turned this up after a casual look in the drawer, here, and—"

But Egbert had seen the eye in Ken's hand, and I had ceased to exist for him. His face quivered with sudden excitement, and he took the small object from Ken and hurried from the room without another word. We followed him, but he went straight out the front door, and when we opened it to peer after him we saw him disappearing into the elevator.

"I think he knows it belongs to John," Ken muttered thoughtfully. "It has some other significance for him too. But where is he off to? Why didn't he take it in to John?"

Mary came up the hall, her heels tapping briskly, and announced, "Lucy has something for us to eat—as usual—and it's all ready. But where is that man Egbert? I want to complain—"

"He's gone," Ken told her. "Anyway, he wasn't the one who locked you in."

"Well, if he didn't, somebody did, and I want that sort of thing stopped."

"He knows all about it, Mary," I said patiently, "and if he did it himself he'll never admit it anyway, and there's really no use in bothering."

She half turned away from me and, put her handkerchief against her eyes, and her body was suddenly shaking with sobs. "I can't stand it," she whispered in a strangling voice. "People overrunning my apartment like this, and Homer refusing to come back and help me."

I silently offered a spare handkerchief, and Ken put his arm across her shoulders. She continued to cry until Lucy appeared from the kitchen and called in loud dismay, "For heaven's sake, has someone hit her over the head too?"

Mary dried her eyes at once and said with cold dignity, "I am all right now—it's just that there has been so much."

She offered the explanation to Ken and me, and ignored Lucy, who merely shrugged and led the way to the dining room. She had a nice little spread laid out, but the sight of the food made me dizzy and I turned away and said I was going back to bed.

Back in the bedroom, I found that I was too restless to lie down, so I slipped into a cool yellow dress that matched Lucy's ribbon and made my way quietly to the little balcony. Light streamed out from the Emerson living room, and although I resisted the temptation for a while, in the end I found myself stepping over the low barrier and peering in through the open French doors.

I was considerably startled to find John sitting in a chair directly beside the door, and he looked up and saw me before I had a chance to back away.

"I—er—saw your light," I murmured confusedly. "Thought I'd drop in and say hello."

John scowled at me, but Mrs. Budd got up from a chair across the room and came forward. "Come in, dear—do. We were just sitting here."

John got to his feet reluctantly and swung a chair around for me, and then asked abruptly, "What's the matter?" because I was staring so intently at his eyes.

I was badly rattled, and instead of being clever and using finesse, I blurted out, "We found your black eye for you. At least I did—all by myself—and then Ken took half the credit."

Mrs. Budd gaped at me, but John's face tightened, and he let a moment pass before he asked quietly, "What do you mean?"

"Your black eye—the one you were looking for—we found it in Mary's apartment, but Egbert took it away from us. I don't know why he didn't bring it to you."

"But how in the world did it get over there?" Mrs. Budd wondered, her eyes round with surprise.

John frowned. "I don't know how I came to lose the confounded thing—or how it got in there. Incidentally, how did you come to know about it?"

"I don't know anything about it," I admitted frankly, "except that I heard you looking for a black eye—and then I found one."

He was silent for a moment before he asked, "Where—where was it?"

"Well, I—er—I suppose Egbert will tell you all about it," I fumbled.

"Now look here," he said with sudden firmness, "that man Egbert is a slick customer, and he'll twist things to suit his own little theories if he happens to feel like it. I lost that eye lately—apparently it fell out of this pocket where I always keep it, in case anything happens to the new one."

I looked up at him and said in honest astonishment, "Do you mean to tell me that one of your eyes is false?"

He nodded. "I thought you must have known—but it's a good job, isn't it?"

"It's wonderful," I murmured, staring, and found that I could pick it out, now that I knew. I had heard that the workmanship on things of that sort had improved enormously, but it was very hard to believe that that eye could not see.

"That's why I've kept it secret," he explained. "There were only a handful of people who knew about it. But that one you found—the first one—was not such a good piece of work. In the first place it was black, instead of being dark brown, and it was an imperfect fit—it made me wink constantly. So I had another one made, and it seems to be perfect."

But you never let anything go to waste, I thought, looking him over coolly, not even a false eye that wouldn't fit. You got rid of those two women by blaming the whole thing on the black eye that made you wink.

I wanted badly to laugh, but I shut my teeth together and swallowed it down.

"Now where did you find the thing?" John asked grimly.

"Oh—well, as a matter of fact, it was in Mary's room somewhere."

"In that drawer under the bed, I suppose," he said quietly. I nodded.

He sat down rather suddenly, at though the strength had gone out of his legs, and said feverishly, "It must have dropped out of my pocket when I examined the drawer that time."

"When was that?"

He pressed his thumb and forefinger against his eyes and gave his head a quick shake. "It was just before Betty disappeared. Homer had called me in to help him move the large bureau in Mary's room, and while we were busy with it Mary called him. I had nothing to do for a few minutes, so I wandered over and examined the bed—and I remember that I opened the drawer and looked inside."

"Didn't you find that it was difficult to open?"

"No," he said, and gave me a glance of faint surprise. "It came out quite easily."

"What was inside?"

"Just a blanket," he said indifferently.

Just a blanket. The same one that was used to cover Betty later on, I thought, and the black eye must have caught in one of the folds.

John stood up, ran a smoothing hand over his hair, and drew a long deep breath. "What are you doing this evening—you and that yellow ribbon?"

"I'm going to bed. What else?"

"No," he said. "It's hot and stuffy inside—and it's a pity to waste that array of yellow. Let us step out—if only to the corner drugstore."

I felt quite impressed at being dated by the fancy Emerson, although I figured that it had become automatic with him, by now, and he couldn't help himself—and anyway, a stroll to the corner drugstore wasn't anything to tell the girls about.

He came over and closed his hand around my elbow. "Come on."

"Isn't it a bit late?" I asked feebly—but I had decided to go, and he knew it.

"Not quite twelve," he murmured, and began to urge me gently from the room.

I said some sort of a hasty farewell to Mrs. Budd, but she was looking down at her hands, which were twisted tightly together, and she gave no sign of having heard me.

Outside in the hall, I suggested that the corner drugstore might be closed, but John merely said, "We'll avoid the elevator—might run into someone. We can walk down the stairs."

We clattered down the five flights and went out a side door onto a back street. The air felt cool and fresh, and I breathed it in gratefully and ignored the slight discomfort in my head. I had a faintly guilty feeling that I should have been in bed, but I couldn't help enjoying the walk after so much confinement.

John still had a guiding hand on my arm, and he said, "There's a little place around the corner, here, where we can get anything to drink all the way down to coffee."

I nodded. "I'll start at the coffee, then, and work up if it seems to be indicated."

He laughed, and it seemed to me that it was the first easy, relaxed sound I had heard from him.

The little place turned out to be comfortable enough, and I ordered coffee, and John bourbon and water, which he downed almost at a gulp. He began in earnest, then, to make himself agreeable, and I could see easily enough how he had come to be the local glamor boy.

When I got a chance—which was not for some time—I asked him what he was going to use as an excuse to get rid of his girlfriends—now that he had no winking eye.

He had been leaning toward me, but he sat back stiffly in his chair and asked in some annoyance what I thought I was talking about.

"Well," I said mildly, "I heard you twice telling the ladies that they had taken your black eye too seriously."

He began to tap irritably on the table with the amber glass mixing stem that had come with his drink.

"That was only a joke," he said sulkily. "Who were the girls anyway?"

"One was the widow Manchester in the drugstore on Tuesday, the other was on Monday night—someone in your living room—only I didn't see her."

The cloud lifted from his face, and he said in a relieved voice, "Oh, I was only joking with both of them—and they knew it."

"And they both knew about your false eye. Dotty Manchester would, I suppose—her husband having been in the eye business, in a manner of speaking—but who was the other one?"

John downed his second drink, closed his hand over mine, and murmured, "Quiet."

I became conscious of a presence at my elbow, and turned my head to find a young girl who could certainly have given Alice a run for her money. She had a long golden bob, cornflower-blue eyes, and a curving scarlet mouth. Looking further, I discovered smooth, shapely brown legs ending in cream-colored sandals to match a slick, brief, cream-colored dress. I observed— while I admired in silence—that she was glaring at John, and that John's face had become impersonal and guarded. The silence had begun to assume an ugly shape, when John said with apparent ease, "Hello there, June. Sit down and have a drink."

"No, thanks, darling, I wouldn't dream of intruding," the girl said nastily, and I noticed that her hands were clenched tightly at her sides. "I suppose you older men have to take a girl out every day for three weeks and then drop her cold, just to prove to yourselves that you're still young."

She flounced off, and I considered John in the role of an older man—and then glanced after her retreating form. Certainly she was young enough, not more than eighteen.

John was laughing. "These kids—if they can't find any other rough spot to chisel off they'll always take a poke at your age."

"They're easier to get rid of, though, aren't they?"

He made some sort of dignified protest, but I had stopped listening. It had occurred to me suddenly that this girl had really identified the other—the one who had been in John's living room and who knew he had a false eye, which she had taken too seriously. It was Suzy.

CHAPTER TWENTY-NINE

OF COURSE it was Suzy—it must have been. John had been trying to brush Dotty off for some time, and had started to take Suzy out on her day off. This June must have come next—and Suzy had seen them together—all of which cleared up the obscure places in Suzy's little notebook.

John, still toying with the glass stem, evidently saw the expression of distaste on my face. He slumped back into his chair, looking suddenly tired, and said, "It's easy enough for you to look virtuous and disapproving. Betty would have nothing to do with me for the last six months—and I've been lonely."

I couldn't blame Betty, but John looked so miserable that I felt a faint pity for him.

"I'll admit that I don't approve," I said, smiling at him, "but I didn't mean to look virtuous. But we'd better go—it's late."

He protested that we'd only just come, but I insisted, and he gave in sulkily. We walked back almost in silence, and I did some furious thinking. John had an easy enough explanation for his eye having been in that drawer—and it could be true, too. I wondered whether Mary would back up his story. And what had poor little Suzy done that was so deadly? She'd seen Homer—that was all—and not his dead body, either.

I was tired to the point of exhaustion by the time we had climbed the five flights of stairs, and then I had to go through the Emerson apartment because

I didn't have any key and did not want to wake anyone up to let me in. Walking down the long hall, with John at my side, I came out in a cold sweat of fear. The place was only dimly lighted—and John could easily have done those murders—and if I knew more than was good for me, here was his chance. When he put his hand on my arm I gasped and pulled away from him.

"Easy," he said, giving me an oblique glance. "You're jumpy."

I swallowed and admitted that I was. He helped me over the barrier on the balcony, and his last words were a remark about the yellow ribbon being very fetching.

I made my way into the living room, wondering if they had sent the fire engines after me, since I must have been missed, because Lucy was sleeping in with me.

I was wrong, as it happened, for they were all still in the dining room and seemed to be having a hot argument. I had to listen for quite a while before I was able to make head or tail of the discussion.

It seemed that Mary wanted to call in a private detective to find Homer, and Ken thought it was ridiculous and that the private detective would merely get under Egbert's feet and perhaps trip him up. Lucy's angle was that Egbert had already tripped over his own feet, and anyway, she had always wanted to meet a private detective. Mary immediately made it plain that if she did get in a private detective Lucy would have to leave, since she didn't intend to hire him just so that he could spend his time flirting with Lucy. Whereupon Ken objected violently to Lucy's leaving and declared that he would not get his proper food if she were not there. Mary's voice, sounding decidedly offended, asked Ken if he didn't suppose she could cook, and Ken replied tactlessly that he had no doubt of it, but it would remind him too much of the Army three rigid meals a day, and no extras. Lucy, he declared, served up something every hour or so, and that was more to his liking. Lucy chimed in again and said certainly! A soldier needed a little extra food on his furlough. Mary, hotting up nicely, observed that a little extra food was one thing, but that shoveling it in at all hours of the day was another, and hardly less than revolting.

I walked in at that point, determined to have my innings.

"How do you expect an invalid to sleep," I asked, "with all this noise going on?"

They looked me over coldly, and Mary suggested that I might sleep better if I tried getting undressed first. I changed the subject hastily and told them that Mary could certainly wait until morning before calling in her private investigator, but that under no circumstances was Lucy to go, and that Ken was to eat every hour on the hour—further, I was ashamed of all of them, arguing like that and making a noise over nothing. I left in a hurry, after that, and retired to my room, where I undressed and went to bed.

I had broken it up, though, for presently I heard dishes clattering in the kitchen, and then they came into the hall and dispersed. Lucy slipped into the bedroom, closed the door behind her, and turned on me. "Well!" she exclaimed, on a long, laughing breath. "You certainly slapped Mary's ears back—telling her what to do in her own home!"

"It's good for her," I said, yawning. "It takes her mind off the fearful mess people make by wearing their shoes around the house."

She gave a shriek of laughter and then went over to the mirror to examine her face.

"It's after one o'clock," I said, yawning again. "Why don't you go to bed?"

"I will," she murmured absently. "Give me time."

She was still working on her face when I went to sleep, and when I woke up, some time later, she seemed to be in the bathroom, for I could hear the water running. The room was dark, except for one small lamp on the bureau adorned with a dark green shade that kept most of the electricity to itself. I was about to turn over when my eye fell on the little clock beneath the lamp, and I saw that it was almost four o'clock. I hesitated, frowning, and wondering whether Lucy were ill, and decided after a moment to stay awake until she came back. It was a mistake, because instantly I started to think about Homer and the whole sorry business, and I could not stop myself.

Where was Homer anyway? Egbert had only pretended to look for the body to appease me, and he'd gone flying off as soon as he had the black eye. Poor John—that eye was going to give him more trouble than ever it had when it was in his head. But perhaps that body I touched had been Betty, as I had thought at first, and Egbert had put her back in the drawer for some reason of his own—only he'd have to have wrapped her up again, and how could he? And why? The thing was absurd.

Lucy came back just then, and I asked her if anything were wrong.

"No," she said, yawning, "I just can't sleep—too much excitement, I guess. I've been washing out some of my underclothes to make me good and tired, so maybe I can get off now."

She flopped onto the studio couch, and I turned over, but neither of us could get to sleep. We turned and twisted for a while, and then Lucy flounced off the couch and declared that it was too hot there.

"But where can you go?" I asked.

"I'll bet it's cooler in the living room—only you'll have to come with me."

"Why?"

"Don't be silly," said Lucy. "I'd be scared to death. Poor Suzy died in there."

"We can't go in there anyway," I said, rumpling my hair fretfully. "Mary would have to have the divans restuffed and dry-cleaned, if we slept on them all night."

"It's morning already," Lucy pointed out. "And anyway, Homer slept on one of her sacred divans."

"I don't believe it—he wouldn't have dared."

"You mean he wouldn't have dared in the days before he got a little independent and decided to live a life of his own—without being told every minute of the day what to do and when to do it." She was over at the mirror now, carefully patting at the faint suggestion she had of a second chin.

"Listen," I said, "whatever has happened to Homer, he still hangs around here, haunting the place."

Lucy ran a thoughtful finger around the line of her jaw and said, "Not the last couple of days—not since Mary has been back."

Well, that was true, and I thought it over for a while but didn't come to any conclusion.

"You can try this bed," I said to Lucy after a while, "and I'll take the couch. I think it's cooler here."

She demurred for a conventional interval and then agreed, and I climbed into the couch.

It was hot, all right—there didn't seem to be a breath of air around it—and I tossed in damp discomfort. I was quite illogically annoyed with Lucy, too, because she went to sleep almost at once in my bed. I flopped around onto my back and saw that the gray square of the window was growing lighter. The various objects in the room began to emerge from total darkness—and then my eyes slid around to the door, and I thought I saw it open slightly. I was instantly in a cold sweat, and I stared in terror with my breath coming short, but there was no sound, and I was able to convince myself, after a while, that the door had not moved at all.

My thoughts slipped to the wrapped-up mummy and the feel of cold marble—like flesh under my fingers—and I gasped and flung off the sheet. Then I decided that it wasn't all that hot and pulled the sheet up again.

No, it wasn't the heat, so much. It was stuffy. I needed more air. I got up and tugged at the couch until it was about two feet away from the wall, hoping that the noise would wake Lucy. But it didn't. The thing moved smoothly, and I reflected bitterly that you could depend on Mary to have furniture that moved smoothly,

I lay down again and breathed deeply a couple of times to see whether there was any improvement, but I couldn't be sure one way or the other. I began to toss around again, and at last I nearly went over the edge on the wall side, because I had forgotten the space there. I flung an arm out to save myself, and glanced downward—and instantly froze with horror. Something lay along the floor between the couch and the wall—something long, and still, and securely wrapped in what I knew would be a pinkish-colored material.

CHAPTER THIRTY

I FLUNG MYSELF off the couch, half fell onto the floor, and stumbled to my feet. I tried to call Lucy, but my throat seemed to have closed up, and I made only an odd croaking sound. Somehow I found myself at the door, but I was afraid to go out into the dark hall—and then quite suddenly my voice came back, and I let out a scream that chilled me to the bone.

It must have scared the others, too, because Lucy gave forth a terrified yell not three seconds later, and Mary and Ken were in the room with us before the echoes had died away. My own scream seemed to have calmed me a little, and I was able to pat Lucy's quivering shoulder while I told the others, almost steadily, to look behind the couch.

Mary, quite automatically, had started to push the couch back against the wall, but as I spoke she stopped and looked down at it as though seeing it for the first time. Ken was already looking behind it, but he said nothing and made no exclamation of any kind, and I had a sudden cold fear that he found nothing—that the dreadful thing was gone again.

But Mary peered around his shoulder and immediately began to moan, "Oh, God! Oh, God! What is it—who is it? Quickly, Ken—see what it is."

Lucy got up and went over to take a look, although I tried to hold her back. After one glance she went off into her own peculiar brand of hysterics, but this time it didn't last very long. Ken picked up a glass of water, and his obvious intention of flinging it at her startled her into silence. He took the opportunity to tell her that she'd get it right in the face if she didn't keep quiet.

She said, "All right, all right—but get the police quickly."

Ken nodded and went off to the telephone, and Mary turned to me with a look of agonizing fear on her face. She's afraid it's Homer, I thought, and it is, too—it must be.

I took her arm firmly and urged her from the room, while Lucy followed so closely that she was treading on our heels.

In the hall Mary stopped, swung around on Lucy, and cried hysterically, "If you go out into the kitchen and start making something I'll scream."

I said, "Nonsense! A good hot cup of coffee is what you need."

But Lucy had no intention of leaving us, and we went on to the living room, where I established Mary in a chair.

"But we ought to go back there," she whispered. "We must find out what it is—who it is. Oh, God! Eugenia, it can't be—"

"You stay where you are," I said firmly. "You'll do no good by running around and getting in Egbert's way. He'll be here soon, and then we'll find out what it is."

"You mean *who*," Lucy shrilled. *"Who* it is. My God! What's going on here anyway!"

"Shut up, Lucy," I said out of the corner of my mouth. "If I have to throw water on you it'll be a pailful."

She subsided sulkily into a chair and looked at Mary, who lay with her head dropped back and her, eyes closed.

"I'm leaving here," Lucy muttered. "First thing in the morning."

Mary opened her eyes. "Why not now? The sooner the better."

They started to quarrel, and I decided that it would do them both good and slipped out into the hall.

Ken was standing near the front door, smoking a cigarette and dropping ashes onto the rug, and I went up and joined him.

"It must be Homer—in there?"

He nodded rather absently.

"Have you looked?"

"Nope. Instructions were to touch nothing."

He handed me a cigarette, and we fell silent, smoking and dropping ashes onto the rug until we heard the clang of the elevator door out in the hall. Ken opened the door, then, and Egbert marched in.

He nodded at us briefly, but when his eye fell on me he started back and blushed all over his face. I looked down at myself in some perplexity, and then realized, with dawning shame, that I had forgotten to put on my dressing gown and was standing before the two of them in a not quite knee-length pajama top.

In my confusion I turned on Ken. "You might have told me—naturally I was too upset to notice."

Ken merely stared at me and asked, "What in hell are you talking about?" and I flew into my room and jammed my arms into the robe.

Egbert and Ken followed me and proceeded to pull the couch farther out from the wall. I caught a glimpse of the wrapped form and the pinkish material before I turned my eyes away, feeling a little sick.

"I told you to look for him, earlier," I muttered to Egbert. "I told you it must be around somewhere, but you wouldn't believe me."

"I'm sorry," Egbert said formally. "I did try to check up on your statement, but you will remember that you were receiving medical attention in this room, and I did not want to disturb you."

"Very proper," I murmured. "After all, I'm perishable, but he'll keep."

But Egbert had stopped listening to me and was busy unwinding yards of pinkish material.

I had just caught a view of Homer's face when I heard a stirring behind me and turned to find Mary and Lucy in the room. I took a quick step toward Mary, but I was too late—she had already seen. Her face looked pinched and frozen, and somehow unbelieving. Lucy, with no sign of her usual hysterics, tried to urge her from the room, but Mary shook her off without being aware of her and whispered, "Homer."

Ken turned his head and saw us. "Here!" he said sharply. "Take Mary out of this."

He came toward us as Mary darted forward, crying, "Homer, Homer—he can't be dead—he isn't. Why don't you get a doctor—quickly !"

Egbert barred her way with an outstretched arm and gave us an appealing look, and Lucy and I went over and led her away. She must have realized, then, that Homer was dead, for she came with us without further protest.

But she would not go to bed. She said excitedly, "Don't be silly—I shall have to see to things. There's so much to be done. It's so dreadful. Homer never hurt a living soul. . . . Dreadful. . . . I can't face it. And I thought he had come back. He was here—right here on Tuesday—don't you remember?"

She sat down on the antique couch in the hall and began to cry quietly. After a while she gave a vague glance at the couch, got up immediately and smoothed the cushion, and then made for the living room. Lucy and I followed watchfully, and when she flung herself into a chair and abandoned herself to hysterical weeping we sat down on each side of her.

Ken presently came and looked in at us. He said that Egbert would like to ask us some questions, and Lucy shrugged.

"He can have Gene and me, if he wants us, but he'll have to let Mary alone. Look at her."

Ken went and leaned over Mary and talked gently to her, but she seemed hardly conscious of him, so he patted her shoulder and went away again,

I glanced at Lucy, who was running her thumbnail back and forth across the arm of her chair, and then at Mary, who was still drowned in tears, and I stood up abruptly.

"Go and make some coffee, Lucy. I'll stay here with her. She ought to be left to cry it out—it's the best thing she can do."

Lucy gave me a look of gratitude and relief and hurried off to the kitchen, and I began to pace the room. It was quite light outside now, and I had to suppress a longing that was almost a physical pain to go out into the sunshine and never come back. I glanced at Mary and was shocked by a sudden desire to scream out at her to shut up. To make up for the ugly impulse I went over and tried to offer her some sympathy, but she shook me off, so I went to her bedroom and got her a couple of clean handkerchiefs, because it was the only thing I could think of.

When I got back I was a bit startled by her appearance. She had thrown her head back and her face was ghastly pale. The tears still slid over her cheeks but she no longer made any effort to wipe them away.

I went back to my room, where I fund Ken and Egbert talking in low voices, while the body of Homer lay covered with a sheet. I kept my eyes away from it while I told Ken about Mary. He nodded, said something to Egbert in an undertone, and accompanied me back to the living room. He looked Mary over and then decided, "I'll give her a sedative."

He prepared a concoction from the prescription he had brought for me and forced Mary to take it by sheer power of will. He raised her from the chair and half carried her to a couch, where he made her lie down, despite a faint, involuntary protest. She did give me a glance of appeal and indicated her slippers, and I hastily removed them, because I knew she'd never rest if they were messing up the cushions. I covered her with a light blanket, and she settled down and seemed to go to sleep almost at once.

I gave Ken a doubtful look and said, "That must have been a pretty powerful sedative," but he shook his head.

"It was only something to relax her—wouldn't even have put her to sleep. She's been under a terrific strain since Homer disappeared—and now she knows where he is, even if he's dead. I expect she'll sleep for a long time."

"Yes," I muttered, "I see. The medical corps really did a job on you, didn't it?"

Lucy came in bearing a large tray, and we silently steered her back into the dining room, where we sat down at the table. I felt that I had never wanted coffee so much before in my life, and I was well into my second cup when Egbert drifted in.

He looked us over with a certain amount of perplexity and asked, "Were any of you playing a practical joke on Tuesday, when Mr. Fredon's pipe was found smoking, and when his things appeared here and there—with Suzy saying he was out in the kitchen?"

We stared at him in dead silence, and he added mildly, "Because he's been dead for quite some time."

CHAPTER THIRTY-ONE

"DO YOU MEAN HE—he was dead before Tuesday?" Lucy whispered.

Egbert nodded and moved in on us. He sat down at the table and put his elbows on it, while Lucy offered him coffee.

"Somebody was deliberately trying to give the impression that Mr. Fredon was still alive—after he had been killed."

"I can't see any reason for that," Ken muttered.

Egbert glanced around at us and asked, "Any of you have an idea?"

We had none, so he went on, "Suzy must have been in on it, since she came and announced that Mr. Fredon was out there."

"Why, yes," I agreed slowly, "but when we couldn't find him she seemed anxious that we search the place, and said something about looking under things—which was peculiar when you come to think of it. Maybe she had found him dead, I mean—and wanted someone else to make the discovery."

Egbert, with a patient sigh for my lame brain, asked, "Then why did she light his pipe and pretend that he had been smoking it?"

"Well, maybe she didn't," I protested. "After all, she was killed herself—that same night, too. Someone else probably heard Suzy say that Homer was out in the kitchen and then lit up the pipe to—to give some atmosphere."

Egbert, still patient, shook his head. "Before all that a pair of Mr. Fredon's shoes was found in the hall. The idea that he was still alive was presented long before Suzy said he was in the kitchen."

Ken stirred, rumpled his hair, and gave his head a shake. "All right," he said, "how's this? Suzy had stumbled across the body at some time and figured she knew who had done it—only she was afraid to say anything. She thought it over and decided somebody ought to know, so she set about giving the impression that he had returned in order that people would start looking for him. She started with the shoes and, when that didn't work, tried the pipe and saying he was there, so that the place would surely be searched."

"Yes, that's it," I said eagerly. "Because when she told us he was there she kept looking up the hall at the front door, so that we wouldn't think he was slipping out while she was talking to us. Then there were those busts out in the hall—I suppose she turned them around the way Homer liked them—and when we finally decided that he had played hide-and-seek with us and got out she told us we'd better search under things, and Mrs. Budd asked her not to be ridiculous."

Egbert sighed. "In the end I suppose she put those things on the couch, to give the impression that Mr. Fredon had slept there—and that was when she was murdered—somehow made to take poison. The couch was left that way, and of course it looked as though Mr. Fredon had done the murder. Apparently there was some imperative reason for keeping his body hidden."

"Betty was hidden too," Lucy said with a shiver.

Egbert nodded. "But even after she was found there seemed to be a frantic effort to keep the other one hidden."

Ken, who had been making patterns on the tablecloth with his coffee spoon, looked up and said, "That's simple enough. After Suzy had made it appear that Homer was in and out of the place it was important to keep him hidden so that everyone would think he had done the murders."

I glanced at Egbert's impassive face and knew that he was trying to get something out of us—some faint suggestion of a motive, probably—because after all, what reason had anyone to kill Betty and Homer? I was pretty sure that John had been fooling around with poor little Suzy, and perhaps she had thought John had done the murders. So she kept quiet about it, but her conscience troubled her, and she tried to get us to search the place. I wondered if Homer's body had been in the drawer with Betty's—and if so, why it had been removed to the bin.

"What about those vegetables?" I asked suddenly. "The stuff that was in the storage bin in the kitchen. Where is it now?"

"Oh, those were all radishes," Lucy said. "Seems it's been a good year for radishes, or something, and everybody's been growing the things. Mary didn't grow any, but her neighbors kept giving her radishes, and she brought them all down, because she hates to waste anything. There were so many that she put them into the bin, but she said she was going to clear them out of there today. As a matter of fact I helped her take them out tonight—we put them in a box."

"Was the freezing unit on?" Egbert asked.

Lucy shook her head.

"Why not?"

"Mary said it wasn't necessary—said we'd eat the radishes up quickly—and I've been using them at every meal, but there's an awful wad of them." She paused to swallow down a yawn and then asked with a little shudder, "Was *he* under those radishes?"

Egbert shrugged, frowned, and got to his feet.

"I must speak to Mrs. Fredon as soon as she wakes."

He went off and left us looking at one another without much to say.

"Oh, God!" I muttered after a while. "I can't stay here. I'd rather go to jail."

"I'll gladly share a cell with you," Lucy moaned.

Ken divided a glance of utter disgust between us. "Shut up! Both of you! You're not helping anyone by going on like that—and why don't you think of Mary? She'll need all we can give her when she wakes up."

Lucy and I looked suitably ashamed and began meekly to shift the dishes into the kitchen. When we had washed them and put them away; Ken suggested that we take a nap, and offered to keep an eye on Mary while we rested.

"You needn't think I'm ever going to lie on that couch again," Lucy declared, with a shudder so violent that she had to pull her girdle down after it.

I agreed to lie on the couch but insisted that it would have to be moved to another part of the room, and Ken said impatiently, "All right, come on and I'll help you to move the thing."

In the hall we came upon Egbert, slinking around with a carrot in his hand.

"What on earth is he doing now?" Lucy bawled. "I declare, I think the man's touched."

"You can't touch pitch without being defiled," Egbert observed bitterly and somewhat obscurely. "I'm trying to decide why there should be a carrot in the desk here."

"People chew on them, sometimes, when they are writing out checks," I murmured, trying to look innocent. "It has a calming effect."

Lucy giggled, and Egbert gave me a narrow, cold, calculating glance that scared me straight into my room. Lucy followed at my heels, but Ken apparently forgot about helping me to move the couch, for he stayed out in the hall.

I heard him start on Egbert, using his sergeant's voice.

"I'd like to know just what progress you've made. For instance, why did Mrs. Emerson and Mr. Fredon spend a night in Binghamton?"

Egbert, evidently impressed by Ken's rather obvious sergeant tactics, answered quite mildly that he did not know. He had made every possible effort to clear up their movements there and had failed. If he could solve that one little thing, he added plaintively, he could break the case without delay.

"They had a late lunch and then went out in the car and were gone for over four hours before they returned to the hotel. There is absolutely no trace of where they went or what they did. I cannot find that either of them had any friends in the vicinity—or any business associates—and yet, there it is."

"Can't Emerson throw any light on it?" Ken demanded.

"He insists he knows nothing about it, and Mrs. Budd backs him up. They declare that they cannot imagine what Mrs. Emerson went for—except that it was not to elope with Fredon."

"What about the friend in New York that Betty was supposed to be visiting?"

"She was not expecting her that weekend and insists that Mrs. Emerson would certainly have made arrangements beforehand if she had planned to come."

The inspector sounded like Pfc. Egbert by this time, and Ken was thundering his questions.

He was silent for a moment, and then he asked, "What about Mary? Are you quite sure she can't explain the Binghamton trip?"

"She continues to insist that her husband never went there at all. Says the woman in the apartment below heard him walking around; he would certainly never have made such a trip without letting her know; and what possible reason would he have had for accompanying Mrs. Emerson to Bing-hamton anyway?"

"Have you made any effort to find out who was walking around the apart-ment?" Ken roared.

"Oh yes," said Egbert in the too quiet voice of one about to score a point. "I know who was here, of course, but it is not very enlightening. It was merely Mrs. Budd doing a little prying."

CHAPTER THIRTY-TWO

LUCY RAISED HER EYEBROWS at me, and I thought of John losing his eye in that drawer.

"Mrs. Emerson," Egbert was saying, "told her mother that Mr. Fredon was driving to Binghamton and had offered her a lift as far as New York, so that Mrs. Budd knew the apartment was empty, and she was in here both Saturday and Sunday. She saves her face by explaining that she thought she heard a noise, and since Mr. Fredon had carelessly left the balcony doors unlocked, he might just as easily have left the front door unlocked, or the gas turned on, or something of that sort. So she went in to check up. She says. However, she was there on Sunday only until one o'clock—when her dinner was ready—and she did not go back in the afternoon."

"It was that afternoon that Betty and Homer came back," Ken said. "What time did Mary get in?"

"Nine o'clock. And at a few minutes after, she went in to the Emersons' and asked if they had seen her husband, as he wasn't there. Mrs. Budd re-marked that she guessed he had not yet returned from Binghamton, and Mrs. Fredon demanded to know what she was talking about and denied that her husband had gone to Binghamton. I believe there was a slight tiff. At any rate Mrs. Fredon returned to her own apartment and, according to her statement, spent the night worrying until the next morning, when Mrs. Budd came run-ning in with that postcard. Mrs. Fredon says she believed in the elopement until she thought it over, when she became convinced that her husband would never have run off with Mrs. Emerson."

"What did Emerson and Mrs. Budd believe?" Ken asked.

"You know what they thought," Egbert replied—and sounded as though he were on the verge of revolt. "Emerson supposed his wife was covering up her elopement with someone else, and Mrs. Budd believed that her daughter was trying to teach her son-in-law a lesson."

Lucy giggled shrilly just then, and the conversation in the hall ceased abruptly. I yawned, flopped onto the couch, and was still wondering whether

I felt squeamish about it when I went off to sleep.

I woke some time later and saw that Lucy was still asleep. I lay on my back, looking at the ceiling, and found myself wondering drowsily why Egbert hadn't arrested John—because he must know all about John and Suzy—and the black eye. But it was the motive, of course—there just wasn't any. John had no need to kill Betty to get rid of her: she wanted a divorce anyway. I knew that he was very fond of the little girl, but with Betty dead, the money would stop, and John was faced with the support of the child—to say nothing of Mrs. Budd. No motive there, and certainly Mrs. Budd had none. Mary had apparently been quite satisfied with Homer, and she'd have to cut down her expenses now, since his insurance would never give her as much as his salary had been. Probably she would have to part with some of her sacred furniture, which would half kill her. Lucy seemed to be nothing but an interested on-looker. Ken had been fond of Betty. There was always Dotty Manchester, of course, who wanted Betty out of the way but who could hardly have been interested in Homer. And then Suzy—poor little Suzy—who had been killed because she had discovered Homer and wanted someone else to discover him too.

Maybe J. X. Boxton was responsible for the whole thing. Perhaps his business had made him a bit callous about making dead bodies out of live ones, and the motive was that he was experimenting with a new method of embalming. He realized that people in more ordinary occupations are a bit squeamish about dead bodies, so he nailed them up in the drawer, where he hoped nobody would ever find them.

I got up, at that point, and went in to take a cold bath, hoping it would clear my brain. It was only eleven o'clock, but I could not get back to sleep, and I had a restless desire to be up and out.

I wanted to take the bandage off my head but decided that Ken would be hurt, so I left it, and arranged the yellow ribbon over it again.

Lucy was still asleep, so I went out quietly. In the living room Mary lay on the couch where Ken and I had placed her, and seemed hardly to have moved. Not far away Ken was sleeping soundly on two chairs and looked thoroughly uncomfortable.

I hesitated and then backed quietly into the hall and crept out the front door. I went down the five flights of stairs and left the apartment by way of the rear exit. I had to sneak past a group of men, but they were all watching a fight between two little boys and did not notice me.

I walked for some distance, breathing in the fresh air and enjoying the exercise, and finally I went into a drugstore for a rest and a cool drink. The drink turned out to be a pineapple squash or something of the sort, and although it was a bit too sweet I enjoyed it until I found that I had forgotten to bring my purse and had no money to pay for it.

I sat there, wondering what the procedure was and whether I had an honest face, when I caught sight of Dotty Manchester sitting by herself and eating some sort of mess.

At the same time I realized that this was the drugstore in which I had overheard her conversation with John Emerson. Perhaps it was a regular hangout of hers, I thought, or possibly John came here regularly, and she was hoping to run across him. It seemed to me that she was eating slowly, with one eye on the door.

I joined her with a bright word of greeting and then discovered that she didn't know me and needed a little reminding. When it was all cleared up she became quite cordial and asked me to sit down with her. I explained my predicament, and she gave the hearty, full-bodied laugh that seems to go with certain blondes, and handed me some money. She settled down and became inquisitive after that, but none of our troubles seemed to interest her greatly, except as they touched John. So I concentrated on John, and she blossomed like a flower and was shortly doing most of the talking herself.

"You know, I was sorry about Betty," she said in a low voice, marking a pattern on her paper doily with a shining crimson thumbnail, "it was dreadful! But she was a deep one—she must have been in some sort of trouble, because nobody would kill her like that without a reason. I hear she was all wrapped up like a mummy?"

I nodded.

"Well, I think it must have been revenge. She was interested in that sort of thing—Egyptology, is it?—and she used to go to museums to study mummies and things like that, so I think somebody took a horrible sort of revenge and wrapped her up that way."

"Seems a queer thing to do, though," I murmured.

Dotty pushed the scarred doily away and leaned closer to me.

"She was hard as nails—and mean to John. She led him an awful life, and he took it like a gentleman. Of course she didn't understand him."

She seemed to be getting off the track a bit, so I tried to ease her back on.

"It's too bad about that eye of his," I suggested.

She drew back, looking startled. "But how did you know about it? He's so very sensitive."

I shrugged and asked, "How did it happen?"

"Well, my dear, it was most unfortunate. An automobile accident—and a flying sliver of glass. My husband had to remove the eye; he couldn't save it. But you'd never know, the way he looks now, would you?"

"No," I agreed, "you wouldn't. What about the first one—the black eye?"

"Oh, that was all John's nonsense," she declared impatiently. "It was perfectly all right, but John insisted it made him wink, and he was always carrying on about it being black instead of dark brown. It really was absurd, and my husband would have been furious if he had lived—he was very proud of that job. John had another one made, and that seemed to satisfy him."

She seemed suddenly to remember at that point that she hadn't been keeping an eye on the door, and she stopped talking abruptly and gave a careful look around, but John was nowhere in sight.

As soon as I could get her attention I said a graceful good-by and made my way out. I headed straight for the apartment, because without money I was lost, but I was determined to get my purse and come out again at once.

I had a little difficulty getting in. There was a janitor guarding the back door, and argument proved fruitless until I told him that I had come to clean for Mrs. Fredon and the madam would cut up rough if I failed to appear. He passed me through, after that, and I climbed the five flights and went panting in the front door, which I found unlocked.

I came face to face with Mary, who had a cold, grim, flint-eyed look about her.

She asked, "Where have you been?" and without waiting for an answer declared, "I'm going to find out who killed Homer, and I shall not rest until I do. I was going to phone that man Egbert—I can't find him anywhere—but perhaps you'll do it for me. Here's the number—Ken gave it to me—and I think he said he could be reached there at any time. I simply must see him."

She pressed a slip of paper into my hand, and I retired, sighing, to the little phone closet. I put the piece of paper down on a magazine that lay beside the phone—and then paused to wonder why a magazine should be lying in the telephone booth in Mary's orderly apartment. I looked more attentively—and then stopped breathing for a moment.

In amongst the hair of the beautiful blonde who adorned the cover was a Binghamton telephone number—and just below was written: "The Black Eye."

CHAPTER THIRTY-THREE

I PUT MY CALL THROUGH and was told that Egbert would contact Mrs. Fredon as soon as Egbert was contacted. That seemed fair enough, so I hung up and sat there for a while, frowning at the magazine.

I heard Mary fussing out in the hall, and after considering it for a moment I picked up the magazine and went out to find her searching through the desk.

"Mary—?" I began, but she broke in feverishly: "I'm going through Homer's things—getting his affairs together—and I shall show them to that Egbert. He'll see then—he must see—that Homer's life was an open book. He should be searching for a maniac, because no one in his right mind could have wanted to kill Homer."

"Mary, look. What was this magazine doing in there beside the phone? You don't usually have magazines slopping around the place."

"Magazine?" she repeated vaguely. "Where? Oh—that. No, no, leave that in there—or wait, I'll get a newer one. I always leave a magazine there. Sometimes you have to wait, you know—or you get people like Lucy on the phone talking for hours about nothing."

She trotted off to get a more recent number, and I looked after her with a faint sigh of relief. She'd be all right, I thought. She was working off her shock and grief by running around and trying to do something about it.

I looked at my magazine again and wondered what it could possibly mean. The Binghamton number probably held the explanation of why Betty and Homer had made a trip there, but what did John's black eye have to do with it? I'd have to give the magazine to Egbert, I thought regretfully—and yet I wanted to call that number myself. I had no right to do it, of course—Egbert would be furious—and anyway, what would I say when the call was answered?

Lucy came into the hall and exclaimed, "Gene! Where in the world have you been? You missed lunch."

"I had some pineapple squash," I said absently.

"I can fix you something in two minutes," she offered amiably.

"No, thanks. Where's Ken?"

"He went out to market—and to look for you. He's taking Mary's car."

I had a sudden, exciting impulse, and I asked quickly, "How long has he been gone?"

"Just left. Why don't you go after him? Because I forgot flour—get a small bag—cake flour."

I tucked the magazine under my arm, and with Lucy shrieking directions about how to find the garage, I flew out the door and down the stairs. I just made it, for he had the car headed down the driveway as I panted up and hailed him. He stopped, leaned over and opened the door, and as I climbed in, asked abruptly, "Where have you been?"

"Making a daisy chain. Listen—how long does it take to get to Binghamton from here?"

"Why do you want to know?" he asked suspiciously.

"Stop the car for a minute, will you, and look at this."

He glanced at the magazine and muttered, "I should have insisted on having your head X-rayed."

"Maybe so, but stop the car anyway."

He drew up to the curb, and I exhibited my prize. He looked at it for some time and then said slowly, "This must be given to Egbert at once."

"Oh yes, of course," I agreed meekly. "But we could copy the number and then run up to Binghamton and call it."

"I don't think," he said in a discouraged voice, "that all that wool in your head would show up in an X ray, after all. Don't you see that Egbert could find out the address belonging to this number without warning them first by making a call?"

"Oh, shut up!" I said in exasperation. "And stop being such a good boy. You don't want to go back to that miserable apartment, do you? Let's drive on up now, and we can phone Egbert and let him follow us."

He began to show signs of weakening, but he glanced at the dashboard and murmured, "Gasoline."

"Well, drive to the station, for heaven's sake, and we'll go by train. Be quicker anyway."

He started the car up again and headed in the direction of the station. "This is absolute birdseed," he observed after a while, "but it might just save my furlough from utter deterioration."

We made the station in five minutes, and there Ken picked up information which shortly landed us in a train for New York. I had relaxed into a seat and was beginning to recover my breath when Ken remarked mildly that I didn't seem to be dressed, exactly, for an overnight trip.

"Overnight?" I echoed hollowly.

"We won't get there before early evening—and after we've attended to our business we won't have time to get back tonight, so you might as well make up your mind to it. Myself, I think it's a very nice idea—and remember, it was your suggestion."

"Don't get any ideas," I said sharply. "If we have to stay all night, then we have to—the same way that Betty and Homer did."

He slumped down in his seat, swatted at a fly, and presently suggested weakly, "Maybe we could get married somewhere."

"Maybe not—we can't afford it. I forgot to bring my purse, and what you can lend me, over and above train fares, etcetera, will have to be spent for a toothbrush and—"

"And nothing," he said, changing to his sergeant's voice. "I won't buy you a thing except dinner. You'll have to brush your teeth with your fingers"

"I'll do without the toothbrush," I agreed uneasily, "if you insist. But I must have a little powder and lipstick."

He was immediately restored to high good humor. "Nothing doing. I shall be interested to see what you look like without the disguise."

But even the impending horror of facial nudity couldn't keep me down for long. It was sheer delight to be well away from Mary's apartment, and there was an added zest in the possibility that at any minute a hand with a cop attached might fall on my shoulder, while a voice snarled, "Trying to make a dash for it, eh?"

However, we arrived in Binghamton unmolested, and Ken insisted that we have dinner before doing any telephoning.

"As far as I'm concerned," he declared; "this trip is pure pleasure until Egbert catches up with us—which ought to be at any minute. So let's delay business as long as possible."

He held a chair for me, and I sat down, shaking my head. "That's not my way—and I didn't come here for pleasure. I'd like to get the whole horrid mess cleared up, so that I needn't ever go back to Mary's dreadful apartment."

But Ken was already deep in a serious study of the menu and had stopped listening to me. I glanced over it, but there was nothing that appealed to me particularly, so I pushed it aside.

"I'll have what you have. No sense both of us wasting time over it, and this sort of thing is your specialty anyhow."

He laid the menu aside and asked, "What are you saying?"

"Nothing—except that if you can afford it I'll have the same."

A waiter loomed up at that point, and Ken took him in hand and poured out a mass of confusing instructions about our meal. The waiter's face froze over, but he stood by valiantly and, when Ken at last gave a name to the dish, stolidly wrote it down.

I left them to it and fell to studying the magazine again. The writing was not very obvious among the swirls of hair, and I was inclined to think that Egbert had missed it. On the other hand, of course, there was a decided possibility that he had already followed it up; in which case I was going to look pretty silly. And maybe I was going to look pretty silly anyway.

Ken finished with the waiter and became gay and amusing for my benefit. When the meal arrived he was a bit annoyed because I was unable to plow all the way through it, but after he had finished my remains himself he cheered up.

"As long as it's not wasted," he said philosophically, "I don't mind. But food shouldn't be wasted these days."

"It's a moot point," I argued, "whether it's more wasted in a garbage can or lying in a rubber tire around your middle. Listen, let's go and phone now."

"Count me out," he said nastily. "If there's going to be any phoning you'll do it. This was your idea. I only came along for the ride."

I stood up in a huff and said, "All right, I'll attend to it myself," but as I flounced past him he caught at my dress.

"You'll need at least a nickel, and you'd better take a pencil and a piece of paper. You might want to write something down."

I waited while he fumbled for and then produced these articles, and marched off with my head in the air.

In the phone booth I hesitated, with the nickel clutched in a clammy hand, and wondered what I was going to say. I was sweating and my stomach was turning over, and since nothing whatever occurred to me I dropped the nickel in and went ahead with my mind a blank.

A man's voice answered, and after I had swallowed twice I heard myself blurt out, "Have you the black eye there?"

It was a moment before he replied, and when he did his voice sounded distinctly angry.

"I have told you before that I will not have the princess referred to as the Black Eye."

CHAPTER THIRTY-FOUR

FROM THAT POINT ON I spoke more by instinct than anything else, for I don't believe my reason was functioning. I said, "I'm sorry, I'd forgotten. Could I—er—may I see—the princess?"

"Well . . . " The voice was reluctant now. "I suppose so. But I don't know why you should want to see her again."

"Oh. I mean I don't want to see her myself. It's—they're friends of mine. These friends of mine want to see her."

The voice took an upturn to cheerfulness. "Ah. With a view to purchase?"

"Yes. Yes, that's it."

"Very well. When may I expect them?"

"Tonight," I said promptly. "Give me the address again. I—I've forgotten it."

This didn't seem to surprise him much, and he gave me an address which I carefully wrote on my piece of paper. He asked for the names of my friends then, and I gave him Ken's and my own and hung up, feeling very clever.

I put on a lot of superiority when I told Ken the tale, but he didn't seem to be much impressed.

"You mean we're going to some unknown address with a view to purchasing a princess? Are you nuts, or was he?"

"You're wasting time," I said, practically hopping from one foot to the other. "Come on, will you? We'll soon find out what it is."

Ken settled himself more comfortably in his chair and lit a cigarette.

"Now wait a minute. I told you I just came along for the ride, but I think I'll have to take action after all. I'm going to phone Egbert."

"You'll do nothing of the sort," I said furiously. "I'm sick and tired of Egbert and his clean little face all washed behind the ears. I'm doing this thing myself. I found the magazine, didn't I?"

Ken squinted at me through a haze of cigarette smoke and asked calmly, "You wish to go and poke your nose into that address all by yourself?"

I deflated a little and admitted, "Well, I'd like you to come along. Why do you have to be such a pig about it?"

"I'm trying to be reasonable. You won't know where to fit this in, but Egbert has all the other pieces, and he'll know where it belongs."

"What more does he know about it than I do?" I exploded.

"He has all the facts at his finger tips."

"Yes," I agreed bitterly, "and all he can do is play tiddlywinks with them. We've been there all through the thing, haven't we? Egbert got all the facts he has from us anyway—he asks us every inch of the way."

Ken shook his head. "He gets out of us what we know—which is only part of the picture. For instance, do you know how those murders were committed?"

"Why—yes. They were poisoned."

"Who told you?"

I thought for a while and then said lamely, "Everyone knows it."

"Everyone thinks it, but it must have been an odd sort of poison. Suzy seemed peaceful enough—she wasn't, apparently, sick or in pain beforehand."

"Then—then what was it? There was no blood on her."

"How do you know that? You didn't really examine her, and neither did I—nor did we really examine Betty or Homer—but Egbert did. You and I don't know how they were killed."

"All right, so Egbert knows how they were killed, and we don't. But he still wants a motive—and if you'll only come with me, maybe we can give him one."

"I've been thinking about it quite a lot," Ken said, ignoring me. "Who the devil could have poisoned her anyway? She'd gone home with Emerson and Mrs. Budd—and of course we don't know when she came back—but you know when Mary came in."

I nodded, diverted in spite of myself. "Mary and I didn't go into the living room until we'd had coffee, so I suppose Suzy might have come in while we were in the kitchen."

"Somebody could have shot her . . . gun with a silencer . . . not much blood. Nobody heard anything."

"You're drooling," I said coldly. "Why would Egbert keep it a secret if she'd been shot?"

"Maybe he's looking for the gun and thinks he'll have a better chance of finding it if everyone else isn't looking too."

I realized that he was stalling, and I said abruptly, "Either you're coming with me or you're not—make up your mind. Because I'm going anyway."

He began to toy with a knife, and I became conscious of a woman at the next table who was staring at me. I looked full at her, and she averted her eyes, and I automatically put a hand to my hair. I discovered that the yellow ribbon had slipped back off the bandage, and I pulled it forward again, at the same time cussing furiously at Ken. "Why didn't you tell me that, silly-look-ing bandage was showing?"

He glanced up. "It isn't. But now that you mention it, I really ought to change that dressing."

"You won't touch it," I snapped, and added with sudden inspiration, "at least not until we get back."

"Don't be silly," he said, with purpose glinting in his eye. "It ought to be looked at and changed. It's dangerous to neglect a thing like that."

"When we come back."

He gave a gusty sigh and threw the knife he had been playing with half across the table. "This is going to mean trouble—for both of us."

"Get the bill," I said, tapping my foot. "Come on—get it."

"You can't get a waiter to come at the drop of a hat these days. He'll come when he's ready and not before."

"You're not even trying to catch his eye."

"Quite useless. You can't catch a waiter's eye. Sometimes he gives it to you in an amiable moment, but you can't catch it."

"Well, for heaven's sake watch him, then, in case he decides to give."

The waiter presently approached of his own accord, and Ken paid the bill, although he gave forth with a low whistle when he saw the total. In the lobby he wandered over to an array of postcards and started looking through them.

"Why don't you buy one and send it to Mary, saying we've eloped?" I asked facetiously.

"Good idea. I shall."

He did too, although by the time he got to the point of slipping it into the mailbox I was frantically trying to stop him—without success.

"No sooner said than done," he observed, dusting off his hands.

I gave a vexed sigh and headed for the entrance. "I'm going straight out front there—now—and hail a taxi and give him this address. You can come with me or not, but I'm off."

He came, but he was shaking his head, with disapproval bristling all over him. Once in the taxi, he drew a breath that came from the bottom of his shoes and handed out a battered cigarette.

"You might as well know that I don't like any part of this."

"Astonishing," I murmured. "I had thought you were all eagerness."

"Save your sarcasm. You'll need all your wits when we get there. This is your show."

We lapsed into silence, and I discovered that I was decidedly nervous. I twisted my hands together and stared out of the window, hoping that I looked more composed than I felt. We left the city and passed through a good residential section which presently changed to more modest surroundings. The cab drew up at last before a rather old house that had certainly seen better days. Ken paid off and then let out a few fruity curses, after the taxi had gone, because he had not told the man to wait.

"We'll have to use the fellow's telephone to call another," he muttered.

"Oh, come on!" I said impatiently. "Stop all these delaying actions, will you? We'll get back to civilization somehow."

Ken set his jaw and took my arm. "Come on then," he said with sudden decision. "If I lose my stripes over this I'll have it out of your hide somehow."

"I shall make it up to you gladly. I'll write you letters and send you boxes of foolishments."

Ken rang the doorbell, and presently the door was opened by an elderly man in shirtsleeves. He had iron-gray hair and wore spectacles with thick lenses.

"Oh." He pushed the glasses up onto his forehead and blinked at us.

"I believe we're expected," Ken announced in his sergeant's voice. "We've come to see the princess."

"Oh yes, yes—of course. Mrs. Emerson gave me your names, but I'm afraid I've forgotten."

I wondered, shuddering, whether he ever read the newspapers, but Ken gave our names, and he nodded and said, "Come in."

We passed through a hall and living room that were dark and musty and crowded with drab old furniture, and out onto a side porch that had been completely glassed in. It looked like a miniature museum. It was crowded with peculiar objects, and I had a vague idea that the things were Egyptian. There was a long coffin-shaped box in the middle of the floor, and the man shuffled, straight over and knelt down beside it.

"She's a very fine specimen," he said, and stroked the lid with loving hands. "Mrs. Emerson calls her the Black Eye. I don't know why, but I don't like it. After all, she is a princess. I have her entire history. Here, now . . ."

He lifted the lid, and Ken and I peered in.

A confusion of colors, with a serene painted face staring up at us—it was an Egyptian mummy.

CHAPTER THIRTY-FIVE

KEN EASED HIS ARM away from me, and I discovered that I was digging my fingers into it with all my strength.

The man was fussing lovingly with his treasure. "See, I'll show you. I wouldn't sell her—not for anything in the world—if I didn't need the money."

He carefully pulled the portrait away and exposed the wrapped mummy underneath. I thought instantly of Homer and Betty, examining this thing, probably with absorbed interest, and then going home to be killed and wrapped in the same way, except that their bindings were pinkish material intended for curtain ruffles, and the princess was bound in ancient, yellowed stuff that was crumbling with age.

I had a sudden attack of nausea and turned away, pretending an interest in the other objects that cluttered the place. I heard Ken telling the man that we were grateful for his courtesy: the princess was an unusually fine specimen, and we, would think it over and let him know. Unfortunately we had no time, just then, to study her history—I think Ken called it a pedigree—but we would do so later, when our engagements were less pressing.

The man was peeved and pleased all at once, and it was obvious that he was caught between his love for the princess and his need for money. He rumpled his hair and said fretfully, "Yes, yes—take your time. Only I don't understand about Mrs. Emerson and Mr. Fredon. He intended to buy her—he said so, definitely. Mrs. Emerson wanted her, too, but she had not the money."

Ken said well, you never knew, did you, and after a final exchange of courtesies and farewells we left the place and headed down the street. Ken was whistling softly, and I still felt pretty sick.

"If we can find some sort of a main street we may be able to pick up a taxi," he observed presently.

I nodded, and he glanced down at me. "Forget it," he said briefly. "Look at that house over there—says 'Justice of the Peace.' Let's go in and get married."

I felt better at once. My stomach seemed to settle, and I said firmly, "No. Girls who get married without being engaged never get the ring—and no matter how long it takes them to have a baby, people always whisper, 'I told you so.' "

"Well," he said mildly, "I told Mary in that postcard that we had eloped, and it always looks better if you're married when you return from an elopement. Besides, this may be your only chance. I might not ask you again."

"We have to take so many chances in the course of a lifetime," I said carelessly. "Look, isn't that a trolley line on the next street?"

It was, and upon inquiry we were told that it would take us back to the city. Once we were in the lighted trolley, with other passengers around us, I found that I could discuss the thing again without the sick, frightened feeling that I'd had before.

"There's one thing I can't understand," Ken said, "and that's why Homer was in the bin and Betty left in the drawer for us to discover."

"But I don't think she was intended to be discovered," I protested. "She was hidden away in that drawer—and nailed in, too."

"All right, but why was Homer in the bin? And who put him there? It isn't easy to lift a dead body."

"Practically impossible, isn't it?"

"Well, we're taught to lift things in the Army—but you have to know how."

"Nobody around there is in the Army, except you," I pointed out.

"I'd push your head down into your neck if we were alone," he said conversationally. "But the thing is, why were they not both put into the drawer? That's what I don't get."

"Mary told me that that bed is going up to the country—she's just waiting until a van is going up that way—and so of course they should both have been in the drawer. Once they were in the cottage, they could have been disposed of somehow."

"Does Mary invite many people up there?" Ken asked.

"Oh yes, at regular intervals, a few at a time. The sort of people who keep their feet off couches."

He nodded and said thoughtfully, "I've been up there twice, with a decent time elapsing in between."

"I've been invited twice, but I didn't go,"

We fell silent, and I tried to think of a reason why Betty was in the drawer and Homer in the bin, but nothing came to me, so I gave it up.

Ken must have been thinking of the bin, too, because after a while he asked, "What is that bin doing in Mary's kitchen anyway?"

"She had it made for her beloved cottage. She'd seen one advertised and liked the idea, but she's so fussy that hers was made to order—a different size and shape, and with removable partitions and—I guess those partitions must have been removed. Anyway, she found it worked very well—vegetables and fruit and chicken—things like that but when gas rationing came she couldn't get up to the country so much to get the stuff, so she had it moved to the apartment, and she says it's been wonderful. Declared that every fruit and vegetable she and Homer ate last winter was out of season."

"That must have been exciting as all hell," Ken said. "But I don't see how Egbert could have missed Homer in there, even if he was strewn with radishes."

"Ahh—Egbert couldn't find the hole in a doughnut."

But Ken shook his head and said, "No. There's something wrong with it."

Back at the hotel, Ken wanted to sit around for a while and talk, but I was tired, and I went straight up to my room. It was heavenly, that hotel room. It was small and hot, and the furniture was nondescript, but I could close the door and be alone and undisturbed and at peace. I went to bed and turned out the light and knew nothing whatever until I woke up to find the sun streaming in at the window.

I took a long, leisurely bath and removed Ken's bandage and happily threw it away. I could not see my wound, but it felt all right—a rough surface and a little tender to the touch.

I longed for fresh clothes as I dressed, and then realized, with real horror, that I had no makeup at all with me. I stood looking into the mirror at my bare, clean face, wondering how I could possibly show myself in public, but in the end I had to go down to the lobby that way, because there was nothing else to do.

I found Ken comfortably established in an armchair with a newspaper, and he looked up and then gave me an astonished stare.

"What is it? What have you done to yourself?"

I gave a short, bitter laugh. "This is the real me. Now maybe you'll give me a few coppers while I run to the nearest drugstore and get some of the essentials."

"'Oh." He looked a bit disconcerted but recovered himself manfully. "Certainly not. You look quite nice that way."

"Please!" I begged. "Just give me a quarter. I can get some sort of a lipstick for a quarter."

He folded his paper and tucked it under his arm. "Not so much as a nickel, sister, but I'll buy you breakfast if you want to come along."

He started toward the dining room, and I tagged after him, whining, "Surely you don't want to be seen in a public restaurant with me looking like this."

He selected a table and held a chair for me, and I sank into it with my cheeks burning. I presently stole a glance around to see how many people were staring at me and was relieved to find that no one was paying me the slightest attention.

"Where's your pretty yellow ribbon?" Ken asked chattily.

I put a hand on my hair, which I had had to comb with my fingers, and gave him an ugly look. "I don't care for yellow bows—or any other color either. Lucy can have them."

He was suddenly stricken with memory, and he bleated agitatedly, "The bandage—what have you done with that bandage?"

"I threw it away. Head's cured."

"You had no right to touch it—you should have let me do it—and I'll have to put a fresh bandage on."

He wanted to examine the wound then and there, but I hissed him back into his seat.

"You leave it alone," I whispered furiously. "I'll let you put on a bandage and the yellow ribbon, too, after breakfast, if you'll buy me some cosmetics and a comb."

"You're forgetting that you made a bargain with me last night. I was to change the dressing after we got back from that fantastic trip, only I forgot. But you're going to pay up this morning."

I poured coffee, and ate and drank in silence, hoping that he would forget again, but of course he didn't. As soon as the meal was over he went to a drugstore and bought a few supplies. In the end he broke down under my anguished entreaties and allowed me to select a small compact of powder, a lipstick, and a pocket comb.

On our return to the hotel we found that we had barely time to catch a train, and Ken hastily paid the bills for both our rooms, while I stood by trying to look like his sister. We flew out, caught a taxi, and raced to the station—and then found that the train was late. We went into the waiting room and sat down, and I eagerly hauled out the compact and lipstick and went to work. I had already used the comb while we were swaying around in the taxi. When I had finished I gave a sigh of the most exquisite relief and stowed the precious articles in the pocket of my dress, along with the yellow ribbon.

I turned to say something to Ken and froze with horror. He had a small box of ointment open on one knee and was gravely cutting a length of bandage with a penknife.

"Oh, God!" I whispered. "Not here. Please!"

"If you can brazenly paint your face in a public waiting room," he said severely, "I can certainly put a necessary bandage on your head."

I could see that argument was useless, and already several people were looking at us curiously, so I shut my eyes, gritted my teeth, and allowed him to go to work. When at last he had ceased to fumble with my head I opened my eyes again and saw that he was admiring his handiwork, quite oblivious to the little ring of people who had gathered around us. I quickly pulled out the yellow ribbon and tied it on, despite his protest that the bandage was so neat this time that there was really no necessity for covering it.

I turned my head away in stony silence and fixed my eyes on the doorway, ignoring Ken and also the people who had been entertained at my humiliating expense.

As I stared grimly a lone man appeared in the doorway and began methodically to sort out the crowd with his eyes.

It was Bartholomew Egbert.

CHAPTER THIRTY-SIX

I FELT KEN'S HAND on my arm, and he pulled me quickly to my feet. We slipped unobtrusively through the crowd and were actually only a few feet away from Egbert when we sped through the door and out to the platform, but he had his back turned and was looking down at the far end of the waiting room.

We stood close together behind a post in the broiling sun, and when I protested Ken said, "He'll be along to see if we're taking this train—and I don't want him to catch us."

"What are we going to say when he finally tracks us down?"

"We can tell him we were off visiting some aunts," Ken said, "and we'll leave the magazine where he'll be sure to find it."

"That's fine," I agreed, "except for two things. First, I must have lost the magazine somewhere, as I don't seem to have it with me—"

"Of all the irresponsible, cloth-headed idiots!" Ken exploded. "Why can't you hold on to your things?"

"I'll make up another magazine for Egbert that'll be just as good," I soothed him. "Anyway, secondly, Egbert will want the names and addresses of our Binghamton aunts, and what are you going to do about that?"

But he had ceased to listen to me and was muttering, "You certainly couldn't tell that Emerson had a false eye just by looking at him."

"No," I said thoughtfully, "but they make a very expert job of things like that these days—and he kept it such a secret."

I remembered the glassy-looking object that we had picked up in the drawer, and decided that it was no wonder John had got another, for that one could never have looked as natural as whatever he was wearing. And then, suddenly, I had a doubt about John's false black eye—and almost immediately Ken put it into words.

"I don't believe it," he said flatly. "That eye we picked up could never look like the one he's wearing for the simple reason that he never did wear that piece of glass."

"Of course," I breathed excitedly. "But why—why would he pretend he'd had two eyes?"

"Money. Betty had the money, and she was getting a bit tired of him, but she could hardly refuse him an eye. When he found out how much an eye cost he thought it was good enough to do over again, so he started to wink and to complain that the eye didn't fit him and was the wrong color anyway. She gave him money for a new one, and he had that bit of glass made up to show her—and somehow it got into the drawer of Mary's bed."

"Yes, somehow—and he made a pretty lame excuse—"

The train came in, and we made a dash for it. We saw Egbert, but he did not appear to see us, and inside the coach we slid low in our seat and breathed lightly until the train was well out of the station again.

"Although I don't know why it matters," I said reasonably, once the danger was past, "because Egbert can easily prove that we were in Binghamton. He has only to glance over the hotel register."

Ken settled himself comfortably. "I don't want him to catch us just yet. I want to enjoy this interlude as long as it lasts. When we get back we can clear away the debris."

We gazed at the passing scene for a while, but I couldn't get my mind away from John, and I presently suggested, "That might be the motive Egbert's looking for. John was found out, and Betty told Homer and threatened a divorce—everything brought out into the open, and John faced the loss of his wife and daughter—and the money, too—so he killed Homer and Betty in a rage."

"Nah," Ken said sleepily. "John would figure that he could always hold Betty if he turned on all the charm. He has plenty of it."

Well, that was true, of course, and I couldn't argue against it. But after all, somebody had killed them, and it seemed to me that mine was the best motive yet.

"I wonder why Betty called that mummy the Black Eye?" I murmured half to myself.

"Simple," Ken said, looking superior. "I knew Betty, you see—I know what she was like. She gave the thing that name because John's eye had cost so much that she couldn't afford to buy it."

I hadn't thought of that, and I didn't want to be impressed by it because Ken's tone was so smug, but I couldn't think of anything to refute it.

"Homer had the money to buy it, I suppose," said Ken, "but he probably had to ask Mary first if he could."

"I don't think Mary would have minded. Anything antique is usually all right with her."

We both laughed a little, but Ken shook his head. "Nope, you're wrong. Mary would spend a large sum on a chair that couldn't safely be sat on, but I'm sure she'd object to Homer going around spending money on foolishness."

We laughed again, and presently I put our single thought into words.

"But she would hardly murder Betty and Homer because they were proposing to buy a mummy. Besides, Homer wouldn't have bought it without her consent. He'd just have said, 'No, dear, just as you say.' "

"You're right in a general way," Ken conceded, "but those mild men stand up to their wives every ten years or so and get quite stubborn. I knew a man once—"

"Spare me," I murmured. "I think I'll take a nap."

"Go ahead," Ken agreed amiably. "Be a good time for a little sleep while I'm telling this story. It's not very interesting, and you won't miss much."

As a matter of fact I did go to sleep, although I hadn't really intended to, and I slept so soundly that Ken had to nudge me awake when it was time to change trains.

We arrived back at Mary's apartment in the late afternoon and went in through the back entrance. Ken had a key, and as we came into the hall the place seemed quiet, although we could hear someone moving around in the kitchen. We didn't bother to investigate—we had a polite scuffle as to who should get into the bathroom first. I won, and I took a long cool shower, and then went to my room for a complete change of clothes. I had to put the yellow ribbon back on because of the bandage, and I wondered despairingly whether I'd have to wear the thing until the end of Ken's furlough.

I went on out to the kitchen, prepared for a series of shrieks from Lucy as to where we had been, but she was not there. Ken was lounging against the table, and Mary stood at the stove cooking something.

It was apparent that Mary had not yet received the postcard about our supposed elopement, and Ken was trying to do a little reasonable explaining.

"We really didn't think you'd mind. It was just one of those things—spur of the moment—and we—er—needed a break from all this trouble."

"I need one myself," Mary said in an injured voice, "far more than you did, I'm sure. And it looked so bad, you know—not even telephoning—and of course Lucy will spread it far and wide, and put the worst interpretation on it."

"We should have telephoned," Ken agreed easily, "but you know how it is. I was tired and ready to turn in when I got back to the hotel, and I suppose Gene felt the same, way."

"Well, yes, but New York isn't so far away, and Eugenia could have phoned from her apartment."

"Quite right. She should have, and I should have. We're sorry, Mary."

He sounded more impatient than sorry, and I realized that he had made up some tale about our jaunt. I wondered if he intended to tell it—whatever it was—to Egbert, and I wanted to warn him that that would be silly.

"Where's Lucy?" Ken asked.

Mary broke some eggs into a bowl and avoided looking at either of us. "She's gone home."

Ken fastened his attention on her and asked, "Why did she go?"

Mary began to beat the eggs briskly and made no reply.

"Did you quarrel with her?"

Mary frowned, dumped her mixture into a pot, and then turned to face us with sudden color in her cheeks.

"There was no quarrel. Lucy left in a hurry when she realized that I knew she had killed my husband."

CHAPTER THIRTY-SEVEN

KEN HAD BEEN TOYING with a knife that lay on the table, and it fell with a sudden sharp clatter to the floor.

Mary said, "Tch," and stooped and picked it up.

"I don't think you ought to make an accusation like that unless you're absolutely sure," I told her soberly.

"I am sure," she said calmly, "and I'll tell you why. Lucy owed Homer a large sum of money. She had expected, when she borrowed it, to pay it back in six months—or that's what she said—and that was four years ago. She didn't know that I knew anything about it, but of course I did—I told Homer to lend it to her at the time. Anyway, Homer was pressing her for it just lately, although I don't know why, and Lucy couldn't pay. I know her circumstances, and I told Homer that she didn't have it, but he wouldn't listen to me—said he needed the money. Now Lucy's been getting along all right financially, but for her to try to raise a sum like that would be disastrous. She'd have to sell everything she owns, and then it wouldn't be enough. So she killed him, and I suppose Betty knew about it and saw her do it, and Betty had to be killed too. You see, it was as simple as that. If Homer were dead he wouldn't dun her any more, and if his body were never found no one would know that he had been murdered."

"You're taking entirely too much for granted," Ken muttered. "Why would she wrap them up like that?"

Mary had put her eggs into a pot and was scrambling them, and I saw that she had some coffee bubbling cheerfully in a silex. She glanced at the coffee and turned the gas out under it before she replied, "It was to preserve them, of course. Homer often talked about mummies and such things, and Lucy always showed interest."

"But why preserve them?"

"Don't you see, she didn't want them to be discovered—ever. She knew I was sending that bed up to the cottage as soon as I could get a van, and if they were nailed into the drawer she could take her time about disposing of them when she came up to visit—so she gave them the injection and then wrapped them up to make sure."

"Have you told Egbert all this?" Ken asked gravely.

Mary shook her head, frowning. "I don't know where he is, but the next time he comes here I shall tell him everything. Lucy must be properly punished—such a selfish, conceited woman. Brushing people out of her way like flies, and thinking she can simply enjoy herself without paying for it."

"I can't believe all this," Ken said, looking unusually serious. "Lucy isn't like that—it's out of character. Let's go into the living room and talk it over. I'm sure you're wrong."

Mary pushed the eggs off the flame and turned to slip some bread into the toaster. "Wait until I get this together—you must be hungry, and we might as well eat, while we're talking."

Ken got a tray from one of the cupboards and began to pile plates and cups onto it. "We'll take it into the living room and eat from our laps," he said. "It's cooler in there."

"Oh no, no," Mary protested, shocked. "It gets crumbs around, and it's so messy. Take the tray into the dining room, Ken."

But Ken had the entire meal loaded onto the tray, and he bore it straight to the living room, so that Mary had perforce to follow or go hungry. She established herself in a straight chair, and Ken said, "I'll personally go down on my hands and knees and retrieve all crumbs after the feast; so smooth out your brow."

She gave him a faint, patient smile, and sighed. "I think you'll find it quite good. I really do cook as well as Lucy, even though she never would admit it." She leaned back in her chair and shook her head a little. "The unutterable gall of the woman—coming here and cooking for us, after what she did."

"But, Mary—" Ken began.

Her eyes flashed. "Now you listen to me, Ken Smith. I would never have thought it of her, myself—never—but I can see it all now. Lucy is selfish and lazy, and good clothes and easy living mean everything to her. She simply would not face giving up what she had, in order to try and pay Homer what she owed him. Perhaps she didn't plan it too far ahead, but when Homer got that stuff from Mr. Boxton it probably gave her the idea. She would kill Homer, embalm him, and put him in the drawer.

"I am convinced that she came over here, that Sunday, knowing that I had gone to the cottage. I suppose Homer let her in, and she found Betty with him. She had always hated Betty, and anyway, she could not afford to wait, so she cooked one of her little meals for them, and they ate it, and died. She did the embalming job on them and wrapped them in that curtain material, so that they would not decompose in the drawer. She must have been worried when she heard that the moving company wouldn't take the bed up until they had a full load—and I know that when I told her about you two she advised me against letting you stay here—and you can see why. Anyhow, when I asked her to chaperon you, she came rushing right over—naturally.

"She must have been terrified when she found evidences of Homer around the place—knowing as she did that he was dead."

Mary paused, gave a little shudder, and moistened her lips.

"She must have caught Suzy lighting Homer's pipe during the party, and she knew at once that Suzy had found them. She was frantic, I expect, and she realized that she should have nailed up the drawer after putting them into it. You remember, Eugenia, you saw it slightly open. Anyway, she nailed it up then—it would be easy because the holes were already there, and the nails would fit right in. I guess it was the next night that you said something about opening the drawer, and I told you to leave it alone. Lucy must have heard and been afraid that you would open it anyway, so in her panic she tried to move them to the bin in the kitchen, but had time only for Homer—"

"No," I interrupted, "that would have been impossible. There was a man on guard in the hall."

"I know, but my room has two doors—one out into the main hall, and the other into the foyer, right next to the kitchen."

"But we were with her," I protested. "I was anyway. I know—"

"We were all asleep by eleven-thirty," Mary interrupted impatiently, "including, no doubt, that policeman in the hall. Anyway, she crept across behind him to my room and got Homer into the bin, taking him through that other door, and then she realized that they both would not fit. All those radishes had to go in, too, so that they would be completely covered. She had no time to think of another place for Betty, so she nailed the drawer again and hoped for the best. At least if Homer weren't found there would be no obvious motive for Lucy to have killed Betty—it would look more like my doing—"

Ken made a restless movement, seemed on the verge of an exclamation, and then relaxed back into his chair with his eyes on Mary's face. I dropped my head against the back of my chair, feeling tired and confused.

"You remember," Mary continued, "that I said I'd have to clean out the bin? Well, Lucy came to me directly afterward and said she was going out and made me promise not to clean the bin until she got back. She persuaded me to take a nap, which I badly needed, and when Eugenia and I were both in our rooms she came back, locked us in, and put Homer back in the drawer."

"But how?" Ken asked. "How could she possibly manage it by herself?"

"I imagine she put a sort of strap through those bindings—it would make it much easier to pull the body around. Of course it would take a strong back—but she has one.

"Later, she got back just in time to see Eugenia kneeling down with a hand already in that drawer—and without waiting for anything, she picked up that silver box and hit her over the head. Lucky for you, Eugenia, that it was only a light box and did no more than knock you out."

I moved my head restlessly on the back of my chair, and Ken murmured, "But there's something more—"

"Oh yes." Mary nodded. "After she had dealt with Eugenia she had to move Homer again, so she put him under the studio couch where she was sleeping—he couldn't be seen there unless someone were to get down on hands and knees and look under. But even Lucy lost her nerve when she tried to sleep there, so she got Eugenia to change—never dreaming, of course, that Eugenia would pull the couch away from the wall. Lucy undoubtedly hoped to get Homer back into the drawer in time for the movers, who are coming tomorrow."

Mary stopped talking and leaned back, looking white and exhausted. Ken got up and began to pace the room and I poured more coffee for myself. After a while Mary started to nibble at her toast and scrambled eggs, and I knew she was excited when I saw that she was dropping crumbs onto her lap.

Ken suddenly stopped in front of her and said, "I can't believe it. For instance, why was Suzy killed and left for anyone to discover—in order to cover up the murders of Homer and Betty?"

Mary was silent for a moment, and then she looked up at him.

"No, of course not—that would have been silly. Oh no—Suzy's death was an accident."

CHAPTER THIRTY-EIGHT

THERE WAS THE SOUND of a footstep on the balcony, and Egbert stepped into the room.

Mary started, looked up, and colored angrily. "Mr. Egbert, I object to your coming into my apartment in that informal way. If you have any business here you can ring the doorbell and wait until you are admitted."

Egbert nodded with the utmost aplomb and said, "Certainly, Mrs. Fredon. I was talking to Mrs. Budd and Emerson, and it seemed simpler to come through this way."

"I must ask you not to do it again," Mary said crossly. "How long have you been out there—listening?"

"I heard your story," Egbert admitted without embarrassment. "I'd like to discuss it with you."

"It was not for your ears. I have no proof of any of this, and you can hardly arrest Lucy on the strength of my opinions."

"I know my business;" Egbert said, exhibiting a touch of hauteur himself. "Do you know the exact amount that was owed to your husband by Mrs. Davis?"

"No, I do not." Mary pressed her fingers against her eyes for a moment and drew a long, slow breath. "I know only that it was quite a large sum."

"It seems a little odd," Egbert suggested. "You and your husband had two joint accounts—one savings and one checking. I should think, therefore, that you'd have known exactly what was loaned to Mrs. Davis."

"No, no," Mary said wearily. "Homer cashed some bonds—it had nothing to do with the bank accounts."

"Why did he want the money back just lately?"

"I don't know."

"Yes, you do," said Egbert. "He wanted to buy an Egyptian mummy."

Mary rested her head against the back of her chair and closed her eyes.

"He wanted to buy a mummy," Egbert continued smoothly, "and you disapproved—but he was going to buy it anyway."

Mary gave a little sigh. "I dislike airing these things—but you seem to know about it. He had his heart set on that mummy, and he would not listen to me. He had made up his mind to buy it."

"It was all right for you to spend ridiculous sums on antiques, but you fought your husband implacably when he wanted an antique of his own," Egbert said, giving her a cold eye.

Mary drew herself up and iced over. "I feel in duty bound to answer your official questions, Mr. Egbert, but I am not interested in your insulting opinions. I bought necessary furniture for my home, but I had no wish to live in daily contact with a corpse reposing in a coffin—no matter how old it might be."

Egbert brushed it aside and said, "I am interested in knowing why you borrowed money from John Emerson to buy that antique bed."

Mary was furious. Hot color stained her face and neck, and her eyes flashed. "I cannot understand John telling you that—he was to have kept it an absolute secret. He'd no right to tell you, and I'll never trust him again."

"Be that as it may," said Egbert, "why did you borrow from him?"

"I see no reason why I should tell you."

"I know your bank balances are pretty low," Egbert continued, "but you have a fortune in securities, so why didn't you use some of that for your bed?"

Mary, her color still high and drumming nervously on the arms of her chair with her fingers, said nothing and stared at the floor.

Egbert regarded her for a moment of silence and then went on.

"You must have wanted that bed pretty badly to offer him such heavy interest on the sum you borrowed."

Mary glanced up and said rather weakly, "How can you think anybody could borrow from John? He never had a nickel."

"No. But he gouged a goodly sum out of his wife recently, by pretending that he needed a new false eye, claiming that the one he had did not fit and was too black, so he'd have to have another one. The cost of the new eye was not enough for him, so he invented a series of treatments necessary to make the new eye fit properly. Since his own oculist—a family friend—had died, he figured, correctly, that he could get away with this. As far as the color is concerned, Mr. Emerson still thinks his eye is too black—he was complaining about that before he got the idea of the new one—so he had to announce that the new one was a shade lighter. Evidently he was believed." Egbert paused to shrug.

"I knew nothing of that until just lately," Mary declared. "Mrs. Budd told me in confidence about his new false eye, and it crossed my mind that perhaps he was faking and that was how he had got the money. Previously I had happened to meet him at the galleries where I first saw the bed. It is a beautiful piece, and I told him how much I wanted it but that I hadn't the cash. He offered to lend me the amount, and I was to give him fifty dollars a month until it was paid off with good interest. I didn't know why he wanted to do it that way until I learned that Betty was going to divorce him—and then I realized that the fifty, added to the little he makes, would keep him for a while, so that he, wouldn't need to rush straight into another marriage with a woman of means."

Egbert nodded. "But you haven't told me why you didn't cash some of the securities to buy your bed."

Mary shrugged. "Homer and I had agreed not to touch those for any purpose. They brought us a steady income, and neither one of us could cash any of them without the other's consent."

"So how did Mr. Fredon expect to pay for his mummy?"

"I've already told you," said Mary, "that he was trying to get Lucy to pay up."

"Yes. Certainly. But you and I both know that Mrs. Davis could not pay even if she wanted to."

"She could have sold everything she owned," Mary said angrily.

"What, for instance? She has no car and no property—she hasn't even jewelry or a mink coat. There's an insurance policy that pays her seventy a month, but she can't get any sort of an advance on it—and if she'd assigned the seventy over to Mr. Fredon, he'd have had to wait for some time before he'd have had enough to buy his mummy—if it was still for sale."

Mary looked at him for a moment, frowning, and with her lips compressed. "Couldn't she have borrowed the money," she said at last, "and signed over the seventy a month as security?"

"I shouldn't care to lend on that sort of security," Egbert replied smoothly. "That money stops the instant she dies."

"Then I don't know how she could have paid," Mary said in exasperation, "and I don't know how Homer intended to pay for his mummy."

"Then perhaps you do know why Suzy's death was an accident," Egbert suggested.

Mary looked down at her drumming fingers and up again. "I'm tired," she said suddenly. "I want to go to bed—I need sleep."

"Yes, certainly," said Egbert, always the gentleman. "But you will answer my question first?"

"Lucy came over here that Sunday afternoon and made some fudge, and she mixed it with morphine pills which were supposed to be nuts. After Betty and Homer had eaten some she put it away in a box on one of the shelves in the kitchen—and Suzy found it and ate some, The poor child was frantically trying to get someone to search the apartment so that the bodies would be found. And now I'm going to bed."

"Mrs. Davis never eats fudge herself?" Egbert asked.

"No." Mary got to her feet. "She's vain about her figure."

Egbert took a step toward her. "I knew Mrs. Davis had made that fudge, but it seemed odd that she would come over here to make fudge for Mr. Fredon when you were not at home. What excuse would she have given?"

Mary stopped on her way to the door and turned back. "I asked her to come. I know that she's lonely sometimes, and Homer was fond of her candy. I never dreamed that he was going up to Binghamton with Betty, of course. So Lucy came in the afternoon, just after they had got back, and made that fudge—and poisoned it, too."

Egbert nodded. "The elevator man said that Mrs. Davis had come in just after Mr. Fredon and Mrs. Emerson. Mrs. Davis declares that she got the nuts out of a labeled tin where you always kept them—and she further states that they ate only one piece each, and she wondered why—she thought there was something wrong with her cooking. She left shortly afterward, as she had a date, and she says that she came only as a favor to you, because you were so insistent—"

Mary came farther back into the room. "How could she say such a thing! It was merely a suggestion, and she clutched at it eagerly."

"I visited your cottage in the country, Mrs. Fredon," Egbert said with apparent irrelevance. "Lovely place."

Mary stood and looked at him in silence.

"Of course Mrs. Davis was right—the curtain material was the wrong color."

"It was nothing of the sort," Mary whispered.

"Yes, I think so—but it doesn't matter now. I believe that Mr. Fredon was ordinarily a patient man, but he was so angry when you borrowed money to buy that bed that he went straight off and sold the cottage in order to have money to buy his mummy."

The color in Mary's face drained away until it was a dead white. She stood absolutely still for a moment and then suddenly screamed, "No! Oh no!" She flew at Egbert and caught wildly at his coat. "He couldn't have—he wouldn't do it—he wasn't going to do anything before Monday—"

Egbert freed himself from her grasp and said mildly, "Then he changed his mind, because I have the proof here in my pocket."

He pulled out an assortment of papers, but Mary did not look at them. She had turned away from him, and her face was livid with rage.

"The monster!" she whispered hoarsely. "Oh, the damnable monster! If only he were here I wouldn't give him such an easy death as I did."

CHAPTER THIRTY-NINE

I DON'T THINK Mary quite realized what she had said. She paid very little attention to Egbert and two of his men, who stepped in from the balcony when they formally placed her under arrest.

Lucy had crept in after the two men, and she stared at Mary with eyes that were round with horror. I sat frozen in my chair, feeling dazed and a bit sick, while Ken stood with his hands jammed into his pockets and the line of his jaw rigid.

When Mary was presently led away by Egbert's men she came to life again and began hysterically to protest her innocence and to accuse Lucy. When she had gone, at last, a blank silence fell upon us until Egbert came back into the room and—elaborately casual—lit a cigarette.

Lucy turned her bulging eyes on him and exclaimed, "Oh, Mr. Egbert, are you sure? I mean, I don't see how she could have done it. She—she wasn't here."

"No," said Egbert. "You did it yourself with that fudge you made for them."

Lucy opened her mouth to scream, and Egbert said hastily, "Don't get excited—Mrs. Fredon tricked you. If you remember, she told you that she had a new kind of nut to mix in with your fudge, and she put those little morphine tablets in the box that was labeled 'Nuts.' You merely took her word for it and mixed them in."

But Lucy was not to be balked, and she went into a nice little bout of hysterics. After we had cleared her up a little she sobbed, "I thought they didn't look like nuts, but Mary said they were, and insisted that I make the fudge with them. She said they were a new kind and Homer was very fond of them. I ought to wear my glasses when I'm cooking! I wondered why they ate only one piece each—I couldn't understand it, because the fudge looked all right. Are you sure that's what killed them? I had to leave about fifteen minutes after they ate it, and they were perfectly all right then."

Egbert nodded. "Mrs. Fredon knew you had that date, and she told you not to come until about three quarters of an hour before you'd have to leave."

He was obviously afraid of Lucy's hysterics, and he turned away from her and spoke to Ken and me.

"Mrs. Fredon put what was left of the fudge away in a box, thinking, no doubt, that it might come in handy again—but she disposed of it when Suzy took some by accident."

"There are several things I wish you'd explain," Ken began, but Egbert broke in on him.

"There's one thing I don't understand. Why did you go up to Binghamton and interfere with my investigation?"

Ken shrugged. "Don't blame me—I was merely escorting my girlfriend around. I had nothing to do with it."

Lucy, trying to mop up tears without getting too much of her mascara off, said, "Ken! You're a cad."

"It's quite all right," I said easily. "He's afraid of Mr. Egbert, and I'm not."

Egbert gave me a cold stare. "I'd like to know where you got that Binghamton address."

I could see that it rankled, and I opened my mouth to tell him, but Ken spoke first.

"I don't see how Mary could have pulled Homer out of the bin, that night."

"Nonsense," said Egbert, looking bored. "The so-called weaker sex has astounding strength when the need arises."

"Do you mean that the story Mary just told us is true, except that it was herself instead of Lucy?" I asked.

"Yes," said Egbert. "Now where did you——"

"But why? How could she do such a thing? She was fond of Homer."

"Mildly, perhaps, but her real passion was her cottage and all the furniture there and in this apartment. She got so wrapped up in her possessions that she went and borrowed a large sum in order to buy the fancy bed—Napoleon, or something, they call it—and she had just bought two chairs that set her back a trifle of seven hundred-odd dollars. Her husband usually did what he was told, but that was too much even for him, so he put his foot down and said no more antiques. But she'd made this home-beautiful business her very life, so she figured she'd have to find the money for the bed behind his back. She got it from Emerson, as you know, but Mr. Fredon found out about it, and he went into one of those calm, stubborn tempers that are apt to crop out in mild people. He promptly made arrangements to sell the cottage, which was in his name alone—and he meant to sell it furnished, too. He intended to use the money to pay off John Emerson and buy that mummy.

"Mrs. Fredon raved and threatened, but she couldn't budge him. He contacted a buyer and finally decided to let the whole thing go at something of a sacrifice—and that was the last straw for his wife. She'd always been able to make him wear a yellow necktie—or sit down, or stand up—but when she borrowed money he felt that his honor was at stake. It had to be paid back immediately—and he was going to throw the mummy into punish her. Now will you please tell me—"

"Wait a minute," I interrupted. "Who locked Mary and me into our rooms? And incidentally, what about the postcard that came from Binghamton saying that Betty and Homer had eloped?"

"Mrs. Emerson sent that postcard as a joke," Egbert said, curling his lip. "I believe there are people who regard that sort of thing as humorous."

I caught Ken winking at me, and blushed, while Egbert went on, "It was Mrs. Fredon who locked you in your room. She had to get her husband's body back into the drawer, because the moving people had said they'd be calling for the bed soon, and she was anxious to keep his death secret, so that he would be blamed for the other deaths. She locked you in to keep you out of the way, and, when she had finished, locked herself in, and pushed the key out under the door."

Ken said, "What about his life insurance, if his body was never found?"

"I believe she could have collected after seven years, and in the meantime she had all those rainy-day securities. She'd have been able to keep up this apartment and the cottage."

Lucy had dried up by this time, and she said earnestly, "It just doesn't seem possible that anyone could do such dreadful things for the sake of a cottage and some worm-eaten furniture."

"Oh yes," said Egbert in the voice of one who has seen enough to believe anything. "Some people get almost mental about their homes—get into a passion if anything is disarranged or soiled. Mrs. Fredon was one of the worst. Now—"

"How did you come to pass over Homer when he was in the bin?" Ken asked innocently.

Egbert looked annoyed and murmured, "Mac did the bin, and reported that it was full of radishes, so when I looked myself I took his word for it that there was nothing else there."

"But, Mr. Egbert," Lucy cried, "I think you're wonderful! How did you ever find out about it all—about Mary and the house and the bed?"

Egbert stopped brooding about Mac, the vegetable fancier, and cheered up. "Emerson knew all about it," he said modestly. "That is, he knew that Mr. Fredon was selling the cottage to pay him back and buy the mummy. When the two failed to return from Binghamton, as he thought, he supposed that Mr. Fredon had left his wife and that Mrs. Emerson had gone off with someone else. Mrs. Emerson had been unaware of the loan he had made to Mrs.

Fredon, and he thought she had found out about it. Suzy was bothering him too—making extraordinary hinting remarks that meant nothing to him. Of course we can only guess about Suzy, but it seems pretty clear that she discovered the bodies in that bed and thought that Emerson, with whom she was in love, had done it. She couldn't bring herself to tell on him and wanted someone else to make the discovery, so she set about making things look as if Mr. Fredon had come home, so that a search of the apartment would be made."

"How did she find the bodies in the first place?" I wondered.

"She was often sent in here to help with the housework," Egbert explained, "and Mrs. Budd used such opportunities to come in too—when Mrs. Fredon was out—and do a little snooping. Mrs. Fredon made the mistake of not nailing the drawer up at once, and in the meantime Suzy was sent in to do some dusting while the apartment was empty. She discovered the bodies then. She didn't know what to do at first, but when you all came to stay she started by turning the busts in the hall the way Mr. Fredon liked them, then put the golf shoes in the hall and Mr. Fredon's pipe in the living room, and at the party she unlocked Mrs. Fredon's door, knowing that Mrs. Fredon often kept it locked, and Mr. Fredon knew where she kept the key—but nobody paid much attention to these things, so she lighted his pipe and then went out and said he was in the kitchen. Apparently the last thing Suzy did was to arrange the couch to look as though Mr. Fredon had slept there, and then that loaded fudge she had eaten began to affect her. I suppose she sat down for a minute and promptly went out like a light. She'd been working, and probably holding off the desire for sleep as long as she could—but she'd eaten more of the candy than the other two. Mrs. Emerson and Mr. Fredon must have been unconscious when Mrs. Fredon returned—and she left them to die while she went to the Emerson apartment, pretending to be concerned about Mr. Fredon's whereabouts. I think she was scared, when she returned this time and realized that she had not nailed the drawer, and she no doubt attended to it at once."

"Seems odd that Mary would let us come and stay in her apartment, when it was loaded like that," Ken commented.

Egbert sighed impatiently. "She didn't want to stay here herself, I'm sure, with only two bodies for company, so she went to the cottage. She'd offered to put you up during your furlough some long time ago—and you turned up at a most inconvenient time. She had to do something—she didn't want you here alone, poking into things, and she didn't want to be here herself, so when she ran into Miss Gates she promptly invited her out. She realized that there'd have to be a chaperon of some sort, so she got Mrs. Davis to take over—and then phoned Miss Gates to lock the door of her bedroom. It was about then that she heard gossip to the effect that Mrs. Emerson would never have eloped with Mr. Fredon, so she came out boldly and announced that her husband would never have gone off with Mrs. Emerson. At the same time she heard about the party you'd arranged, and it scared her. Too many people around—and also, her antiques might be injured—so she came back. Now—"

"I think you're wonderful," Lucy breathed. "Simply wonderful. But why did she accuse me? I've never borrowed a sou from Homer. Why, the old tightwad wouldn't have parted with a nickel."

Egbert rumpled his smooth hair in an exasperated sort of way, but talked over Lucy's head to Ken and me.

"She was alarmed. The professor in Binghamton had called her and asked if Mr. Fredon were still interested in the mummy, as two people had looked at her with a view to purchase, and he must have given her your names. So she decided to tell you the whole story, only substituting Mrs. Davis for herself. The telephone was tapped, and the conversation reported to me. I wanted to hear what she'd say to you, because on top of the fact that you'd seen the mummy, Emerson had started a little polite blackmailing on her. He knew his glass eye had been planted in that drawer, and since he knew all about the mummy and Mr. Fredon's intentions regarding the cottage, he was convinced that Mrs. Fredon had killed them. She had seen the black eye once, and he knew that she must have found it and planted it in the drawer as an added protection to herself.

"I returned from Binghamton shortly after you did and went through the Emerson apartment to the balcony. Mrs. Davis had gone in there instead of going home, and she attached herself to me. And now tell me how you found that Binghamton address."

"I agree with Lucy," I said admiringly. "I think you're wonderful. Only you don't seem to search very well. The telephone number was written on the cover of a magazine in the telephone closet—for all to see."

Egbert closed his eyes for a moment and murmured, "Mac!" He opened them again and shook his head. "Manpower shortage," he muttered, and added, "He's consistent, anyway—made a clean sweep. Missed Mr. Fredon in the bin, the magazine in the telephone closet, and the eye in the drawer. Due for a promotion."

"Why," Lucy cooed, "that shows that you're even smarter than I thought—having to solve the thing with such bungling assistance. What ever made you suspect Mary?"

Egbert stood up a little straighter and smoothed his hair back into place.

"It was when she said she didn't know whether any of her husband's clothes were missing. She wasn't the type not to know every stitch belonging to Mr. Fredon, so then I investigated the possibility of her ever having had any morphine and found she had—plenty—in tablet form, which her husband had obtained for some of his amateur experiments. Then I confronted Mrs. Davis, who I knew had been here that Sunday, and found out about the fudge. After that I had only to find the motive."

He bowed to Lucy, glared at Ken and me, and took himself off.

Lucy sighed. "I was so scared about having been here that Sunday I kept it a dead secret, but that Egbert's long nose found out about it. Oh well," she finished up brightly, "no sense sitting around here glooming. Where shall we spend the rest of our vacation?"

Ken and I looked at her, while she tapped at her teeth with a brilliant fingernail.

"Oh, I know. Why not? We'll go to my apartment."

"Lucy," I said patiently, "your apartment has one room."

"No—not exactly. I have one room, and then the kitchen. There isn't a reason in the world why Ken can't sleep in the kitchen."

I started to laugh, but Ken turned around with sudden energy.

"Certainly I can sleep in the kitchen. Come on, girls." He took each of us by an arm and pushed us toward the bedroom we'd been sharing.

"Pack your gear," he said, "and don't waste time over it—and don't forget your makeup, either. I'm the type that likes to be fooled. I was nearly fooled into cutting my furlough short to visit with a blonde near camp. But you dames will do as well, if not better."

THE END

About The Rue Morgue Press

The Rue Morgue vintage mystery line is designed to bring back into print those books that were favorites of readers between the turn of the century and the 1960s. The editors welcome suggests for reprints. To receive our catalog or make suggestions, write The Rue Morgue Press, P.O. Box 4119, Boulder, Colorado (1-800-669-6214). The Rue Morgue Press tries to keep all of its titles in print, though some books may go temporarily out of print for up to six months. The following list details the titles available as of September 2001.

Catalog of Rue Morgue Press titles January 2002

Titles are listed by author. All books are quality trade paperbacks measuring 9 by 6 inches, usually with full-color covers and printed on paper designed not to yellow or deteriorate. These are permanent books.

Joanna Cannan. The books by this English writer are among our most popular titles. Modern reviewers favorably compared our two Cannan reprints with the best books of the Golden Age of detective fiction. "Worthy of being discussed in the same breath with an Agatha Christie or a Josephine Tey."—Sally Fellows, Mystery News. "First-rate Golden Age detection with a likeable detective, a complex and believable murderer, and a level of style and craft that bears comparison with Sayers, Allingham, and Marsh."—Jon L. Breen, *Ellery Queen's Mystery Magazine.* Set in the late 1930s in a village that was a fictionalized version of Oxfordshire, both titles feature young Scotland Yard inspector Guy Northeast. *They Rang Up the Police* (0-915230-27-5, 156 pages, $14.00) and *Death at The Dog* (0-915230-23-2, 156 pages, $14.00).

Glyn Carr. The author is really Showell Styles, one of the foremost English mountain climbers of his era as well as one of that sport's most celebrated historians. Carr turned to crime fiction when he realized that mountains provided a ideal setting for committing murders. The 15 books featuring Shakespearean actor Abercrombie "Filthy" Lewker are set on peaks scattered around the globe, although the author returned again and again to his favorite climbs in Wales, where his first mystery, published in 1951, *Death on Milestone Buttress* (0-915230-29-1, 187 pages, $14.00), is set. Lewker is a marvelous Falstaffian character whose exploits have been praised by such discerning critics as Jacques Barzun and Wendell Hertig Taylor in *A Catalogue of Crime.* Other critics have been just as kind: "You'll get a taste of the Welsh countryside, will encounter names replete with consonants, will be exposed to numerous snippets from Shakespeare and will find Carr's novel a worthy representative of the cozies of two generations ago."—*I Love a Mystery.*

Clyde B. Clason. Clason has been praised not only for his elaborate plots and skillful use of the locked room gambit but also for his scholarship. He may be one of the few mystery authors—and no doubt the first—to provide a full bibliography of his sources. *The Man from Tibet* (0-915230-17-8, 220 pages, $14.00) is one of his best and highly recommended by the dean of locked room mystery scholars, Robert Adey, as "highly original." It's also one of the first popular novels to make use of Tibetan culture. Locked inside the Tibetan room of his Chicago apartment, the rich antiquarian was overheard repeating a forbidden occult chant under the watchful eyes of Buddhist gods. When the doors were opened, it appeared that he had succumbed to a heart attack. But the elderly Roman historian and sometime amateur sleuth Theocritus Lucius Westborough is convinced that Adam Merriweather's death was anything but natural and that the weapon was an eight century Tibetan manuscript.

Joan Coggin. *Who Killed the Curate?* Meet Lady Lupin Lorrimer Hastings, the young, lovely, scatterbrained and kindhearted newlywed wife to the vicar of St. Marks Parish in Glanville, Sussex. When it comes to matters clerical, she literally doesn't know Jews from Jesuits and she's hopelessly at sea at the meetings of the Mothers' Union, Girl Guides, or Temperance Society but she's determined to make husband Andrew proud of her—or, at least, not to embarass him too badly. So when Andrew's curate is poisoned, Lady Lupin enlists the help of her old society pals, Duds and Tommy Lethbridge, as well as Andrew's nephew, a British secret service agent, to get at the truth. Lupin refuses to believe Diane Lloyd, the 38-year-old author of children's and detective stories could have done the deed, and casts her net out over the other parishioners. All the suspects seem so nice, much more so than the victim, and Lupin announces she'll help the killer escape if only he or she confesses. Imagine Gracie Allen of Burns and Allen or Pauline Collins of *No, Honestly* as a sleuth and you might get a tiny idea of what Lupin is like. Set at Christmas 1937 and first published in England in 1944, this is the first American appearance of *Who Killed the Curate?* "Coggin writes in the spirit of Nancy Mitford and E.M. Delafield. But the books are mysteries, so that makes them perfect."—Katherine Hall Page. (0-915230-44-5, $14.00).

Manning Coles. The two English writers who collaborated as Coles are best known for those witty spy novels featuring Tommy Hambledon, but they also wrote four delightful—and funny—ghost novels. *The Far Traveller* (0-915230-35-6, 154 pages, $14.00) is a stand-alone novel in which a film company unknowingly hires the ghost of a long-dead German graf to play himself in a movie. "I laughed until I hurt. I liked it so much, I went back to page 1 and read it a second time."—Peggy Itzen, *Cozies, Capers & Crimes.* The other three books feature two cousins, one English, one American, and their spectral pet monkey who got a little drunk and tried to stop—futilely and fatally—a German advance outside a small French village during the 1870 Franco-Prussian War. Flash forward to the 1950s where this comic trio of friendly ghosts rematerialize to aid relatives in danger in *Brief Candles* (0-915230-24-0, 156 pages, $14.00), *Happy Returns* (0-915230-31-3, 156 pages, $14.00) and *Come and Go* (0-915230-34-8, 155 pages, $14.00).

Norbert Davis. There have been a lot of dogs in mystery fiction, from Baynard Kendrick's guide dog to Virginia Lanier's bloodhounds, but there's never been one quite like Carstairs. Doan, a short, chubby Los Angeles private eye, won Carstairs in a crap game, but there never is any question as to who the boss is in this relationship. Carstairs isn't just any Great Dane. He is so big that Doan figures he really ought to be considered another species. He scorns baby talk and belly rubs—unless administered by a pretty girl—and growls whenever Doan has a drink. His full name is Dougal's Laird Carstairs and as a sleuth he rarely barks up the wrong tree. He's down in Mexico with Doan, ostensibly to convince a missing fugitive that he would do well to stay put. The case is complicated by three murders, assorted villains, and a horrific earthquake that cuts the mountainous little village of Los Altos off from the rest of Mexico. Doan and Carstairs aren't the only unusual visitors to Los Altos. There's Patricia Van Osdel, a ravishing blonde whose father made millions from flypaper, and Captain Emile Perona, a Mexican policeman whose long-ago Spanish ancestor helped establish Los Altos. It's that ancestor who brings teacher Janet Martin to Mexico along with a stolen book that may contain the key to a secret hidden for hundreds of years in the village church. Written in the snappy hardboiled style of the day, *The Mouse in the Mountain* (0-915230-41-0, 151 pages, $14.00) was first published in 1943 and followed by two other Doan and Carstairs novels. "Each of these is fast-paced, occasionally lyrical in a hard-edged way, and often quite funny. Davis, in fact, was one of the few writers to successfully blend the so-called hardboiled story with farcical humor."—Bill Pronzini, *1001 Midnights*. Pick of the Month at The Sleuth of Baker Street in Toronto. Four star review in *Romantic Times*. "A laugh a minute romp…hilarious dialogue and descriptions…utterly engaging, downright fun read…fetch this one! Highly recommended."—Michele A. Reed, *I Love a Mystery*.

Elizabeth Dean. Dean wrote only three mysteries, but in Emma Marsh she created one of the first independent female sleuths in the genre. Written in the screwball style of the 1930s, *Murder is a Collector's Item* (0-915230-19-4, $14.00) is described in a review in *Deadly Pleasures* by award-winning mystery writer Sujata Massey as a story that "froths over with the same effervescent humor as the best Hepburn-Grant films." Like the second book in the trilogy, *Murder is a Serious Business* (0-915230-28-3, 254 pages, $14.95), it's set in a Boston antique store just as the Great Depression is drawing to a close. *Murder a Mile High* (0-915230-39-9, 188 pages, $14.00), moves to the Central City Opera House in the Colorado mountains, where Emma has been summoned by am old chum, the opera's reigning diva. Emma not only has to find a murderer, she may also have to catch a Nazi spy. A reviewer for a Central City area newspaper warmly greeted this reprint: "An endearing glimpse of Central City and Denver during World War II. . . . the dialogue twists and turns. . . . reads like a Nick and Nora movie. . . . charming."—*The Mountain-Ear*. "Fascinating."—*Romantic Times*.

Constance & Gwenyth Little. These two Australian-born sisters from New Jersey have developed almost a cult following among mystery readers. Critic Diane Plumley, writing in *Dastardly Deeds*, called their 21 mysteries "celluloid comedy written on paper." Each book, published between 1938 and 1953, was a stand-alone, but there was no mistaking a Little heroine. She hated housework, wasn't averse to a little gold-digging (so long as she called the shots), and couldn't help antagonizing cops and potential beaux. The Rue Morgue Press intends to reprint all of their books. Currently available: *The Black Coat* (0-915230-40-2, 155 pages, $14.00), *Black Corridors* (0-915230-33-X, 155 pages, $14.00), *The Black Gloves* (0-915230-20-8, 185 pages, $14.00), *Black-Headed Pins* (0-915230-25-9, 155 pages, $14.00), *The Black Honeymoon* (0-915230-21-6, 187 pages, $14.00), *The Black Paw* (0-915230-37-2, 156 pages, $14.00), *The Black Stocking* (0-915230-30-5, 154 pages, $14.00), *Great Black Kanba* (0-915230-22-4, 156 pages, $14.00), and *The Grey Mist Murders* (0-915230-26-7, 153 pages, $14.00).

Marlys Millhiser. Our only non-vintage mystery, *The Mirror* (0-915230-15-1, 303 pages, $17.95) is our all-time bestselling book, now in a sixth printing. How could you not be intrigued by a novel in which "you find the main character marrying her own grandfather and giving birth to her own mother," as one reviewer put it of this supernatural, time-travel (sort-of) piece of wonderful make-believe set both in the mountains above Boulder, Colorado, at the turn of the century and in the city itself in 1978. Internet book services list scores of rave reviews from readers who often call it the "best book I've ever read."

James Norman. The marvelously titled *Murder, Chop Chop* (0-915230-16-X, 189 pages, $13.00) is a wonderful example of the eccentric detective novel. "The book has the butter-wouldn't-melt-in-his-mouth cool of Rick in *Casablanca*."—*The Rocky Mountain News.* "Amuses the reader no end."—*Mystery News.* "This long out-of-print masterpiece is intricately plotted, full of eccentric characters and very humorous indeed. Highly recommended."—*Mysteries by Mail.* Meet Gimiendo Hernandez Quinto, a gigantic Mexican who once rode with Pancho Villa and who now trains *guerrilleros* for the Nationalist Chinese government when he isn't solving murders. At his side is a beautiful Eurasian known as Mountain of Virtue, a woman as dangerous to men as she is irresistible. Together they look into the murder of Abe Harrow, an ambulance driver who appears to have died at three different times. First published in 1942.

Sheila Pim. *Ellery Queen's Mystery Magazine* said of these wonderful Irish village mysteries that Pim "depicts with style and humor everyday life." *Booklist* said they were in "the best tradition of Agatha Christie." *Common or Garden Crime* (0-915230-36-4, 157 pages, $14.00) is set in neutral Ireland during World War II when Lucy Bex must use her knowledge of gardening to keep the wrong person from going to the gallows.

Beekeeper Edward Gildea uses his knowledge of bees and plants to do the same thing in *A Hive of Suspects* (0-915230-38-0, 155 pages, $14.00). *Creeping Venom* (0-915230-42-9, 155 pages, $14.00) mixes politics and religion into a deadly mixture.

Charlotte Murray Russell. Spinster sleuth Jane Amanda Edwards tangles with a murderer and Nazi spies in *The Message of the Mute Dog* (0-915230-43-7, 156 pages, $14.00), a culinary cozy set just before Pearl Harbor. Our earlier title, *Cook Up a Crime*, is currently out of print.

Juanita Sheridan. Sheridan was one of the most colorful figures in the history of detective fiction, as you can see from Tom and Enid Schantz's introduction to *The Chinese Chop* (0-915230-32-1, 155 pages, $14.00). Her books are equally colorful, as well as showing how mysteries with female protagonists began changing after World War II. The postwar housing crunch finds Janice Cameron, newly arrived in New York City from Hawaii, without a place to live until she answers an ad for a room-mate. It turns out the advertiser is an acquaintance from Hawaii, Lily Wu, whom critic Anthony Boucher (for whom Bouchercon, the World Mystery Convention, is named) described as an "exquisitely blended prod-uct of Eastern and Western cultures" and the only female sleuth that he "was devotedly in love with," citing "that odd mixture of respect for her professional skills and delight in her personal charms." First published in 1949, this ground-breaking book was the first of four to feature Lily and be told by her Watson, Janice, a first-time novelist. No sooner do Lily and Janice move into a rooming house in Washington Square than a corpse is found in the basement. In Lily Wu, Sheridan created one of the most believable—and memorable—female sleuths of her day. "Highly recommended."—*I Love a Mystery*. "This well-written. . .enjoyable variant of the boarding house whodunit and a vivid portrait of the post WWII New York City housing shortage, puts to lie the common misconception that strong, self-reliant, non-spinster-or-comic sleuths didn't appear on the scene until the 1970s. Chinese-American Lily Wu and her novelist Watson, Janice Cameron, are young and feminine but not dependent on men."—*Ellery Queen's Mystery Magazine*. Look for more books in this series in 2002.